FOR THE
GREATER GOOD

LISA WARING

Order this book online at www.trafford.com
or email orders@trafford.com

Most Trafford titles are also available at major online book retailers.

Printed in the United States of America.

ISBN: 978-1-4907-2731-8 (sc)
ISBN: 978-1-4907-2730-1 (hc)
ISBN: 978-1-4907-2732-5 (e)

Library of Congress Control Number: 2014902381

Trafford rev. 03/07/2014

 www.trafford.com

North America & international
toll-free: 1 888 232 4444 (USA & Canada)
fax: 812 355 4082

CHAPTER 1

LAZARUS RECLINED QUIETLY IN the shadows of the Ambassador's empty office. He glanced at his watch, crossed his legs and waited . . .

Ambassador David Falconbridge was late. As he entered the embassy, he cursed under his breath. That woman would be the end of him. She was like a drug and it took everything he had just to wrench his body away from her. He knew he was in over his head but couldn't help himself. He smiled nervously at his staff and nodded to each one before heading to his office. Did they know? he thought. Could they tell? He cursed to himself again.

The Ambassador unlocked his office, entered and closed the door. He took a deep breath and ran his hands through his greying hair.

"You're late," a voice from the back corner stated dryly.

"Who the hell are you?" Falconbridge barked, "and how the hell did you get into my office?" There was a long pause.

"The Agency has become aware of you latest dalliance," Lazarus replied. "It's not happy with you Mr. Ambassador." He smiled. "Did you ever wonder why such a beautiful, sexy young thing would be interested in an aging diplomat?"

Falconbridge felt a cold chill go down his spine and he tried to swallow. His throat was dry with the sick realization that his world was crumbling. His thoughts went to the bottle of bourbon tucked into the back of his bottom desk drawer.

"Go ahead," Lazarus suggested as if reading his mind. "If you think a stiff drink will help. By all means go ahead." The diplomat retreated behind his desk and with shaking hands retrieved the bottle. Lazarus rose and approached. "Fortunately for you Mr. Ambassador, your presence is crucial at some very important negotiations. It seems I am not at liberty to take direct action because of it." Cold blue eyes communicated a threat across the desk. "It will be in your best interest to make sure that continues." He paused for effect. "Are we on the same page, Mr. Ambassador?"

Falconbridge's gaze remained steady but he nodded. He hadn't gotten where he was by being timid or backing down. After returning the bourbon to its hiding place, the Ambassador placed both hands palms down on his desk. Taking a deep breath he prepared himself for what was coming next.

"Its over," ordered Lazarus. "You will not call her, see her or communicate with her in any way." He leaned forward leaving little space between himself and the man seated before him. "Believe me Mr. Ambassador you don't want me to have to make a second visit. Am I making myself clear?"

Falconbridge nodded.

"Am I making myself clear?" Lazarus repeated.

". . . Yes."

Once alone, David Falconbridge dialled her number. He had to warn her; she didn't answer.

Lazarus was calm and rational. Killing the girl had been necessary. No one would ever find her. The diplomat had picked the wrong woman with which to become involved. She worked for a foreign government and was extracting sensitive secrets from her lover without his knowledge. Lazarus didn't know which government; it didn't matter. His assignment was to first verify the Agency's suspicions and then, if necessary, take care of the problem.

He'd dined near the couple many times in the city's numerous high end restaurants. Lazarus had carefully listened for any evidence of political misconduct. Amidst much small talk and flirtation, a gradual drawing out of information began. Little things to start, insignificant in manner but once the line of inappropriate familiarity had been crossed the progression was inevitable. The Ambassador wanted to impress her and because of it sealed both their fate.

As Lazarus stepped into the street his cell phone began to vibrate. He paused, considering the call before reaching into his pocket. He'd learned over time to answer promptly.

It was a text message,

"Alabaster."

He stopped; Priority One. Lazarus went directly to his small rented house and awaited instruction. He didn't have to wait long.

Questioning the Agency had long since been extracted from Lazarus' nature, replaced with pass codes, combinations, protocol and the many techniques of the "trade." He could speak 12 languages and transform himself into whomever he needed to be. He did what they told him to do and became who they wanted him to become. He was a chameleon and a very good one. So good that the people he influenced had no idea they were being manipulated and that the man who'd arrived in their lives was anything but what he seemed to be.

It'd started very early in his life. They'd found him at age 7 and immediately recognized his incredible abilities. A new teacher arrived at his school with a special interest in the gifted child. She watched him carefully and once the decision had been made to act, she began to form a plan of recruitment.

The boy became ill. His mother worried. He'd stopped eating and became increasingly weak. After 3 days, he was brought to the hospital where he was immediately put into quarantine. He languished for 3 more days, while his mother watched through the window of an adjacent room. The medical staff prepared her for the worse, but when the end finally came the loss was devastating and complete. She had lost her son to juvenile meningitis and the community had been lucky he'd been the only fatality.

Once the package arrived Lazarus placed the bags on the bed and went to the washroom sink. He looked in the mirror as he splashed cold water on his face. He took a deep breath, inhaling and exhaling slowly.

The briefcase was locked but with a set passcode he quickly opened it. Inside was an envelope, wallet and plane ticket. The envelope contained a passport and a brief identity summary. Albert Dalute', hockey player, returning to the US after failure at tryouts in Sweden. He'd spent 2 weeks in Barcelona with his girlfriend before heading home. Inside the passport was a picture of Lazarus and in the wallet, ID that supported the document. In its pockets the wallet had two hundred dollars American, a few Spanish coins, several Swedish café receipts and a picture of a raven haired girl signed on the back *"To Al, love you always, Margareta."* The plane ticket was in Dalute's name, destination Spokane, Washington. Departure time: 10:00 am the following day.

Lazarus stood, closed his eyes and began the mental process of becoming Albert Dalute'. He was intrigued; a hockey player would be a new role for the young man. Lazarus would be no more; his belongings, identification, mannerisms and even the fingerprints that he'd left around his small room would be wiped clean. When finished, it would as if Lazarus had never existed.

*   *   *

Talbot

It was the only inviting room in the entire compound. The leather chair and sofa beckoned occupants to recline in comfort. Plush carpet blanketed the floor and two large skylights filled the room with soft, natural light. The space was tastefully decorated and valuable paintings that had not been seen by the public for generations were placed carefully around the room. The side walls contained large wooden cabinets, some with large file drawers, and others with floor to ceiling doors. All were locked. Near the back wall, a large oak desk stood with authority, surrounded by book filled shelves. Three high backed chairs faced the man seated behind it.

"This really puts us in a very difficult situation." Talbot stated. The two men sitting opposite shifted in their seats. The young woman across from his right remained still, looking straight at him. She was petite, yet commanding. Her long, dark hair framed her face and her bright green eyes fixed on him. They made Calvin Talbot feel very small; something he was not accustomed to. *He*, was the one people listened to, the one who could make others feel insignificant. Swallowing hard and breaking eye contact, he continued, "You must understand that without Adam in the field our effectiveness is greatly diminished."

"His talents will be utilized to the fullest if we decide to take him," the man Talbot knew as Smith replied. "We need to observe him first. This decision will not be made lightly."

"Besides," Smith's partner inserted, "we have been told that there would be full co-operation from the Agency. Your concerns are of no consequence."

Talbot put his elbows on his desk and inhaled deeply. He wanted to get this over with as soon as possible. He didn't like these guys coming in and undermining his operation. He'd never heard of Global Security (GS) but when the guys in charge told him to co-operate there were no other options.

"His plane arrives today at 3pm," Talbot informed them. "A helicopter will meet him at the airport and bring him directly here. Shall I set up a meeting for later this evening?"

"Absolutely," Smith replied, "but we'd like to observe Adam for a few hours in order to facilitate the best possible meeting scenario." The two men rose from their seats. "We'll continue to need your full co-operation in this matter. We expect full access to the compound and its facilities."

"It's not like I have much of a choice. Everything is at your disposal, but please don't disrupt ongoing operations." Talbot also rose. He glanced over at the girl and their eyes met. He froze, unable to move. Her gaze surrounded him and she looked at him expectantly. The moment passed and she looked away, following her colleagues out of the office.

Calvin Talbot sat, closed his eyes and tried to shake off his uneasiness. With a deep breath Talbot considered losing Adam. It bothered him. The young man was his pride and joy. Not that Talbot was emotionally attached; on the contrary, he was professionally invested. Talbot had been the boy's handler from the beginning: from the first day he arrived at the compound.

* * *

The drug had done its job. The child appeared lifeless and remained unresponsive for several days. The Ministry had red flagged the child's school assessment and forwarded the file to the Agency. Talbot had never seen scores quite like the ones presented. Most potential candidates had elevated scores in one or two areas, this boy's levels were off the charts in every category. If things went well, this kid would help Calvin Talbot. The boy would ensure Talbot's proper place within the Agency.

It was a slow process—made easier by the boy's young age, imagination and thirst for knowledge. During that first meeting Adam had been promised exciting things, experiences any child would dream of, but only if he behaved and did what he was told. It was hard. He'd reacted as any child when told of the terrible accident that claimed the life of his mother. He missed her, but was assured he would be well taken care of. Soon, his mother's face began to fade. He was like a sponge. By the time Adam was twelve years old he could speak 5 languages and knew more than the average university professor.

It also seemed the youngster had the amazing ability to convincingly transform himself. This gift was encouraged and cultivated until Adam could take on many different characteristics and mannerisms. He was trained in disguises and instructed in many professions. As a teenager he travelled the world with Talbot, learning everything. By age 17 his training was complete. He'd learned 11 languages and could be dropped almost anywhere in the world where he'd become invisible.

Of course there'd been a trade off. Talbot made some tough decisions along the way and Adam himself did not exist. He'd been wiped clean and reprogrammed. Ever compliant, he did everything expected, questioned nothing and was lost. Talbot had planned it all along. Adam was his masterpiece.

The young man had lived several dozen different lives in the last few years. The subjects were always new and fresh. With little down time, Adam was kept too busy to become distracted. His roles started slow. The first was a young prisoner helping to build a new structure on the Compound; a runaway from Montreal, Canada. He was a francophone who spoke very little English. Adam convincingly became the troubled young man working off the last of a robbery sentence. Talbot had watched carefully and his star student had passed with flying colours. He'd stayed in character and proved himself ready for the next task.

Adam's next role was as a Russian taxi cab driver. He played the part for 2 months. His assignment had been to live the man's life 24-7. He was put on a bus to New York with instructions to board with a Russian immigrant family. With only $50, a Russian passport and directions to the Doranacov's house, Adam managed to find a job and become immersed in the immigrant community. He made friends and garnered the affections of the oldest daughter. Every laugh and hand held was calculated in order to win the trust of those around him. There'd been no mission, but it hadn't been about a mission. It had been a test to see if Adam had what it took and he did.

The assignments went on from there. At first they were just roles to play but then important missions for the Agency: espionage, infiltration of terrorist factions, collecting data, planting information, but mostly, as in Barcelona, taking care of business. He'd been all over the world and had never disappointed Talbot.

Recently, Adam had been in the Sudan with Doctors without Borders. The Agency needed a man on the front lines. Stationed there for 3 months as a British physician, Adam had met a girl. She was also doctor and they had become very close. He played his part well, enjoying another man's life to the fullest but using everyone and every situation to further the cause of the Agency. When the word came down, he left it behind without a second thought. Doctor Jacob Morris ceased to exist and Lazarus De'Angelo headed for Barcelona.

*　　*　　*

As a child Adam was insatiable. His young mind would take in whatever was presented and as the boy learned it became clear that the Compound's educational programs wouldn't adequately meet the developing genius' needs. Yes, Adam was a genius; the superior test scores continued to rise and the more he learned, the more he seemed able to learn. Medicine, Law, Physics, everything came easily. His education was not only academic. He was immersed in assorted trades and cultures. Once taught, Talbot would move Adam onto the next subject until it became more and more difficult to present him new material. That's when the travelling and role playing began.

It got to the point when Adam was Adam only during training periods and eventually even that part of him was lost. His wants, needs and dreams all ceased to be. He became so accustomed to instruction and imposed purpose that his own purpose no longer existed.

Albert Dalute' shifted positions in the small airplane seat and grinned to himself. He began to consider who or what would meet him at the airport and what this life had in store for him. Content Albert finally did doze off.

*　*　*

Talbot's suit didn't fit and it bothered him. He unbuttoned the jacket and loosened his belt. What had happened? Everything was going so well a week ago. He climbed into the helicopter, buckled in and settled down for the ride to the airport. He'd tried to tell GS how to handle Adam, after all he knew the young man better than anyone. He also knew what it took to control him. They wouldn't listen. Smith and Johnson wanted to observe Talbot's masterpiece without outside influence.

As he looked out the window he thought about the girl, where did she fit in? She hadn't spoken a word, but the whole situation somehow revolved around her. Talbot was worried. He'd spent years working toward Adam's development and taken great risk to keep the young man in check. If the lengths he'd taken became known, there'd be trouble. He was hoping the whole thing would blow over and that Adam wouldn't turn out to be the one they were looking for, but deep down he knew different. He couldn't shake the sense of foreboding that GS had brought with them.

*　*　*

Albert attempted to stretch his legs as the plane landed in Boston. There would be a brief stop before boarding his flight to Spokane. He rubbed his sore knee and glanced again at the address on his driver's license. If there were no further instructions he would take a cab home. It would be a new city for him and getting to know it would be a bit of an adventure. As the seatbelt light turned off with a chime, the plane came to a stop at the terminal.

"Would you please help me get my bag from the overhead compartment?" asked the elderly woman next to him. She'd been quiet for most of the trip, allowing Albert to sleep. "My grandson will meet in the airport, but I am not use to travelling alone." She gathered her things into her bag. "My old bones are getting far too old for this silliness."

The young man stood as the aisle cleared of passengers. Making one last check in his pockets to ensure he was not leaving anything behind, Albert rescued the old woman's bag from the overhead compartment and offered to carry it off the plane.

"Thank you young man," she replied. "May you reap what you have sown." Albert smiled as he helped the woman from her seat.

"Let's go and see if we can find your grandson," the hockey player suggested.

The terminal was crowded, but Albert spotted Talbot immediately. He quickly found a luggage cart for the woman's bag and apologized for not helping her find her grandson. "I have to go, my uncle is here to pick me up," he lied. "Have a wonderful visit with your family."

Talbot walked straight toward Albert. "There's a helicopter waiting for us," he stated. Talbot then looked toward the customs officer and nodded. The man in uniform tipped his hat and waved both Albert and Talbot through. The two men did not speak. Albert disappeared and Adam fell back into the old pattern of a student following his teacher without question.

The helicopter ride was equally silent, but Adam knew where they were headed. They'd made the same trip countless times upon their return from travelling overseas. He was going back to the Compound; a place he'd hoped never to see again. It didn't bring back good memories. Most of his time there had been filled acquiring new knowledge but Adam's mind returned to thoughts of the first days and his mother. He imagined her face. He'd drawn it many times in the beginning, hiding the sketches; but as time wore on Adam had become distracted. Years had passed since he'd imagined her smile, her touch, her smell. She always smelled of lilacs. Adam realized the reason for his ease on the plane; the old woman next to him had smelled like lilacs. He shook his head as a piercing pain shot through his temple. He blinked, inhaled deeply and the pain dissipated.

Arriving at the Compound, Adam became stoic and in control. His mind dictated his thoughts and actions. He'd been well trained. Talbot should have felt reassured but he didn't. He knew bringing Adam back was a mistake, but one he couldn't avoid. Director Ackerman had been insistent that all co-operation be afforded to GS, without question.

The Compound was a sprawling complex. Mountain fenced the facility to the back and thick forest hedged the rest. Smatterings of trees hid observation posts throughout its grounds with motion detectors covering the entire area. No one could get in or out without being seen. It could house up to 60 trainees, but was never filled to capacity. The residents could be confined to their room if deemed necessary and surveillance cameras kept track of every occupant. Each conscript had been surgically implanted with a GPS chip and their whereabouts were known at all times. The training programs were individualized to each recruit. By the end of their programs each new operative would be ready for a specific task based on his or her specialized skill set and trained not to question the Agency's authority.

As the two men climbed from their transport, Adam considered why they had brought him back. A young woman met them at the door of the main entrance. She was dressed in typical Compound fashion, a loose fitting, grey uniform with a small Compound Security badge attached to her left shoulder. The old feelings of confinement and lack of control Adam had experienced at the Compound were gone. He'd become a different person, able to take control of any situation and he knew it. His keen senses had already assessed his surroundings and an escape plan began to formulate in his mind. He'd planned long ago how to remove the GPS from his arm. It would be quick, not painless, but quick. His constant assessment and reassessment was mostly out of habit, but it was also a game he played with himself. This game had saved his life many times.

Talbot spoke to the security guard quietly, glanced at Adam then continued down the hallway alone. He had given no instruction to the new arrival and had not participated in any conversation. It was as it had always been. Affection had never been a part of their relationship.

Adam was given an in depth orientation on the way to his new living quarters. It bored him; he already knew everything there was to know about this place. He also knew he was being watched but it didn't matter. The next assignment was all that mattered.

Smith and Johnson sat watching Adam's every move on the security monitor. Cameras followed the young man wherever he went. "He really doesn't look very impressive," stated Johnson, "and he doesn't seem like the same man that was in Barcelona."

"He's not," the girl observed. She sat apart from the two men, carefully examining the figure on the screen. Both turned and looked at her. Her voice was crisp and assertive. Smith and Johnson had been with her for three days and these were the first words she'd uttered.

"He is a chameleon," Smith put forward, mildly amused. "I've watched this guy and lost him more times than I can count."

Johnson cleared his throat and began to pace. He looked at Smith, "We can't stay here long much longer."

"I know." Smith replied. All eyes returned to the image on the screen.

"He is dangerous," the young woman whispered.

*   *   *

Adam absolutely hated the treadmill, but the weather had turned and he needed to run. He'd been antsy since his return. He hadn't recognized many faces; after all it had been five years since he'd been at the Compound. Other than Talbot, Gwendolyn was the only familiar face. She still ruled the Library like a drill sergeant. She'd been one of the few people to reach out to Adam as a child. She'd been old then, but time had been kind to her. As he ran, Adam reflected on their interaction.

Even after so many years the tiny librarian had smiled a little when Adam entered the library, but she'd caught herself and continued on as normal.

"Hello Adam," Gwendolyn greeted as she gazed at him over her spectacles. "Your regular study carol is free." Adam sensed uneasiness. Her look she told him to be careful. She'd said nothing further to him except for a thank you when he'd returned a book before leaving. He considered her behaviour. Something very strange was going on and as usual Gwendolyn knew more than she'd let on. He'd always known that the Compound's walls had eyes but now he felt that they were all focused on him. He hoped for answers soon.

*   *   *

"We've seen enough," Smith stated as he turned from Adam's image on the monitor. "It's time." He'd already called the Director. In thirty minutes, Adam was to meet them in Talbot's office. They'd been watching and had gleaned nothing. Adam hadn't given them anything to work with. He'd rarely spoken and kept to himself.

Talbot sat in his quarters. He wouldn't be part of the interview and was hoping that what transpired in the next few hours wouldn't end his career. Actually, he was hoping it wouldn't end with him in jail or worse. He'd crossed the line with Adam. He'd known better, but when presented with the opportunity he'd jumped at the possibility of complete control. Adam was Talbot's masterpiece. The procedure hadn't been sanctioned and after many failures it'd been banned. He knew if the truth came out everything he'd worked so hard for would be taken away.

GS had no idea of what they were dealing with. Talbot had gone to the Director to argue his case without giving away too much, but to no avail.

"We appreciate a job well done, Cal," Director Ackerman told him firmly. "But now it is time to stand down. These people are out of your league, hell; they're out of my league." Talbot tried to argue. "Listen to me," the Director continued, leaning forward across his desk and looking into Talbot's eyes. "You will not make this difficult." There was a threat in his voice. "You are but a puff of smoke; stand down."

"None of you understand this kid more than I do," Talbot desperately insisted. "I could be of value."

Jonah Ackerman had stood and leaned forward on his desk, supporting his weight on his hands. He'd stared at Talbot menacingly. "Listen you little, little man, you are nothing. They will give you back your little, insignificant office when they are done and you can continue on with your little, insignificant job, but you will stand down!" The Director then stood straight. "If you do not stand down," he'd stated calmly looking at Talbot with what seemed to be an amused grin, "poof, gone," he snapped his fingers. "Just like a puff of smoke." He returned to his seat and opened a file. "Now get out of my office," he'd finished, no longer interested.

Talbot shook his head trying to forget the threatening tone that'd been in Director Ackerman's voice. He went over to the small desk and turned on the computer screen. Instantly his office appeared on the monitor. If he couldn't be a part of the interview at least he could watch.

*   *   *

Adam was almost ready to meet with Talbot. He closed his eyes, took a deep breath and became the student. His handler had never given him much credit but young man had figured Talbot out years ago. Adam became exactly what his handler expected, just as always. It was easier that way. He looked in the mirror and fixed his hair. Talbot was weak. The student would listen, be captivated by every word and then comply. He'd been trained so well; every choice was calculated. The end justified the means. His entire purpose was to be in the field for the Agency.

With his shoulders hunched forward and a tentative look on his face, Adam left his room and headed toward Talbot's office. He knew something strange was going on; why else would they have brought him back to the Compound? He shuffled his feet and made sure his collar was slightly crooked. The uneasy feeling that began in the library intensified. When he rounded the corner to the office a large man in a dark suit stood waiting. He obviously wasn't from the Compound. The man stepped aside and opened the office door.

As Adam stepped into the office the student instantly disappeared. The chair behind the big desk was empty; Talbot nowhere to be seen. The man that sat on the couch rose to his feet and the other closed the door as he followed Adam in from the corridor. They were dressed alike and had the same haircut. Both looked to be in their late 40s. Adam took in a deep breath, stretched to his full height, straightened his collar and smoothed his hair. He stood with authority and presence. His eyes assessed the entire room and he stepped aside to allow his doorman to join his partner.

"We have been waiting a very long time to meet you Adam," The man from the couch said as he took his seat. "My name is Smith, this is Johnson." He gestured for Adam to have a seat in the chair facing the sofa. The doorman joined his partner. Adam complied.

"It wasn't our first choice to bring you back here," Johnson began, "but we had to be sure you were the right man for the job."

Adam turned and looked intently into Smith's eyes, dismissing Johnson entirely. Smith was clearly the one in charge. "Smith and Johnson how original," Adam mused. "And *now*, are you sure I am the right man?" he inquired.

"Not quite," Johnson explained rather nervously, attempting to regain Adam's attention. "There is someone we would like you to meet." He became flustered as Adam's gaze didn't waver from Smith's face. He could feel the colour rising in his cheeks.

The two other men studied one another carefully. Surprisingly, Smith couldn't read Adam, but the GS agent was both amused and impressed. The young man was all of 24 years old and had managed to manipulate Johnson without effort. There was something about him. He'd read the kid's file and watched him for countless hours, but this was something more. It was as if he could feel Adam's presence. It was tangible. Perhaps it was all true and he was exactly who and what they thought he was. Several minutes passed and the two men continued to assess one another. Smith finally leaned back and smiled, as did Adam. The posturing was over and Adam had prevailed. *She's right,* Smith thought, *this kid is dangerous.* He looked over at Johnson. "No kid gloves needed," he decided. "We don't have a lot of time, let's quit wasting it."

* * *

The girl observed the activity in Talbot's office with amazement. She'd watched Adam transform. He entered the room as a ruffled youth and became what seemed to be a dark force, totally in control. She marveled as things quickly unfolded. Was he able to read people that well or was there something more? As she turned from the images on the screen, she chewed her lip. She'd read his file and knew what he was capable of. How was she going to be able to work with him, knowing all the terrible things he'd done? She almost hoped they were wrong about him.

Get yourself together, she thought to herself. Taking a deep breath she got up from her seat and smoothed her sweater. She flipped her long hair behind her back and tried to tuck it into her collar. A knot tightened in her chest. At 21 she'd seen too much already. With another deep breath, the girl took a moment to prepare and then reached over and turned off the camera in Talbot's office. As the screen went blank she left the room.

Talbot's screen also went blank and he cursed. He was totally shut out.

CHAPTER 2

WHEN THE GIRL ENTERED, Adam's focus remained on the two men. He wanted to study their reaction to her arrival. Smith's shoulders moved forward and his breathing deepened. He looked from Adam to the girl in anticipation. In contrast, Johnson didn't look directly at her and his shoulders moved back as if trying to stay as far from her as possible; he then quickly left the room, closing the door. It took only fractions of a second for Adam to interpret their body language. It was evident that she was an assignment not a colleague. These men were very uncomfortable and neither was sure as to what was going to happen next. The girl would dictate the course of events.

Adam turned his attention to the new arrival. She was dressed in blue jeans and a red sweater. She stood straight with her shoulders back and her chin up. Long dark hair framed a delicate face. He rose to his feet, careful to remain casual, soaking in every nuance of the young woman that stood before him. He studied the face, recognized it, then tried to brace himself but it was too late.

"This is . . . ." Smith began, but as the girl looked directly into Adam's eyes it as if shockwave struck him full on. The room became cloudy and unfocused. He tried to listen intently, straining to hear her name but sounds became garbled and unintelligible. Adam's knees gave out and he fell back into his chair. Talbot's office melted away and Adam found himself back in a Barcelona café. She'd dropped her bag that day and he picked it up for her.

When he'd looked into her deep green eyes, he felt weak; his heart pounding in his chest. By the time he regained his composure she was gone. It had taken him days to get her out of his head; to stop feeling so exposed. Adam put his head in his hands and started to breathe deliberately; in through his nose, out through his mouth. He was helpless.

The girl involuntarily stepped back as Adam crumpled into his chair. Smith froze, frowning as he looked at her. Both were astonished. The young man that had been such presence only a moment before, now sat doubled over trying to get his wits about him. Smith sprang into action, pulling out his cell phone, speaking quietly into it.

"I'm sorry Adam," the girl whispered as she knelt in front of struggling man, "but we had to know." She put a hand on his shoulder. "Look at me again," she said firmly. Uncertain, Adam's eyes remained downcast, sweat beaded on his brow. His head slowly cleared. He took a deep breath, preparing himself. As he looked up, the girl smiled. "I'm sorry," she repeated. "It was the only way to be certain." Adam searched her face, her eyes, but found no trace of whatever had just happened.

She rose, turned to Smith and nodded in his direction, who in turn headed toward the door. "We'll take care of it," he confirmed as he left. The girl walked over to the couch, smoothed her sweater and sat down. She looked at Adam and waited.

"We've met before," Adam stated having regained some of his composure. "It took me days to get you out of my head." He was no longer sure of which role to play, what would be the most effective. At a loss, Adam waited for an explanation.

She nibbled on her lip before she spoke picking her words carefully. "My name is Aberdeen and there was another compound much like this one," she looked around and continued, "but it had a much different function." She cleared her throat. "In the mid 70's a group of scientists began research with regard to a small gland just behind the hypothalamus. It directly affects visual interpretation and sequencing. They performed experiments to enhance this gland in order to allow test subjects to transmit information through simple eye contact. It was discovered that every person in the entire human population is a transmitter of certain chemicals and light waves but only those test subjects with altered visual cartal glands can receive these signals and with practice, decode them. Or at least that is what we thought. You are the only receiver we know of who has not been enhanced by the program." Aberdeen leaned forward with her elbows on her knees looking at him. "Although your reaction to my transmissions is not typical there can be no other explanation." She sat back, waiting for a reply.

Adam carefully considered her words. His mind started to work; reflect, reconcile what he'd learned and extrapolate conclusions. She waited patiently.

"Okay," Adam finally responded, "but . . . I read body language and variances in speech and behaviour, not minds." He stopped, on his guard and considered his next move. "What just happened and what happened in Barcelona?

Aberdeen smiled. "What you experienced was high intensity, focused information. I'm not sure why you reacted so strongly. In Barcelona we tried to figure out who you were, but for some reason couldn't decode your thoughts. So I played a hunch at the café and after what happened today, there is only one explanation. Your cartal gland was over stimulated. Your brain was not expecting the type of information it received and for some reason you had a visual overload. We don't know why. We think with proper training and practice decoding will become second nature to you." She ran her hands through her hair. "Remember we are dealing with visual interpretation not reading minds." Aberdeen took a deep breath and tried to search his eyes. She could see nothing.

Although she'd told him they couldn't decode his thoughts, Adam was careful not to make eye contact. He was unsure and felt at an extreme disadvantage. He was having a hard time wrapping his brain around it all and the question still remained; what did she want from him?

"We need to leave this place," the girl stated. "The walls have eyes. The Agency has agreed to transfer you to Global Security for the time being. Smith is getting the helicopter ready."

Adam sat back and reflected on what she'd said. The Agency had directed his actions for as long as he could remember. The fact that she was here at the Compound, in Talbot's office, dictated his compliance. He knew how much power and how many resources the Agency commanded; Global Security seemed to supersede all of it. The Agency brought him back here to meet these people for a reason; he knew what he had to do. As he pondered, Smith re-entered the office.

"We've got ten minutes," Smith informed the girl as she rose to her feet. He looked at Adam expectantly. "Are you in?"

Adam also stood. "I'm in," he answered.

Aberdeen became serious. "You will no longer be answering to the Agency, but to GS."

Adam nodded as Smith stepped toward him. "Role up your sleeve, we need to get rid of that GPS. We don't want anyone tracking you." The GS agent produced a small apparatus from his jacket pocket and moved it along Adam's arm. It beeped intermittently until a steady tone announced that Smith had found the imbedded GPS. He placed the device firmly against Adam's skin and pressed a button. A sharp pain was followed by a small, smudge of blood. Smith apologized as he opened the device, extracted the implant from inside and placed it in insulated container.

"No need to apologize," Adam responded. He reached into his pocket and retrieved his cell phone. "I won't need this any longer," the young man stated. He walked over and placed it on Talbot's desk. He then removed his watch and set it next to it.

"You can't bring anything with you," Smith stated.

"I rarely can," Adam replied.

*　　*　　*

Aberdeen sat across from Adam. She hadn't been entirely honest with him, but she suspected he already knew. He'd need to know the truth but that was for others to reveal. She watched him, careful he didn't notice, but he no doubt had. She'd never met someone so closed or hard to read. His eyes scanned the helicopter, absorbing his surroundings. She almost felt guilty for getting him involved, but she reminded herself of how perfect he was for the job. His ability to reinvent himself and the training he'd received from the Agency would aid greatly in the task at hand. Besides she'd read his file; he'd been involved with far more unseemly things than what was ahead.

* * *

She was watching him and he felt very uncomfortable. Adam didn't want to give anything away, so he did not return her look. The more he thought about what she said the more questions he had, but there were no regrets. If the Agency had not wanted him to get involved they wouldn't have allowed a meeting, but Adam was blazing new territory. He had no given perspective and so he had to find his own. It was difficult. He longed to fall into some role that would dictate his behaviour, but he hadn't been given one. As he tried to focus on the things at hand his head began to ache.

* * *

Calvin Talbot spotted Adam's phone the moment he entered his office and realized it was over. Adam was not only gone but out of reach. The cell phone had been Talbot's ace in the hole. It had all been for not. In a few weeks or maybe only a few days, everything would start falling apart.

The right training could accomplish much but Adam had not been typical and to expect unquestioned loyalty and obedience from someone of his intelligence was unrealistic. The strength of his will had been apparent from the moment he'd arrived at the Compound and at 16 he'd become defiant. The decision to place the device at the base of his skull hadn't been an easy one. 60% survived the surgery and only 33% of those avoided diminished mental capacity.

Again Adam hadn't been typical. He recovered quickly and the only marked changes were those that'd been intended. His genius and adaptability remained intact. Adam had become the perfect operative. He questioned nothing. He breathed, ate and slept for the Agency. Low frequency electrical charges numbed the part of his brain that endangered his effectiveness. He was both loyal and utterly fearless, but as per usual Adam's reaction was unexpected. His brain began to compensate so it became necessary to regularly change the frequency of the charge influencing his emotion and behaviour. The small changes caused occasional, brief headaches but there were no other repercussions.

The cell phone and GPS worked in tandem readjusting as one read Adam's ever adapting brain waves and the other changed frequencies in order to regulate his behaviour. Without the frequency changes the real Adam would resurface and Talbot had no idea what would happen after eight years. The feeling of dread surrounding him thickened.

*   *   *

The movement of the helicopter changed and Adam's attention was drawn to the landscape below. By his calculations they'd been in the air for 93 minutes. They'd been flying over water for 51 minutes and the vessel he spotted below seemed alone in the darkening expanse. She had obviously been a luxury yacht before being converted into a stronghold. The craft blended into its surroundings and after a brief survey it was clear to Adam that it was off the radar. A small helicopter already nested upon its deck. Several brightly clothed figures moved to and fro directing Adam's pilot where to set down. No doubt they were in international waters; a perfect hiding place.

Aberdeen and Adam were met on deck. He nodded to Smith as the copter took the GS agent and his partner back into the sky. Adam had been correct; Aberdeen was an assignment not a colleague. His attention switched to his surroundings; three on deck, one probably a woman, all of them busy lashing things securely to the vessel. Everything was covered with light deflecting material. Even the landing pad was quickly re-blanketed once the helicopter was in the air.

"Has everyone arrived?" Aberdeen asked the stocky older man standing in front of her.

"Some time ago," was the reply, "and they are anxious to get started." He looked at Adam. "You must be the fella they're all in an uproar about." He reached out his hand. Adam ignored it, his head now pounding. Unflustered the man made an about face. "You've got 30 minutes," he said, "follow me." He quickly headed toward a cabin door.

Three doors to the left, one to the right, a set of stairs going down, fifteen steps and then turn to an intersecting corridor. As usual, Adam began to map out surroundings and develop a plan, but he struggled with the pain in his temples. The vessel itself was about 120 feet long and he estimated that there were 10 crew plus on board.

"These are your quarters. You'll find everything you need in the cupboard. There's a shower in the head," the stocky man stated to the new comer, "I'll be back to get you in 30 minutes." He opened the door and motioned for Adam to enter.

Aberdeen looked from one man to the other. She sensed something was wrong. "Adam," she asked, "are you alright?" He nodded, grabbing onto the door frame. Showing weakness was never an option. He straightened up.

"Thirty minutes," Adam acknowledged. He turned, entered the room and closed the door. He went directly to the small cot and sat down with his head between his knees. He slowed his breathing which seemed to ease the pain. Although headaches were common they were usually brief and not as intense.

Breathe in, breathe out. Start at the toes. Relax. Take a deep breath. Adam heard the pitch of the engines change as the boat started to move. *Continue to the calves, up to the knees: breathe in, breathe out.* It took Adam 15 minutes to regain control.

He then scanned his small room. It was about 10 foot square. It was tiny but an efficient use of the space. The cot faced the door. To the right, a desk hugged the wall. A bookcase, ceiling high, stood next to it. To the left there was a small basin and mirror, framed by cabinets on either side. The door to the head was ajar. Almost everything was made from wood. The clear grain of the panels echoed the care and workmanship that had gone into the vessel and the brass knobs and handles reflected the light from the small porthole.

Adam calculated that he had thirteen minutes to get himself together. He stood slowly. With another deep breath he went over to the basin, turned on the tap and splashed water onto his face. The image looking back at him from the mirror narrowed its eyes. Composure; that was what Adam needed to find. He had to get a hold of himself. He rummaged through the cabinets and found a change of clothes and quickly changed. After glancing in the mirror and looking through the shaving kit, he resolved that his 5 o'clock shadow would be appropriate. Examining himself again, he straightened his entire 6' frame and pulled back his shoulders. He untucked his over-shirt, unbuttoned it and raised the collar on either side. With a deep breath he ruffled his dark hair slightly and set his jaw. Adam would have to wait to see where all this would lead. In the meantime he did not want to come across as someone who could not hold his own. Being young was usually an advantage, in this situation however, he didn't want his age to be interpreted as weakness.

With his remaining time Adam searched the rest of the room. The desk drawers were empty and the bookshelf was bare except for a few nautical charts, a clock and a small looking glass. He speculated that they were relics from the vessel's former life. As Adam reached for the looking glass there was a crisp knock on the door. He glanced again in the mirror, took a deep breath and reached for the doorknob.

The stocky man had returned. "Are you ready?" he asked, already turning to lead the way.

"I am," replied Adam. The man took three steps down the corridor then suddenly stopped and faced Adam. He looked grave.

"I hope," the older man said, "you aren't wasting our time laddie because time is one thing we don't have." His gaze remained steady, almost pleading.

Adam's experience with the Agency had always been cut and dry; black and white instructions to be carried out expediently. This was desperation and desperation either came from or led to weakness. He'd never become attached or invested in anything. Orders were to be followed, not questioned or stressed over. Adam understood human nature but he had been able to personally avoid it. He did not empathize, but rather used others' emotions to his advantage.

"My name is *Adam*, not laddie" he answered, "and I do not waste time."

"Mine is Flynn. We'd best get going then."

*   *   *

The room had five chairs placed around two small tables. Three seats were filled and Flynn took the forth. The fifth was empty, obviously meant for Adam. There were no windows. The chairs faced a large screened wall filled with the projected image of a man in a white doctor's coat. At the far table, Aberdeen and two men sat quietly talking; in front of the elderly man in the middle chair there was a laptop with the same doctor's image on its screen. Everyone stopped, looked at Adam and waited for him to take a seat.

Adam normally had an extremely high pain tolerance but the concentration he needed to remain in control due to his headache was beginning to concern him. Now was not the time to show weakness and he stumbled slightly as he carefully lowered himself into his chair. Once seated, Adam took a deep breath and was able to clear his head. No one seemed to notice his misstep.

"My name is Dr. Bjorn Erikson and next to me is Ken Munroe," the man with the computer began. "You've already met Aberdeen and Flynn O'Sullivan. We've brought you here because of him," He motioned at the screen. "He was Doctor Anthony Bergstein and he was my friend and colleague for many years. He headed a program that altered test subjects to enhance speechless inter-human communication. As you have experienced, those tests were somewhat successful; of the 43 treated we know of only four that survived with certainty and they are in their late 40s and early 50s." Adam looked at Aberdeen and then back to Dr. Erikson. The old man followed the young man's gaze.

"She was not a test subject," the doctor explained, "She is one of their children." He paused giving Adam a moment to process what he'd just heard; to perhaps come to the real understanding of what it meant. Dr. Erikson then changed the image on the screen. "As is this man," he said.

Adam studied the newly projected figure carefully. He felt everyone's eyes on him, waiting for his reaction. He breathed purposefully and battled not to narrow his eyes or change his body language. The pain in his head had momentarily subsided and he was able to concentrate fully. He wasn't stupid and understood the implications. The man in the image had Adam's eyes and strong jaw line.

"We do not believe the resemblance is coincidental, but short of a DNA test we have no way of proving it and we do not have a sample to compare with yours." The doctor was very matter of fact. "The Agency destroyed all record of where you came from. We know nothing of your parents or where the Agency found you. All we know is that you arrived at the Compound at age 7. We traced children born in North America on your birth date, but could account for everyone. You were either born in another country or someone fudged the date. If your mother was hiding you from Bergstein she would have taken certain measures to keep you safe."

"It seems to be the most likely explanation for your abilities Adam," Aberdeen interjected. "Do you remember anything about your family that could help confirm our suspicions?" she asked.

Adam took a deep breath and closed his eyes. He pictured his mother and considered what he remembered about life before the Compound. The Agency had told him she'd died in a plane crash. They'd showed him the crash site pictures. He recalled the sharp pain it had caused; the pain of loss. But it was just a memory; Adam hadn't felt anything for so long. Even now there were no emotions.

"My school was by the ocean," Adam remembered as he reached over and took a piece of paper and a pen from the stack in front of Flynn. "We lived in a small yellow house at the end of a long driveway. The yard was surrounded by a tall fence. It was just my mother and I." As he spoke Adam began to draw. The others waited patiently. "Her name was Julia, she smelled like lilacs," he continued. An annoying ache from the back of Adam's neck began to distract him. Again he took a deep breath. "The last time I saw her I was in the hospital and very sick." Adam stopped talking but continued to draw.

The others watched Adam. He was silent, concentrating on the image he was creating on the page. When finished he looked at the face he'd sketch and nodded. He then passed the drawing to Flynn. "This is my mother," he said. Flynn looked at it and passed it on to Dr. Erikson.

The doctor studied the drawing. It was a sketch of a young woman. She was smiling, her short curly hair crowned her beautiful face; her eyes flashed. "It's definitely Elena," the doctor confirmed with a smile. "Her hair is different, but it's her." He sat back in his chair. "When Jarvis was unable to decode your thoughts in Barcelona he had his suspicions. We had no idea that she had another child and until now we weren't sure."

"I have many questions" Adam stated. His entire reality had changed. He needed to reconcile it all: to know what was next and what they wanted from him. His head was pounding again and it was when touched his nose that he noticed the blood.

"Something's wrong," Aberdeen exclaimed. Adam looked at her with clouded eyes and then back at his hand. He was confused. *Why was it red? Why was everything happening in slow motion?*

Sounds became garbled and Adam found rising to his feet a struggle. He needed to get some fresh air, but before he could reach the door, the young man collapsed.

It was Flynn who caught him and gently lowered Adam to the floor. Dr. Erikson rushed to his side and checked his vitals. Aberdeen stood back, her face in her hands as she watched blood trickle from the nose of Adam's motionless body. Ken Munroe reached for the intercom and called for help. In moments Adam was on the way to the infirmary.

* * *

"Those Agency dogs, I'd like to get my hands on them. I'd . . ."

"Take it easy Flynn," Munroe said. "We need to stay calm and keep our wits about us." His voice was soft and low as if he were not just talking to the other man, but also to himself.

Adam's implant had shut down and without the outside electrical influences his brain was struggling to compensate. Initially Dr. Erikson feared the young man had succumbed to the same fate of many of the original test subjects. The experiments damaged their brains and over time it'd been too much for them to handle. Thankfully he was wrong. A hastily performed scan had pinpointed the problem immediately. The boy would be fine, but needed time to recuperate.

The three men returned to the meeting room after Adam had been made comfortable and they were all grappling with what had happened. Aberdeen stayed with him. "We'll keep him sedated until tomorrow and then reassess," the ship's doctor informed them as he peeked into the room. "If there are any changes before then I'll let you know immediately." Erikson nodded. The door closed quietly.

Erikson cleared his throat and looked at the two men sitting across the table from him. His eyes were tired and suddenly he looked very old. He was frustrated with the continued obstacles. He'd been on a roller coaster ride in the last few hours; the excitement of finding out Adam was Elena's son and then the stress of his collapse. "We have no idea how much Adam's behaviour had been modified. The implant targeted the areas affecting emotion and self determination. It would seem the Agency felt the need to keep Adam from being Adam. It turns out he is not the man we thought he was. It's no doubt also effected the cartal gland enhancement and the reason he's reacted so strongly to Aberdeen's attempts to communicate."

The trio remained silent for a long time; overwhelmed and only too aware that time was running short.

"It's late. I'm calling it a night," Erikson mumbled. "Hopefully tomorrow will bring better things or we'll have to revisit our options." He looked frustrated. "Goodnight gentleman, I still have to inform Jarvis of the latest developments with our young friend," he said rising to his feet. He turned and left the room. Flynn and Munroe sat for a long time. They knew the options were limited and that the young man resting in the infirmary was their best hope of finding the truth.

$$* \quad * \quad *$$

Aberdeen headed for her quarters. She hadn't stayed with Adam long. When she'd seen the blood, Aberdeen had thought of her mother. Watching the woman who'd raised her gradually slip away had been so hard. The enhancement procedure had been hardest on women and once the lower brain started to degrade, death was only a matter of time. Nose bleeds were but one symptom of breakdown. It'd been difficult after she'd died. Aberdeen had been only 13 and surrounded by men. Her father had never been the same.

Arriving at her room Aberdeen showered, allowing the day's stress to wash down the drain. When Adam collapsed she'd panicked. There were so few of them left and the task at hand was daunting. Finding Adam had given them all a new perspective; hope that they would finally find some answers but for that brief moment all seemed lost.

The girl had been excited when she heard that he may be one of the 2nd generation, but after reading his file and learning of his history she'd had mixed feelings. It seemed to her, Adam was no different than those who had started this whole mess. Decoding him hadn't worked; her father had tried and failed. She wasn't sure why. Was it because of the implant? Or was it Adam's abilities? With the unfolding events she was confused. Aberdeen had never met another child of the experiments. She'd been born after Bergstein had taken the others. When she finally laid her head to her pillow Aberdeen knew that sleep would not come easily.

* * *

Erikson watched Adam for a while before entering the infirmary and although he had physically recovered, the young man's composure had not returned. His face was drawn. As he lay on the cot, pillows propped up his upper body. The young prodigy stared out the porthole.

"I see your awake," Erikson commented as his took a chair next to the bed. Adam, filled with frustration, looked at him. "We didn't know about the implant Adam."

"What implant?"

"It seems the Agency implanted a device at the base of your skull which modified your behaviour," Erikson replied. There was no point sugar coating anything for the boy. He needed to know answers. "It sent varying frequencies to the areas of your brain that regulated emotion and self determination." He allowed Adam to absorb this new information before continuing. "We estimate its been there for at least 7 or 8 years. It shut down last night and you've had quite a battle to re-adapt." Adam looked back out the porthole and said nothing. Erikson waited.

"Can it be reactivated?" Adam asked, overwhelmed.

"I don't know," the older man replied. "It was regulated by something that you no longer have in your possession. It could have been your watch or cell phone or perhaps the device that was removed from your arm." The doctor shook his head. "There's no way of knowing."

"This is too much." Adam put his face in his hands. "I've lost control. Everything is so overwhelming." He began to breathe purposefully; in through his nose, out through his mouth.

"You have the skills to deal with this," Erikson said firmly.

"I'm not sure that I do," responded Adam looking into the doctor's eyes.

"I've been around for many years and have seen more than most." Erikson began. "I can't imagine what you're going through right now, but I do know you can't go back." He put his hand on Adam's shoulder. **"As do you,"** he determined with his eyes. Adam flinched, able to decode his thoughts. "I hate what the Agency has done to you, but at this point you must fall back on your Agency training. I have a lot of answers for you when you are ready. Now I think you need to rest for a while. I'll be back."

Adam closed his eyes and quickly drifted into a fitful sleep. It was filled with disturbing images from his past; the first dreams he'd had in years.

Chapter 3

Dr. Erikson left a message for Adam to meet on the upper observation deck upon his release from the infirmary, but only when he was ready. The young man first went to his quarters for a shower and shave. He didn't recognize the man he saw in the mirror. His reflection looked timid, and confused. Its eyes tortured. The face showed evidence of the nightmares he'd experienced throughout the night.

"This isn't right," Adam said out loud shaking his head. "I can do this." He closed his eyes and inhaled deeply. As he let out his breath, he stood tall, pushing back his shoulders. Adam set his jaw and opened his eyes. A familiar face appeared in the mirror. With a satisfied nod Adam went to meet Erikson.

He found the old man sitting on a deck chair with a book propped up on his chest. On a table next to him there sat a pitcher of iced tea with two glasses. It was half empty. As Adam took a seat, the doctor poured him a drink.

"You seem to have regained your composure," Erikson observed with a smile. "I trust you slept well?"

"No," Adam replied as a matter of fact.

"No, I suppose you didn't," the old man said. "It's a whole new world for you my boy. The implant not only modified your behaviour, it also suppressed your ability to visually decode. That is why Aberdeen affected you so strongly. The device had to compensate and well, as you experienced, it did so rather strongly."

Erikson looked at Adam and considered him carefully. **"Welcome aboard my yacht."**

Adam couldn't help but flinch as the doctor's words appeared before him. "How are you doing that?" he asked.

"I'm actually not doing anything," Erikson answered. "You are simply visually decoding specific light waves and chemicals being released by my brain through my cornea."

Adam was dumbfounded. He ran his hands through his hair. "Can you also decode?" he inquired.

"No Adam," Erikson responded, "but anyone with a little training can transmit focused information. Of the ten successful results Bergstein managed, I knew with certainty of only three that remained. That of course changed when Jarvis found Shane Stevens and the young man we now know is your brother. And then there are you and Aberdeen."

". . . and my mother," Adam added.

"Yes . . . Elena," the Doctor paused for a moment and had a sip of his tea.

"What's to say Bergstein hasn't continued his experiments," Adam considered. "Maybe there are others you don't know about."

"I don't really think there are," Erikson replied. "Before things fell apart he'd tried for months to duplicate the experiment with disastrous results. I could tell his intellect was letting him down. Besides all his research was destroyed in the fire."

"What fire?" Adam asked. "What happened? What happened to my mother?"

"I don't really know," the doctor answered. "The last time she was seen, Bergstein was forcing her into a helicopter at gun point with your new born brother in her arms." He took another sip of tea, putting his book on the table next to him. "I should start at the beginning." Sitting back in his chair, Erikson cleared his throat. "I met Bergstein when we were research assistants in Switzerland. We had both taken summer internships at the Bern University. We hit it off and had a blast. Being young while travelling overseas will bring many adventures and it certainly was the case for me and Anthony. We kept in touch after and met in exotic places occasionally. He was a good friend. It didn't matter how long we'd been apart; we'd start up right where we'd left off. Then for a period of about 5 years I heard nothing from him until one day he called and wanted me to join his research team. He was excited so I knew he was onto something big."

"It took awhile but I cleared my schedule and headed to back Switzerland. Anthony had set up a research clinic high in the mountains. To outsiders it was a retreat for the wealthy. It was very secretive and mysterious. When I arrived he showed me his results but gave me no history and I didn't ask for any. They promised to revolutionize human communication. Enhanced individuals could consistently and accurately pick up messages from a control group and nonverbally communicate with one another. The research was fascinating and I jumped in with both feet. The risk seemed minimal, or at least that is what Anthony led me to believe. We'd been friends for years but I had no idea the lengths to which Anthony would go and had already gone. He gave only limited access to research and even less to his test subjects. As results showed more positive outcomes, Bergstein let his guard down. It was then that people started getting sick and I started nosing around in Bergstein's office. One day, to my horror, I stumbled on the truth."

"Anthony kept copious notes recording each death. He'd lost more than 15 patients in his initial enhancement procedures. He'd injected the cartal gland with a growth hormone causing it to increase production of the needed neurotransmitter; it also made the gland itself grow causing severe brain damage and eventual death. He changed his tactics and shifted his focus to gene therapy." The doctor paused and shook his head.

"Anthony was brilliant, but that brilliance cost so many so much." Erikson looked at Adam. "When I confronted him with my findings he just laughed and said I was weak. He said that it was the results that mattered not how he'd gotten them; that those lost meant nothing compared to the outcome."

"The gene therapy obviously worked and the changes were passed onto offspring or Aberdeen and I wouldn't be here," Adam concluded.

"It did and they were, but it took its toll on many. I discovered Anthony was able to successfully genetically alter 10 individuals. Many were not so lucky. Very few know of this, even the authorities in Switzerland never knew the full scope of what happened. It was the only way to protect those affected." The Doctor swallowed. "The last thing these poor people needed was more scrutiny, testing and unwanted attention." He looked out at the ocean. "You must understand it was very traumatic; not even the victims knew what Anthony was up to." He shook his head again and he was quiet for a long time.

Adam sat silently for several minutes. "I need to know the rest," he insisted quietly. "Finish the story, I need to know." He looked at Erikson and waited.

"Anthony only let me work extensively with Elena and a young French Canadian named Andre'. They were both very young, especially your mother. I'd sat in a couple of sessions with Jarvis and Munroe but I only knew of the others through the snippets of research Anthony afforded my way. It was incredible and exciting work. When it was discovered that Elena was pregnant the atmosphere at the clinic changed. Anthony had brought everyone to the clinic under the pretence of great scientific advancement. They hadn't been disappointed but your mother wanted to go home."

A noise at the door startled both Erikson and Adam. It was Munroe. "Are you okay Doctor?" he said concerned.

"It's okay Ken," answered Erikson. "Sit with us and maybe you can fill in some of the details." Munroe took a deck chair from against the wall and moved it next to Erikson. The three men sat in a small circle. The Doctor leaned forward putting his elbows to his knees.

"That's when I broke into Anthony's office and discovered the truth. I didn't know what to do at first. I was in shock. I needed to tell the others but never had the chance. He returned and there was a confrontation; an ugly one. Anthony was a big man and he physically overpowered me. I'm not sure what happened next but I awoke in a locked room. I knew he was watching me."

"I was there for a few days, without food when Anthony paid me a visit." Erikson relived the terror as he closed his eyes. "I almost didn't recognize him. He'd brought a tray of food and watched amused as I fixated on it. He told me that science was full of men like him, willing to take the necessary steps in order to advance human knowledge; men who were willing to make the tough choices for the greater good. He called me a fool and laughed, handing me the tray. As I ate he gave me a choice. I could help him move forward with his research or become a part of it. I was terrified. He laughed and left.

"I don't know how long I was there and I lost track of time."

Adam stood and went over to the railing to look at the ocean. The others watched him carefully. His own past was gaining perspective and he marvelled at the irony. His mother had somehow saved him from Bergstein only to have the Agency step in and steal him away.

"And then one day the door opened again," Erikson continued. "It was Jarvis and Munroe. The clinic was on fire and Anthony was gone."

"So were Shane, Elena, their newborn and Sophia, my wife," added Munroe. His face was covered in pain and regret. "I watched from my room as Bergstein loaded them into a helicopter. I couldn't help them, the door was locked. The clinic was filling with smoke and we were prisoners. Something had gone terribly wrong." Munroe shook his head, "When my door opened Andre' was bleeding heavily and Flynn was holding him up. Jarvis met us in the hallway. We could already hear the sirens. Jarvis and I went and freed the doctor. Only five of us made it out alive; Andre' died in Flynn's arms."

"By the time we escaped the ceilings were starting to fall in." Erikson continued. "Twelve people died in the fire. When we finally made it outside the fire trucks had arrived."

Adam reclaimed his seat and the three men sat for a long time. They all looked out at the ocean together. The clouds had gotten dark and a cold breeze started to blow.

"So then Bergstein escaped taking the others with him" Adam asked, "for what purpose?

"We're not so sure," Munroe answered. "He was never able to replicate the results. The ten of us were anomalies. Somehow Bergstein had managed to get everything just right, but for some reason could not repeat it. He tried. We do know that he was being funded by someone and no doubt had to produce results."

"That's why he fought so hard to keep you," Adam concluded.

"And that's why the children were so important." Munroe added.

"Children," Adam questioned. "There was more than one?"

Munroe got up and went back inside. Erikson answered, "Sophia was expecting when Anthony took her." He looked at Adam and the young man understood.

"Bergstein built the clinic in the mountains. Money was never an issue. He must have had some very deep pockets backing him but I have never been able to find out whom. He disappeared and the rest of us tried to pick up the pieces and go on. We changed our identities fearful that Anthony and his people would come looking for us. Flynn, Munroe and Jarvis never stopped looking for the one's taken. We parted ways but kept in touch."

". . . And Aberdeen's mother?"

"Angela died going on eight years ago. She started to exhibit the same side effects that took many of the others. Her brain began to breakdown and we lost her." Erikson was finished; physically and emotionally spent. "Jarvis spotted Shane a few months ago and discovered his son not long after. They seem to be working together. He gathered us together with the intention of finding out what they were up to and stopping them if necessary. It was not long after that he spotted you as well."

"So is Shane my father?" asked Adam.

"I believe so," Erikson answered as he rose from his chair. "I'm sorry Adam; this is a lot to absorb. Jarvis arrived this morning while you were still recovering. He can answer some of your questions. He's a good man, very capable but the rest of us, not so much. I'm an old man, too old for all this but I do know that now that we've found the others we need to find the answers we've been looking for," he said. The doctor deeply inhaled. "It's time for these old, tired bones to rest." He put his hand on the young man's shoulder. "None of us asked for this Adam, but we need to finish it and you need to decide for yourself what you are going to do."

Adam stared out at the water for a long time after Erikson left.

* * *

Jarvis met Munroe in the passageway. "I'd thought I might find you here. How did it go?" he inquired.

"The kid knows everything," the other man answered. "Now we wait to see what he's going to do. He's a mess, but doing well at keeping himself together. I still can't read him and can't imagine what he's going through."

Jarvis looked at his friend. **"Are you ok?"** he asked with his eyes.

"No," Munroe replied. **"I'm terrified by what we might find."**

Jarvis nodded and patted Munroe's back. "I've known you a long time and we both knew this day would come." He tried to smile. "It looks to me like you need a drink."

"Not tonight Daniel. I appreciate your concern," replied his friend, "but I can't hide from this one and I need some time." Munroe walked down the passageway alone.

"This needs to end," Jarvis said aloud. He was surprised by the raw emotion in his voice. He leaned against the wall until Erikson came in from the outer deck.

"That young man will want to talk to you," the Doctor informed him, "but by the look of you, now would not be a good time." The old man grabbed Jarvis' arm for support. "Help me to my room; it's been a really long day." The two headed slowly down the corridor.

*   *   *

Aberdeen had spent the day helping Flynn with details. They moved forward believing that Adam would make the right decision and help them. He'd left the infirmary before lunch and headed straight for his quarters. She imagined he had a lot on his mind and needed some time, but part of her wanted the chance to convince him to do the right thing.

She also wanted the chance to talk to him about decoding. She could read things the others couldn't and not even the doctor could explain why. It may be a variance with the enhancement passed to the 2nd generation or an anomaly affecting only her. Her father had returned in the helicopter early in the morning and she'd promised him she'd be patient. The others needed time to figure out how to move forward with Adam.

Knowing about the implant helped; maybe he wasn't a monster. It also explained his collapse in Talbot's office. It had unnerved Aberdeen that he'd reacted to her so strongly.

She looked at her watch and realized why she was so hungry. She'd missed dinner. On her way to the galley she again thought about what had happened to the others after the clinic fire. Aberdeen retrieved her dinner from the ice box and sat down at the table. She took a minute to explore the residual light signatures of those who had been in the galley earlier. The others couldn't do this. She noticed that Adam's signature was not among those who had gathered for dinner; nor was the doctor's. She hoped their meeting had gone well and that Adam understood how much they needed his help.

*   *   *

Adam was enjoying the cool breeze in his hair and the smell of the salt air. He'd been on the ocean many times and observed these things but he had never actually experienced them. The up and down pitch of the boat was soothing. He kept his eyes closed avoiding the overwhelming bombardment of visual information that flooded his mind with strange images. He had no idea how to filter them. He'd avoided eye contact with the doctor and Munroe; it was all too much. He obviously was going to need help from the others.

The Agency was all Adam had known for as long as he could clearly remember. He'd lived and breathed for them. They'd trained him well, provided every resource and modified his behaviour to their own ends. He felt betrayed. Adam did remember a time when he had hopes and dreams but the Agency took them from him. There were no checks or balances and they had the power to do whatever they wanted. The Agency was accountable to no one. It made Adam consider all the assignments he'd had over the years and wonder how many innocent lives were affected by the Agency's so called greater good. Then Global Security showed up and took Adam away to this ship and to these people. The Agency must have known the implant would fail or were they the ones that shut it down hoping he wouldn't recover? He was confused. Why did the Agency let him go?

. . . Then there was the news of his brother and father.

He spent a long time trying to figure things out. There was no question as to whether he would help the others; what else was there for him? He couldn't go back to the Agency. It was the first time in as long as he could remember that he thought about his future and about what he wanted. The fact that he had choices at all was still a little beyond him. Although he had gained control of his life, he'd lost control of everything else.

His newfound emotions were overwhelming. They were raw and he was unpracticed. Deep sadness and confusion bombarded him and his intellect struggled to overcome the onslaught. He realized that he couldn't reason his way out of how he felt and mixed in with all of it was the visual overload that inundated him no matter where he looked. Adam was becoming Adam again, but he had no idea who that was.

A food tray was waiting on his desk when he finally returned to his room. As he sat to eat, Adam caught a shimmering smudge of light and he froze. The image was moving, dissipating, spreading, and almost dissolving into the room around it. There was a lot to learn about the information lingering around. The world had changed for him and not just inwardly. He sat looking down at his meal; chicken, rice and peas. It was still a little warm. He considered the peas and took a bite of the green vegetable, really tasting for the first time in years and crinkled his face. He didn't like them and for a moment he marveled that it mattered. The Agency had stolen so much from him; even his likes and dislikes. He pushed his food away, no longer hungry. What Adam needed to do was run; it helped him clear his mind. In the morning he would go onto the deck, but until then he lay on his bunk frustrated, trying to sleep but knowing another set of disturbing dreams awaited.

* * *

Daniel Jarvis observed Adam. The young man was watching the crew transform the ship back into a yacht. It was obvious what the newcomer was doing. He was trying to come to terms with his new found ability; trying to regulate it. Jarvis remembered the struggles he and the others had gone through. It'd been overwhelming but they had each other and with Bergstein's help, being able to filter through the craziness, freed them to a whole new world.

In the last two days Adam's entire world had changed and no doubt so had he. Jarvis wondered what kind of man Adam was. Their first meeting had been impressive but Jarvis doubted their second encounter would play out the same way. With the implant Adam had been closed; today Jarvis hoped to get a good peg on this new recruit. Being able to trust him was paramount. The others didn't have the skills needed to find out what was going on or come against whoever had financed Bergstein.

* * *

6:45 AM and Adam was hungry. He realized he hadn't eaten much the day before. Breakfast was at 7 so he left his spot on deck to meet what awaited him in the galley. He'd decided not to get invested in these people or their problems. It was the only way he could remain focussed. Adam would help them but it would be like any other assignment. What he needed now was an objective, a plan and a breakdown of the resources available to him. He did not need a bunch of amateurs getting in his way. It was time to take control and quit wasting time. Unfortunately, Adam wasn't sure what to do next. The visual decoding thing was new to him and he hadn't much time to adjust; he really didn't know enough about it to use it effectively. He needed help.

The others were in the galley when he arrived. Breakfast smelled delicious. As he looked at the doctor, Adam could read the old man's weariness. Erikson wasn't well. The evening's rest had not helped him and it occurred to Adam that the doctor's condition was more than just the frailty of age. He was sick and Adam could tell that everyone in the room knew.

Adam took his seat and tried to remain stoic. He was surprised at the concern he felt for this man he'd just met. A blur of confusing images bombarded him as he looked at the others. Adam sat at the table, closed his eyes, and took a deep breath to clear his mind. It was then Jarvis entered the galley.

"Smith?" Adam questioned as he turned to look.

"Actually, my name is Daniel Jarvis," the tall athletic man answered. He looked at the others, quickly assessed the situation then sat next to Aberdeen. "And right now I am really hungry," he said with a smile. "Doctor, would you please pass me the pancakes?" The tension in the room lifted and a strong sense of connection and intimacy replaced it. These people truly cared for one another.

Adam attempted to remain closed, but had no idea how successful he was being. Could these people read what was going through his mind? What images was he sending?

"It's been a while Daniel," Flynn directed at Jarvis. "How's the golf swing?"

"Still better than yours," Jarvis answered with a laugh and a wink at Aberdeen.

Familiar banter continued as the group shared breakfast. Adam watched carefully as the others reconnected. He considered the dynamics of conversation. Aberdeen remained quiet, smiling and acknowledging past events with a nod or quiet laugh. They were all putting on brave faces for Erikson, normalizing their behaviour as if at any morning get together. Their eyes however betrayed them and Adam could decode the underlying sadness and stress that prevailed. It forced him to close his eyes and as he reopened them he saw Jarvis briefly put his arm around Aberdeen's shoulder.

"It's okay, Sugarplum," he told his daughter, "be strong."

"I know Dad," she replied, deciding to distract herself with breakfast.

Adam's eyes began to burn as he watched them. He needed to stop the flood of emotion. He didn't want to become attached to these people. Attachment led to weakness. Adam looked at his plate. He hadn't touched his food. Determined to regain focus he began to eat. He concentrated on the sweet taste of the syrup and the crispness of the bacon. He was hungry and centered his attention on sating his appetite. Every bite was a new experience with taste and texture. Adam started to feel better.

"Enough of this small talk," the Doctor finally declared abruptly. "The boy's had enough time to get his wits about him. It's time to get down to brass tacks; time is short."

"Doctor . . . ," Munroe began.

"Save it Ken," Erikson continued. "I'm a big boy and I know how you are all feeling, but my goal right now is to see this mess to the end. We've been striving toward this for too long to let it fall to the wayside. We need to get moving."

Everyone was silent, allowing the old man to direct his attention to Adam. "You need to decide what you are going to do Adam and you need to do it now. We'll be in port in three days and need to be ready. There is much to do either way." He swallowed looking at the others; each one in turn. "None of you deserve this. I don't deserve this, but who else is there? We know that whoever was funding Bergstein had an agenda. We need to find out what happened to the others. We know they are involved in something big; something that is no doubt big trouble." There was a pause. "Three days people, get busy." Before leaving Erikson glanced over at Adam.

After the doctor left no one spoke for several minutes. The gravity of the situation settled heavily on the group. Jarvis cleared his throat and turned to the few crew men that remained in the galley.

"You guys can head out please," He addressed them. "We need to talk privately. Thank you for breakfast; it was delicious." Jarvis received a crisp nod from both men as they left.

"What time does Abby have to leave, Flynn?" Jarvis asked. His demeanour had changed. All levity was gone. It was obvious Jarvis was in control and there was already a plan in place.

"The lass' interview is at 6 o'clock tomorrow. With this weather, I would say first thing in the morning," Flynn looked at his watch. "Around 7 am." Flynn took out his note pad and jotted something down then looked over at Aberdeen. "Did the passports print successfully?" he asked.

"Yes," Aberdeen answered, "but all the photos can't be added until the team makes sure none of you will be recognized; wardrobe will be arriving in Leith, on Monday morning with Lee and Tina. They'll be there at about 10:30 to work out the details. The hotel has been booked; check in time is 2pm Tuesday." She looked at her Adam. "You need to be at the airport at 1:30 that same day to meet your car."

"Aberdeen will need at least an hour with the kid before she leaves," Munroe added. "There are certain things only she can help him through." Everyone turned and looked at Adam. "The choice is yours kid; it's now or never." Ken urged." We can give you a new identity, and money. We can fly you anywhere in the world. This is only your battle if you make it your battle. Are you in?" he asked.

Adam was amused at how the others referred to him. The lad, boy and kid comments were out of place. It was as if they hadn't read Adam's file. They must know what he was capable of.

Adam looked at each one of their faces. He'd been wrong, these people weren't desperate; they were determined. Smith's arrival had surprised him. Somehow these people had managed to get Adam away from the Agency and they'd watched him in Barcelona without his knowledge. He was usually in control or at least that it what he'd thought. It's what had kept him alive and made him so effective. So much had changed in the last two days and he couldn't help second guessing himself. He would help them, but his nature fought the idea. What the Agency had done had blindsided him. Adam's loyalty would remain tenuous. He would be very careful not to put his life or future in anyone else's hands; including the people that sat before him.

"I'm in," Adam answered, "but when we get your answers I'll take you up on your offer. I'm not looking for a family or storybook ending."

"Agreed," Jarvis replied crisply. "Now moving forward; let's gather in the meeting room in 20 minutes so we can go over details. That will give Adam a chance to get up to speed with what we already have in place and perhaps he can give some input as to what he thinks we may have overlooked. By then, my people should have gotten back to me as to what they have found out about our targets."

"Afterward would be a good time for Ken to spend some time with Adam," Jarvis continued. He turned and looked at the new team member. "You need to get a handle on the ins and outs of decoding." Rising to his feet he reminded his daughter. "Make yourself available at some point along the way Abby; I'm sure there will be questions Munroe can't answer. Alright, see you in 20 minutes everyone."

The group dispersed and Adam found himself sitting alone at the table. He rubbed his face. He took the last drink of his orange juice then left for his quarters.

CHAPTER 4

WHEN ADAM ARRIVED IN the meeting room Flynn was busy typing on a lap top. "Hey Laddie," he acknowledged and motioned to a file on the table. "Have a look in there. It will give you a chance to get up to speed before the others arrive." Flynn nodded and then turned his attention back to the screen in front of him.

Adam got comfortable and opened the file. The first page was an aged newspaper article about the clinic fire. A small picture of a building engulfed by flames was followed by a brief summary of what was headlined as, "Luxury Retreat Ends in Tragedy." There was no mention of Bergstein's research or of the survivors. Adam turned the page.

Several pages followed showing a series of photographs capturing the same three individuals on a least 4 separate occasions. There were others in the photos but it was obvious which three were of interest. From afar one looked strikingly like Adam. The other man was older and it was obvious that he was not someone to be underestimated. The third was a young woman. All were dressed in dark clothes and were clearly providing security for those around them. Below the photographs, the location and date of each was recorded with a brief note naming the others present. They took place over a 2 year period.

Adam put the file down and exhaled. He was very familiar with what the photos had captured and he understood the concerns that Erikson and the others had expressed. He took a moment and considered what they were up against. Adam went back to the file and turned to the next page. Its heading didn't surprise him; The Van Hussen Group. Nothing in the report was new to him, but Adam knew a few things he could add. He'd run into these guys before. Many rather unpleasant activities let straight to their door. They disguised their comings and goings within a handful of humanitarian organizations and societies. On the surface The Van Hussens were always willing to lend a hand and could get things done but there was always a hidden agenda. Non Profit Humanitarian Organizations loved them. Some of the most powerful people in the world were connected to the group and they did indeed have deep pockets.

He turned to the next page. It was a press release: The 2007 Edinburgh World Economic Summit. He finished reading through the rest as the others arrived; the doctor was not among them. When everyone had settled Flynn projected one of the photos on the big screen. It had the best view of the three faces they were all interested in.

"This is outside the Royal Duchess Hotel in Jakarta on July 5th, two years ago." Flynn explained. "It was the first appearance of Shane Stevens we have been able to track. We initially spotted him three months ago at a Cairo hotel." Flynn put up another photograph from the file.

"My people were able to track him from the hotel to an abandoned warehouse outside the city," Jarvis added. "A very influential group of people were meeting there. It was then we discovered that the Van Hussen Group was involved. Go back to the first picture please Flynn," he asked.

"Have a really good look at these faces Adam," Flynn instructed. As the first picture returned to the screen a red laser pointer circled a young man. He was opening a back, passenger car door in front of the hotel entrance. "This is Elena's first son. We have traced him to three different names, all no doubt aliases. If I remember right, he was named Jonathan. He's 26 years old and is a 2nd generation receiver. After your session with Munroe we'll have a better idea of exactly what that might mean. If you exhibit the same abilities as Aberdeen we can only assume that the additional enhanced adaptations are typical to all of the children."

Adam looked carefully at the face on the screen and then went to the same image in the file. The similarities were striking. With a haircut and a few minutes of observing body language and facial expressions Adam could easily be mistaken for his brother.

"And this," Flynn continued as the laser moved to the young woman, "We believe is Sophia's daughter, again a second generation receiver. She is the right age and body type that we would expect. She also looks a lot like Sophia."

Munroe coughed back emotion. The others became quiet and Jarvis walked over to his friend and put his hand on his shoulder. Adam was uncomfortable with the display. He struggled with his own feelings in order to remain objective and in control. He looked carefully again at the man he now knew was his brother and reflected on what could have been. He felt a heaviness that he'd never felt before; regret. Adam put his head in his hands and swallowed hard. He looked at the others. To regain composure, he began to slow his breathing.

"We need to stop this," Adam finally whispered. He took another breath and cleared his throat. "I do not mean to seem callous but we need to set our emotions aside or this is not going to work." He looked at Munroe. "We can only imagine what these people are up to; if you are attached and unable to do what needs to be done you need to walk away now."

"Adam . . ." Aberdeen interjected, "you're out of line."

"No Lass, he's not," Flynn stated. "Time is short. The Doctor was right, none of us deserve this. Ken . . . you don't deserve this, hell, your daughter didn't deserve this, but this is the way it is. These people were stolen from us. We can't change that. We don't know what is ahead but chances are things won't end well, but they do need to end."

Adam stood holding the file in his hand. "I don't know what you've all been going through for the last 25 years," he said, "I cannot imagine." Adam's voice remained calm. He took another deep breath. "I do know that in the last two days everything for me has changed, so much that it is almost overwhelming, . . . but," Adam paused. "Munroe . . ." He searched for words before he continued. "One way or the other, we can save her from this." He lifted the file. "Can you set your feelings aside or at least find a way to use them in order to do that?"

Munroe looked at him and suddenly it was as though Adam had been punched in the stomach. A wave of pain and sadness flooded from the other man's eyes. Tortured images flashed before Adam. He braced himself as he lived through a series of agonizing events that had happened before he was born. He found himself looking out a barred window as the woman he loved was pushed into a helicopter. He could smell smoke and hear screaming. Adam stood his ground; determined but shaken.

The room was silent as the others watched the two men engage. Adam's knees became weak but he battled to remain resolute. With all his strength he fought to not become overwhelmed by Munroe's pain. The longer he stood his ground the less intense the emotion became, until finally Munroe exhaled heavily and looked away.

Adam scanned the room; everything was seemed cloudy again. He could see the others talking but couldn't hear their voices. He felt someone take him by the arm and help him into a chair. Everything had slowed. Adam watched as Jarvis took Munroe by the shoulders and looked at his face. Munroe was nodding but seemed lost. Jarvis glanced over at Adam. His lips were moving but no sound came out. He motioned to Flynn. Adam watched as Flynn and Munroe left. It was like watching a silent movie. He was floating. The sensation ended abruptly and he grabbed onto his chair. As his senses returned he could see the concern on Jarvis.

"What just happened?" Adam gasped. He put his head between his knees trying to fight off nausea.

"Take it easy," Jarvis cautioned, "Give yourself a minute to recover."

"Recover from what?" Adam's breathing was shallow and he was becoming light headed. "What do you people want from me? How much do you thing I can take? I thought you wanted my help." Raw frustration erupted from Adam. "I just want this all to stop." His head was in his hands.

"That should never have happened," Aberdeen sobbed.

"That and everything else," Adam raged breathlessly.

Jarvis looked at his daughter, "Go, check on Ken."

"But Daddy . . ." her tear filled eyes answered.

"Go . . . now," was his firm but gentle reply. Closing the door behind her, she left without another word.

Adam looked at Jarvis. "This is a really bad dream and I keep hoping I'm going to wake up." He shook his head. "But I'm not going to wake up am I?" he asked not expecting an answer. "I don't need to live someone else's nightmare; I'm in one of my own." The young man shook his head. "The ironic thing is that I'd been asleep for eight years. I didn't even remember I liked pancakes until this morning." He sat back in his chair and inhaled deeply. "There are times that I would just switch the implant back on if I could."

Jarvis watched the young man across the table struggling with so much. They'd all been so caught up that they'd forgotten about what he was going through. He remembered their first real meeting in Talbot's office. It had only been two days and since then everything had changed for the kid. He'd seen a glimpse of the strong, confident Adam earlier but now Jarvis didn't know what to do. Adam had to know that everything wasn't always going to be this hard. Jarvis went over to his stack of papers and retrieved a file of photographs from near the bottom of the pile. His people had finally found the letters. He placed it in front of Adam opening it to a photograph.

It took a long while before Adam picked up the photo. Jarvis could see the recognition in the young man's eyes as he studied it. It was of better days; everyone was smiling. Adam brushed his finger over his mother's face and felt deep sadness. He wondered where she was. Standing next to her in the photograph was a young Shane Stevens, his arm around her shoulder. Adam took his time studying the two of them. His father was extremely tall and well proportioned. He looked as though he should be riding atop a dark horse somewhere out on the plains. His jaw was set yet his eyes shone with amusement. Elena's head leaned onto his him like it was created just to be there. Shane held her close. They were happy and obviously in love. Adam closed his eyes; it hurt to think of the things that could have been; for the things that had been stolen.

"I had sent these to my parents many years ago," Jarvis told him. "This is what we remember and we need to know what happened."

Adam looked back at the photograph. Next to his parents Flynn grinned as he held a young woman with long blonde hair. His own hair, tousled, curly and red, gleamed in the sun. Munroe, with his arms tightly wrapped around a beautiful girl with blonde hair, scrunched his face as if straining to hold on. She laughed as she pretended to pull away. Another couple Adam didn't recognize smiled at the camera. On the end was Jarvis. He looked like a teenager. He stood with a crooked smile holding hands with young woman with long braided hair and freckles. She was lovely and she had Aberdeen's eyes; green and penetrating.

"That is how it began," Jarvis remembered. He looked far away; caught up in the past. "That is what life is about; joy, happiness, belonging. It was good. We were young, fearless and in the middle of something extraordinary. We were on top of the world blazing new ground. Dr. Bergstein was amazing. He not only made us able to decode, but he brought us through the experience with hope and expectation. It didn't have to turn out the way it did, but when things started to turn bad, they turned bad quickly."

There were more pictures; images of better times. Adam felt his eyes begin to burn. He put the file down and closed its cover.

"I cannot do this," Adam motioned to the file. "I think my head might explode." He took a deep breath and rubbed his eyes. He waited until his heart stopped pounding in his chest before he continued. "I understand your motivation but at this point more emotion will only be an obstacle; believe me it is so much easier without all the baggage." He shook his head, "so much easier." Adam picked up the file filled with photographs and handed it back to Jarvis. "I don't need this. Getting attached to these people or a past that could have been will not help me. I have read through the plan. If we are going to do this, let's do it. Stuff like what happened earlier will get us all killed. We need to get a handle on it and we need to work out some details. How many people do you have on the outside?"

"Eight," answered Jarvis.

"Eight?" Adam was surprised. "What about Global Security?"

Jarvis looked amused. "Global Security existed for the explicit purpose of getting you away from the Agency."

"Hmmm," Adam paused. He debated as to whether to let his guard down. "Jarvis," he said, "I don't know if this decoding thing is going to help me or make everything more difficult. It's just so much all at once. At another time, in another place . . ."

"I'll order some lunch and get Flynn back in here so we can hammer out some details." Jarvis replied. "Afterward you can spend some time with Aberdeen. I would prefer you meet with Ken but under the circumstances she will do. Hopefully it'll help you feel better about it all." He looked at Adam. **"You and my daughter have an ability to remain closed that I don't understand. I can only assume all of the children are similar."**

"For me, right now, it is fear," Adam answered as he turned away. "At this point I'm not sure I even want to know mess the Agency has left me with." He cleared his throat. "Lunch sounds good," he quickly changed the subject. "I'm hungry."

CHAPTER 5

MUNROE FELT TERRIBLE. FLYNN had been called away but the Doctor had arrived. Aberdeen told him of the events in the meeting room. Erikson sat quietly and listened.

"I don't know what came over me," Ken lamented. "It was a stupid, stupid thing to do. I just wanted him to know and it got so out of hand. I wasn't expecting him to receive as much as he did." Aberdeen sat beside him holding his hand.

"I think it's one of the added adaptations," Aberdeen interjected. "My abilities came gradually when I was young but he is being bombarded with everything at once."

"How did the boy fair?" asked the Doctor.

"Dad stayed with him and Flynn was just called back," Aberdeen replied. "He was pretty shook up when I left. He was disoriented and nauseous for quite a while." Aberdeen was worried; she nibbled on her lip. It'd been so intense, yet Adam stood his ground. She shook her head.

"And you Ken?" the Doctor inquired.

"I'm exhausted . . . but a big weight has been lifted; he took it all," Munroe put his head in his hands. "Adam is the one we should be concerned about. How could I do that to him? Doctor, I don't know what to say."

Erikson was intrigued. "It is what it is Ken. The boy continues to surprise us. The additional enhancements may be consistent in all 2nd generation individuals. Aberdeen what do you think?"

"I think I need to spend some time with him, but time is short."

* * *

Adam was satisfied. Both Jarvis and Flynn had proved to be very smart men. They'd done their homework and everything was in place. The collaboration went well. His whole adult life had been about manipulating people to his own ends or rather to the Agency's ends. This was different. Adam hadn't spent his time calculating his every action or playing a role set before him. He'd brought his expertise forward and shared it as Adam. It was a new experience and it wasn't easy. He still had trust issues with the others and with himself. Now he needed to find Aberdeen, but she made him nervous. He also needed to face Munroe. If he couldn't get a better understanding of decoding, success would be impossible. He found them both sitting on the deck.

"Adam I . . ." Munroe began, rising to his feet.

"Save it," Adam interrupted. He looked him straight in the eye. "What's done is done." He narrowed his gaze. "What happened does not concern me as much as that fact that it happened at all. You will get us all killed if you do not find a way through this. Figure it out or walk away. A loose cannon is not something I am willing to chance." Adam showed no compassion; compassion led to weakness. He was regaining control. "There will be no second chances." It was a threat. Both Munroe and Aberdeen could tell Adam was very serious.

"Now," Adam changed his tone, "I have got to figure this out and I as much as I do not want to admit it, I need help." He shook his head. "For some reason I cannot seem to focus my thoughts in such a way that they can be seen and filtering through the craziness is giving me a headache."

Aberdeen looked at Munroe, **"I'll be back shortly."** She knew the two had to come to terms with what happened and she didn't want to give either the chance to sweep it under the table. Everyone had to work together.

"That is my first question," Adam declared. "Is there a way of transmitting information so that only one person can decode it?"

Aberdeen smiled. "No or at least we haven't figured it out yet and we've been trying a long time. Ken truly is the best person to help you through this." As she departed Aberdeen looked deep into Adam's eyes. He felt exposed. **"Be patient Adam; it's like riding a bike. Once you figure it out there'll be a huge learning curve."**

Once the two men were alone there was an awkward silence. "Adam . . . ," Munroe tried to apologize for a second time.

"I said let it go Munroe," Adam interrupted again. "We need to move on. I have a lot to learn and there is not much time."

*　　*　　*

Aberdeen found Jarvis watching the two men she'd left on deck. She slipped in beside him and tucked herself under his arm. It was the only place she ever felt truly safe.

"Well," her father asked, "is he going to play nicely."

"For now," she replied. "It's strange, as hard as I try I still can't read him. What is he hiding?"

Jarvis took his daughter by the shoulders and looked gravely into her eyes. "Everything," he answered. "If you start feeling comfortable around him I want you to remember what you read in his file. He is dangerous, and even more so now."

"But the Agency, the implant . . ."

"Abby, he's a chameleon." Jarvis was adamant. "I've asked him to pretty much go into the middle of this alone and he didn't even bat an eye. He's not stupid and certainly doesn't have a death wish. You know what he's capable of and what he's done in the past. He's made it very clear that once this is over he'll leave. Don't get attached, he certainly doesn't intend to." It was a warning based on fear, but it was the truth. Jarvis hadn't wanted to get Aberdeen involved in any of this. Adam was right about one thing. Emotions had to be set aside. "I don't want to lose you too, Sugarplum," he said as his held her in his arms. "Don't take any chances in Edinburgh."

*   *   *

After a brief explanation of decoding mechanics, Munroe handed Adam a package.

"You are not the only one who has trouble filtering information," he said, "we all do, except Aberdeen. You still may be able to learn how to control this on your own. Until then . . ." Inside the package was a pair of glasses. "They have three settings," Munroe explained. "Information comes in three waves: ambient thought, emotion and focussed communication. Ambient thought is the most confusing because the average brain jumps around. A person's attention span determines the amount of time they spend thinking about any one thing. We can glean a lot of information about someone by decoding their ambient thought but when there is more than one person it becomes difficult to figure out who is thinking what and when there are many people it becomes impossible."

Munroe took his own glasses out of his pocket. "They work both ways," he continued. "You and Aberdeen seem to have more success with blocking your thoughts; the rest of us depend on these things. Pay attention to my words and thoughts; try to sort through them," Munroe instructed. Adam concentrated. The thoughts were random: playing golf, a rainstorm, driving a car. He looked deeper: sadness, shame, fear, anticipation. "Once you can distinguish the different waves try the glasses."

Two settings filtered emotion or ambient thought, the third both. Focussed thought was not affected. "These are incredible," Adam took the glasses off and studied them.

"Doctor Erikson and I developed them over many years." Munroe informed Adam. "They have made our lives much easier. Be very careful with them; they are not easy to come by and if a decoder cannot see your thoughts they might become suspicious." Munroe got very serious. "Now as for phase two, we need to break down this wall you've put up which makes you unreadable." He squirmed a little in his chair. "You are going to have to trust me. If you can't I'll get Aberdeen, but I don't think you really want that.

This may get messy." Munroe took a moment. "I screwed up earlier and you saw my worst . . . you lived it." He shook his head. "I respect the fact that you haven't thrown it back in my face."

"Munroe," Adam replied, "I have already told you to move on; forget it."

"It's not about apologizing anymore Adam," Munroe insisted. "It's about how this works. You need to figure out how tall your wall can be without affecting your ability to transmit." He leaned closer. **"I've had a wall for years,"** the older man assured Adam, **"and I can help you if you let me."**

*   *   *

They waited for the two men to arrive for dinner. Adam had been told 6 o'clock but they were late. After Aberdeen left to pack, Jarvis had watched them for a while. It hadn't been easy for either of them and now no one at the table spoke. The entire plan hinged on Munroe's success with Adam. As the food arrived so did the two latecomers. They both looked exhausted. Everyone looked at Adam expectantly.

"What's for dinner?" he asked. A collective sigh of relief filled the cabin. Jarvis dismissed the crew with a crisp nod as the group began their meal. Adam was subdued. He kept his eyes on his plate. He'd been sick to his stomach several times and really didn't feel like eating. The things he'd remembered made him angry and he'd had a hard time. He was exhausted. They'd rebuilt his wall but the small glimpse of what he allowed Munroe to see on the other side disturbed him. He realized the wall was not just there to keep the others out but to protect himself. Munroe said it wasn't Adam's fault and that was true, but he'd been there and done those things and he remembered.

"You look like you had a good rest Doctor," Flynn commented as he took a large bowl of carrots from Erikson. "Personally I'll be glad when this is all done so I can beat Daniel in that round of golf he promised me." He winked at Aberdeen. She chuckled softly. "Or maybe we will bring the young lad along and he can show us both a thing and two." Flynn looked over at Adam. **"It's okay Laddie, we are all right here with ya."**

The problem was that didn't help. Adam wanted to be alone; he needed to run. He needed to get rid of a lot of pent up energy; it'd been building for days. Adam took a deep breath to change his countenance. "Pass the carrots," he requested with a grin.

* * *

The wind gently tickled Aberdeen's face as she watched the moon slide softly behind the clouds. Adam would meet with her soon. He'd said very little at dinner and left with Munroe, promising to meet with her at around 8 o'clock. She waited in the small lounge area that looked out onto the observation deck. It was a cool night but she'd opened the window hoping to smell the salty air.

"So why do you want to work in Edinburgh?" Adam asked as he entered, "seems like it is a long way from home."

Aberdeen was confused. "What are you talking about?"

"I want to make sure you are ready," Adam answered. "Believe it or not it is easier to play a role than pretend to be someone." He took the chair next to Aberdeen. "It makes it more believable," Adam continued. "If you react in a way that is natural to the situation based on the character you have become you do not have to make up stuff on the fly. You find yourself acting naturally and thereby you are more convincing."

What he said made sense but Aberdeen still couldn't read Adam and was uncertain. She knew she could hide her thoughts from the others, but always had been able to see theirs. It had frustrated her father for years and now she too was frustrated.

"I need your help," Adam continued. "Munroe tried but he is missing something that you have. Tell me how are we different." Aberdeen took a deep breath.

"My skills are more refined and I can hide my thoughts. Somehow I have the ability to impede the transmissions at their source. I also filter more effectively than the others," Aberdeen replied. "The glasses are helpful but with some practice you should be able to tune out what you don't want without them." She thought for a moment. "It's like concentrating on one voice in a room full of voices or maybe perhaps . . . rather like . . . instead of looking at the smudges on window glass looking through the window at what is beyond. It all comes down to focus." She grinned slightly. "I have spent hours with my father trying to help him get the hang of it but he can't. His brain isn't wired that way." She looked at Adam. "You've obviously figured out how block your thoughts. It's a big advantage but other decoders will wonder why they can't read you and that could be a problem. Wearing the glasses brings up the same issue."

"I need to be able to do more than just block my thoughts," Adam asserted. "I need to be able to manipulate them so the others will only see who I want them to see." Adam rubbed his face. Exhaustion was setting in but there was little time for rest. "With Munroe I could sense I was sending more than he could decode."

"I've noticed a few things over the years," the young woman replied, "but I've had no one to bounce my thoughts off of or at least no one who could understand them."

For the next two hour and a half hours the two played an elaborate game of cat and mouse with their thoughts. Adam was a quick learner and Aberdeen was amazed that most of her suspicions had been true. She felt so energized and imagined that it was how her father and the others must have felt when it had all started. They were blazing new ground. The 2nd generation indeed was unique in their ability to control which thoughts were transmitted.

They explored many possibilities. Adam didn't like surprises and wanted to know exactly what he was up against. They were both able to not only block their thoughts but to mask them. With a little practice even their ambient thought and emotion could be manipulated in such a way as to give the receiver only the information intended.

When Adam was finally satisfied Aberdeen walked to the window. "There's more," she said. "I was unable to decode until I was 14 years old. Dr. Erikson told me it took that long for the cartal gland to mature." She paused. "Not long after that I started noticing strange smudges of light; reflections of objects and people that were no longer there. It's sort of like how a smell lingers and over time dissipates into the air. Everything has a reflective quality to it and that's what I was seeing. They were light signatures left behind." Aberdeen turned and looked at Adam. "Stand beside me and look back at where we were sitting."

Adam rose to his feet and stood next to her. She didn't like being so close. He had a tangible presence and although there was space between them she moved farther away. Aberdeen wanted so much to figure him out, but he remained closed. She'd been so excited when they'd found him but now she just didn't want to feel so small when he was near.

Adam concentrated on the chair he'd left but was unable to see anything out of the ordinary. "I don't see anything," he told her.

"Don't focus on the chair," Aberdeen explained, "Try to blur your vision just slightly. Try to see yourself sitting in the chair." She watched his face for a reaction as Adam followed her instructions.

Slowly he began to notice a change. Adam could see himself. It was like looking at a time lapse photograph; his features blurry and his outline smudged. Aberdeen's image was more hazy than his own and he watched the reflections slowly start to separate and begin to dissolve into their surroundings. The paths he and Aberdeen had taken to the window were but a smear of colour and they too started to dissipate. Adam closed his eyes for a moment to refocus and when he reopened them the images were gone. With a little concentration he could again distinguish the residual light signatures.

"How long will the reflections last," he asked.

"It depends," Aberdeen answered. "If I were to change the lighting it would almost certainly destroy them, but if it remains constant they could last several hours. Of course the more time that passes the harder the images are to distinguish."

"Amazing," Adam shook his head in wonder, "and the others can't do this?"

"No," she replied, "and until now we weren't sure it wasn't just an anomaly. We should assume all of the 2nd generation can see these types of reflections."

"It sure makes going secretly into a room a little more complicated." Adam thought for a moment. "If the others can see me even after I'm gone I'm going to need some sort of flash so I can shut these things down before I leave." He turned to look out the window at the ocean. "Is there anything else I should know?" he asked.

"Yes," she began. "The 1st generation has a weakness. My mother died from it." Adam watched as Aberdeen stood tall and regained control. "The extra stimulation caused by the enhancement works the brain at an accelerated rate," she explained. "After time it starts to breakdown and without treatment eventually leads to death. Yesterday when you collapsed we all thought that's what was happening, but it didn't make sense because the doctor has assured I'm not affected. Our brains are wired for this; we were born this way. The others weren't."

"When is this breakdown expected to happen in the others?" Adam asked.

"It's already started," Aberdeen replied, "but with the proper treatment Dr. Erikson has been able to stop the process. If he had known what was happening to my mother he could have saved her."

Adam absorbed this new information. "What kind of treatment and how long does it last?" His mind was racing.

"It's a drug taken in pill form; a neurotransmitter." she explained. "How often depends on how far the breakdown had progressed prior to treatment. My father takes a pill every 16 days; Flynn about twice a week, Ken needs one daily. There are no side effects of the medication and all are able to fully function despite the deterioration. Although it does seems that decoding is affected by the breakdown of the cartal gland, before my mother died she could not decode at all. Right now the other's abilities seem unaffected." She stopped for a moment, trying to anticipate Adam's next question. "The doses have remained constant from the beginning and no change has been detected to brain integrity in any of them. The Doctor does believe however, if treatment stopped total collapse could happen in as fast as a couple of weeks."

"So we can assume that Shane and Sophia have the same limitations," Adam interjected, "unless Bergstein was able to solve the problem more permanently." His mother's face came to mind as a harsh reality faced him; without intervention she would have died years ago. He paused and swallowed hard. "My mother . . ."

"Adam, I'm so sorry." They were both quiet for a while.

Aberdeen broke the silence. "If anyone could have come up with a permanent solution it is Dr. Erikson. He spent the last eight years working on one."

"Is there any way of knowing how often Shane would need treatment?" Adam questioned. "Every sixteen days is a far cry from daily."

"We can only speculate," Aberdeen replied. "We know that my mother and Sophia were among the first group, so we assume that their deterioration timeline would be similar, although if Bergstein knew about the problem sooner with the treatments Sophia could still be alive. Your father and Flynn received the enhancements at the same time but if the problem was caught earlier or later the frequency of treatment would differ. The math would work but we don't have all the variables."

". . . unless the breakdown was discovered under the same circumstances," Adam concluded, "and treated the same way." Adam shook his head. This was all so hard to wrap his brain around to start with and the more he found out the more incredible the story became. "Is that it?"

"Yes," she replied. "You know . . ." she confided, "I always knew it would come to this but I can't shake the feeling this isn't going to end well. Do you think we can really do this?"

It was a sincere question and Adam considered carefully how to reply. Confidence was such a huge part of success. Lack of it led to weakness and weakness led to failure. **"I would not do it if I didn't.** You concentrate on doing your part and trust that the rest of us will as well." She needed to have confidence in herself as well as the others; as did he. Adam was use to doing things alone; not having to worry if someone had done their part, not leaving his life in someone else's hands. This was all new to him and he didn't like not being in control. **"This is what I do Aberdeen,"** he continued. It was the first time he'd used her name. "It is what I have done for a very long time and I am good at it; too good at it. Failure is not an option and never has been. If I thought it was not going to work I would come up with another plan that would."

She thought for a moment, unsure about quite what to say next. She bit her lip. She had so much wanted a connection with Adam. He was the only one she'd ever met who could see the world as she did and she honestly believed it was her last chance not to feel so alone in the world. Her whole life had been controlled by past events out of her control as had his. Aberdeen wanted her feelings validated. Her emotions were thick in the air; she let down her wall just enough so that Adam would understand. She didn't have the words to express how she felt.

In the past he would have turned on a switch and become everything she needed but now was different time. Adam had no idea where that would lead. Attachment was not an option, he needed to remain distant. This girl could unnerve him so easily and there would be nothing but trouble for him if he didn't stop this now. Compassion was dangerous; it led to weakness as did attachment.

"Adam . . . I . . ." Aberdeen began but couldn't finish. She looked in his eyes hoping to see understanding but found none.

"I am not like you and I cannot give you what you want," Adam stated. He was abrupt. **"You don't know me; you can't."** He took a deep breath and stepped back. "You need to stay away; I am not who you want me to be. I said I would get you people through this mess and I will, but that is all." Adam looked back out at the ocean.

Aberdeen quickly regained her composure. She'd been able to manage until now and she would not leave Adam thinking she was some emotional train wreck. She wasn't. Aberdeen smoothed out her blouse and pushed her hair behind her ears.

Exhaustion overtook Adam as he left Aberdeen but he needed to clear a few things up. He sat at his desk studying the pictures of his targets. He was looking for glasses. He spotted only one pair; they were perched on Shane's head.

* * *

Adam chose to exercise on deck rather than join the others for breakfast. He needed to work a few things out and his body needed to sweat; it had become the only time he felt in control. He was constricted on the boat. He really wanted to run, get his heart rate up and get rid of the stress he felt building inside. From the upper deck he had a good view of the helicopter pad so when the others gathered to say goodbye to Aberdeen he went down to join them.

He watched as she hugged each one in turn and tension pulled at his shoulders as she approached. She had to look up at him. Adam stepped back. Her gaze still unnerved him. **"Remember play the role; don't pretend and don't take any chances."** Aberdeen nodded, smiled at her father and got on the helicopter.

CHAPTER 6

As THE LUXURY YACHT entered port, a small customs vessel came along side and prepared to board her. The passengers and crew were ready. Everyone was on deck with passports in hand. Adam was with the crew, his uniform crisp and clean. Everything was found in order and after a brief search of the vessel its captain was given the okay to proceed into the marina.

At the dock a slim man, his fedora too big for his head, stood next to a large, smiling woman. As the yacht docked she waved and eagerly boarded, brushing Doctor Erikson's cheek with a kiss. Adam stepped back as handshakes and greetings filled the deck. People needed to feel connected. It was something he'd learned early on and was able to use to his advantage. Adam was adept at getting people to do what he wanted and could turn on the charm as needed, but things had changed; he had changed. There was no reason to manipulate the group that mulled around before him. They knew Adam was anxious to get off the yacht and as he greeted the new comers Tina gave him a suitcase in which she assured contained everything a young Russian would be traveling with. Earlier Flynn had given him his papers, money, itinerary, a watch and a cell phone. Before leaving he nodded to Erikson and paused to take a last look at the group before him.

Their affection and willingness to open themselves up gave him pause to think. Comradeship provided people a reason to do things for they wouldn't do otherwise. It was the method the doctor had used to get Adam's help, although not the reason he'd agreed. A mission was a familiar scenario and he needed at least one thing to remain constant in his life. It would take his mind off what was to come; the unknown. Adam smiled at the scene before him and imagined what it would feel like to be a part of it. He set his jaw and inhaled deeply. He didn't belong; that which he had in common with the others was coincidental. Adam didn't need the complication. It would leave him vulnerable and he was unwilling to put himself in that position. Attachment led to weakness.

"**It's an Agency lie,**" Jarvis communicated. Adam had been preoccupied and let his guard down; Jarvis had seen his thoughts. "**There is strength in numbers and most people will give more and try harder if they are personally invested in the outcome.**"

"**I am not most people,**" Adam answered. "**Failure is never an option. I do not try, I do. If one cannot think logically and make decisions based solely on the situation at hand he is likely to second guess his choice and get himself and others killed. One's own emotions must be left out of the equation. The emotions of others become variables.**" He paused and took a long hard look at Jarvis. "Don't try to get inside my head. I will help you but on my terms." He turned and began to walk away.

"This is not about you," Jarvis insisted. He grabbed onto Adam's arm. It was a mistake. With one swift movement Adam twisted his body around and pulled Jarvis toward him. Before the older man realized what was happening he found himself flat on his back with Adam's hand around his throat. Everyone on deck froze and looked toward the commotion.

"**In another place or at another time,**" Adam warned, "**you would be dead. Don't underestimate me.**" He let Jarvis go and helped him to his feet but his eyes held the threat. "Not to worry everyone," he said for all to hear. "It seems the deck is a bit slippery and our friend took a bit of a spill."

"I'm okay," Jarvis declared, as he straightened out his jacket and rubbed his neck. "I will catch up with you all in the meeting room shortly. Adam and I have a few details to work out first." He smiled in assurance and both men waited in uncomfortable silence until they were alone.

"I have no need to meet with the others," Adam replied abruptly. "I'll see at the hotel tomorrow." He turned again to leave.

"Adam wait," Jarvis called after him. The young man stopped, knowing what was coming next. This was not about him at all; it was about Aberdeen. "I need you to promise me something," Jarvis insisted. "I need you to keep my daughter safe."

Adam considered the man standing before him. Jarvis was strong, capable and controlled, yet there was a flaw in his armour. He was proof that personal involvement was a limitation that could not be easily overcome. It may well totally cripple a man, leaving no logical reasoning. Emotion was dangerous and to be avoided. "What if keeping her safe means failure?" asked Adam. He already knew the answer.

"Promise me Adam," Jarvis insisted ignoring his pride. "If you don't, I'll pull the plug on this whole thing right now." He shook his head. "Even if it means failure—I can't bear to lose anyone else, promise me."

Adam thought quickly. He worked out the different scenarios he was up against, carefully going over each aspect and detail of what was ahead. This was not ideal but nothing ever was. **"I promise"**, Adam finally answered, **"but failure is still not an option and never underestimate me again."** With that he turned and left Jarvis standing on deck.

*　*　*

The Agency had trained him well; never take anything for granted. So much so that only weeks after his first assignment away from the Compound, Adam had begun to develop a back up network of resources independent of the Agency. They had no knowledge of it. Not far from the Marina he went into a crowded market and bought a deposable cell phone. Then he found a quiet bench away from the busy shoppers. Adam set his suitcase beside him and dialed a number that he had dialed many times before.

"Pizza," answered the voice on the other end.

"I'm looking for curry do you have any suggestions?" Adam replied.

"Chinese or East Indian?" the voice inquired.

On cue Adam answered, "Hungarian."

"Acknowledged," the voice affirmed.

"It's Franco," Adam continued. "I'm in Edinburgh and I need papers and funds."

The voice remained quiet for but a moment. "Fifteen minutes," it responded and the line went dead.

Adam sat back, closed his eyes and slowed his breathing. The sounds around him became more pronounced and he began to focus on a voice over by the produce section of the market. Its thick brogue filled his ears and his brain began to work through the intricacies of the accent. He listened for dialect and slang. Satisfied Adam switched his attention to the softer more musical voice of the shop keeper. Again he began to work through the intonations of the words spoken. He sat up as his phone rang.

"Hello," he answered.

"Pizza."

"Its Franco," Adam confirmed.

"341 Strathcona Place, ask for Doogan," the voice replied. "He's an unknown; be on your guard." The line went dead.

Adam left the Market via the employees' lounge where he grabbed an over coat and wool cap from the employee coat rack. With his suitcase in hand Adam spoke quietly to himself. As he quickly walked towards the bus stop he practiced the thick Scottish brogue.

Identical, narrow flats lined Strathcona. A set of stairs led up to each entrance; decorative railings and flat numbers were the only way to distinguish between them. Adam only stayed long enough to get what he needed. Although Doogan was an unknown, he knew what he was doing. He asked no questions other than those necessary and sent Adam on his way with two passports which included supporting documents and 15000 Euro. Adam found decoding to be of great benefit. He'd known exactly what the crusty old man was thinking and was able to let his guard down if only just a little. It gave him the opportunity to make a mental list of the things he needed to do before meeting his car at the airport the following day.

*   *   *

Luka Reznikov: age 26, diplomatic translator, nationality: Russian.

Adam took a deep breath. He sat in a small hotel room next to the airport. Four shopping bags filled with the items he'd put on his list sat on the floor. His suitcase's contents covered the bed. Jarvis' people knew what they were doing. Every detail had been looked after; most items had a Russian brand name or label. Included was a small briefcase with 1000 rubbles and a credit card in Reznikov's name from the Hansabank of Estonia. This identity package rivalled anything the Agency had provided. Jarvis was a man with pull and knowledge but Adam was not surprised. It had taken some doing to get him away from the Agency, never mind associate him with it. These people were of means and knew how to get things done. The Economic Conference was one of the most secure venues in the world and they had somehow managed to get on the inside. Adam wondered if there was more to Jarvis than he was letting on. In the long run it didn't matter. Adam would get the job done. It was the down time he struggled with. It gave him time to think and thinking was dangerous.

A lot had happened in the last week and it was catching up to the young man. At 24 years old Adam had been around the world and lived dozens of different lives. He'd never been concerned about what was to come next but now it was all he could think about. He shook his head and ran his hands over his face. He kept trying to convince himself that this was just like any other assignment, but it wasn't. Without the implant Adam's world had become a moment by moment battle with feelings he didn't understand.

Decoding only made matters worse and the episode with Munroe had profoundly changed him. Logically he'd known the roller coaster ride others operated on and had been able to use it to his advantage. Not being bound by a conscience and being unable to truly empathize had made Adam who he was: calculated, detached and deadly. Now, it was only his intellect and training that allowed him to continue. His new reality was almost too much to bear, so he determined to set it aside and move forward as he always had. But he was struggling. The others had gotten to him. He could see they had something; something he wanted to be a part of and it made him feel weak but for Adam weakness was not an option.

He stood and went to the bathroom sink. Again he didn't recognize the face looking back at him. Again, for what seemed the hundredth time over the last week, he splashed cold water on his face and took a long drink from his cupped hands. *Keep it together Adam*, he told himself, *you are stronger than this.* With his heart pounding Adam watched himself in the mirror. He slowed his breathing: *breathe in, breathe out . . . breathe in, breathe out.* He straightened his shoulders and set his jaw. *Better*, he thought. He went to the bed and retrieved a file folder.

Inside was the floor plan of the Atlantic Hilton and Conference Centre. It was where the conference was to be held and where the majority of the players were to stay. The Conference itself would last 4 full days with an opening night for registration. In the first few days Adam would need to get a good idea of how the security would work and where everyone would be stationed. Jarvis would help with that. He had somehow managed to get himself hired as one of the security. With inside information, pin pointing exactly when and where the best place to move in on the targets would be easier.

Aberdeen had done her job well. As one of the personnel coordinators, she had managed to get Adam assigned directly to Kristof Hoffman. He was a major European Economist, and would be accompanied by several of his staff including Shane and Jonathan. Jarvis' people had been able to track them and although neither had ever been directly connected with Hoffman in the past, several of the most powerful and influential people in Europe were known to belong to the Van Hussen group. They had no intel on the girl.

Adam carefully studied the hotel's floor plan and made a mental note of where he and the others were staying. His room was centrally located on the 8th floor and it would be surrounded by rooms filled by members of the Diplomatic Translator's Pool. The targets would be on the 12th floor, three doors down from the elevator. Adam carefully calculated how long it would take to get from one to the other before he switched his attention to the Conference Schedule. It laid out the entire 5 day timetable including smaller brainstorming, information and regional sessions, plus their locations within the Hotel. He still did not have the intel on where Hoffman would be or whether his staff were expected to accompany him.

There were so many variables and unanswered questions. Adam looked up from the page and measured the next few days. There were a lot of things he needed to figure out still and there was so little time. *First things first,* Adam thought to himself, *Luka Reznikov who are you?* Adam considered his new role. *What kind of person would best serve my purpose?*

* * *

The young Russian confidently walked away from his arrival gate, the strap of his satchel draped over his shoulder and his forest green scarf loosely wrapped around his neck. Luka Reznikov's beard was neatly groomed and his eyes sparkled with adventure and daring. Adam had spent at least 45 minutes in front of the mirror deciding how to hold his jaw in order to change the contours of his face. He also kept his eye brows higher making himself look more open. As he entered the baggage area, two young women caught his eye and he smiled. They turned to each other giggling. He approached them, aware of their older female companion standing nearby.

"Hello beautiful ladies," he complimented with a thick Russian accent. "It seems my day has just become a little brighter in light of our acquaintance." He winked at them and extended his hand. "I am Luka and you two lovely ladies are?" His charm was disarming but before either girl could reply their grandmother stepped between them and the flirtatious stranger.

"Excuse me young man," the old woman interjected, "but I am sure you have better things to do then harass young girls at the Airport." Her eyes shot daggers but her thoughts betrayed her; she was amused. Luka flashed his biggest grin.

"Oh my," he mused, "a third lovely lady." He bowed, took the woman's hand and gently pressed it to his lips. "It is my honour to make your acquaintance also." As he straightened he spotted a uniformed driver holding a sign with his name on it. "Unfortunately my car has arrived and I must depart." He gave the girls a quick wink. Retrieving his suitcase from the conveyor belt he flashed them one more smile then headed toward his driver.

*　*　*

Aberdeen was enjoying herself. She was meeting new people and learning new things. She'd been able to match Adam with Hoffman and now was playing the role of a young intern working the job of a lifetime. She knew it would be short lived but she liked her new friends and was enjoying every minute of Alison Mitchell's life. She was behind the registration desk listening to her co-worker and roommate share the story of the previous night's party when she spotted him. He looked so much like Adam it took her breath away; tall, athletic and confident. The features were similar to Adam's but he carried himself differently and there was something else but she couldn't quite put her finger on it. Careful to mask her thoughts, Aberdeen smoothed her suit jacket and took a deep breath. She smiled as his group approached. An older man stepped forward.

"Hello, my name is Kristof Hoffman." His accent was thick.

"Hello Herr Hoffman, we expected you later in the day," Alison replied, "but we are so glad you have arrived safely. We trust your travels have gone well?" She reached into the file drawer behind the desk and retrieved a folder with Hoffman's name on it, then pressed a button on the phone. A young man arrived from the back room.

"Yes all went well," the German replied clumsily searching for the right English words.

Alison introduced the young man and instructed that he would be taking their pictures for ID cards. "The cards must be worn at all times during the Conference," she informed the group, motioning to her own clipped to her lapel. "Anyone not wearing proper identification will be detained by security, until their identity can be confirmed." Aberdeen was careful not to look at Jonathan, but made a mental note of his registered name; Franz Weber. She wanted to study him, compare him with Adam but controlled herself.

She glanced his way quickly. His thoughts were disjointed, unlike the girl's standing next to him; Anika Bauer, Munroe's daughter. Aberdeen still didn't know her given name. The young woman was on her guard watching everyone and everything. She was nervous. Shane followed the group, glasses on; carrying two large suitcases. In all, it was a group of five and as they proceeded to the back room Franz caught Aberdeen's attention. His gaze made her feel uncomfortable.

"If all the girls in Scotland are as pretty as you Alison," he told her after looking at Aberdeen's name tag, "I think I'm going to like it here." She pretended to blush and turned away.

"Jon, quit it," the girl shot at him, **"Don't get distracted. There's too much at stake."** Aberdeen was taken aback; she'd know they could control their transmissions but she was still surprised and took great care avert her eyes and mask her thoughts. It was so strange to see others that could decode. Shane shook his head and smiled gently at Aberdeen. He then put his hand on his son's shoulder and led him to the back room to get their pictures taken. The girl followed along with the others but not before she had a chance to glare at Aberdeen. It wasn't jealousy behind her gaze but before Aberdeen had the chance to figure it out Anikka Bauer was gone.

*   *   *

Registration

The car ride took 35 minutes and Luka arrived at the Conference Centre just after 2 o'clock. Upon entering Adam paused, surveying the scene and comparing the floor plan he'd studied earlier to the landscape before him. The lobby was scattered with incoming dignitaries, participants and security. Several small groups lounged in the chairs clustered throughout the large open area. He quickly counted the security and noted that Jarvis was among them. He was wearing a pair of Erikson's glasses. To the left signs directed those in the Diplomatic Translation Pool to go down the hall and register in a small conference room. Other signs pointed the way for the many other groups expected at the Conference. Behind the front desk stood Aberdeen, politely informing the new arrivals as to where to go. She was relaxed and smiling. Adam paused for a moment to watch her. He narrowed his gaze and rubbed his brow. She was totally absorbed and playing her role perfectly. *Good girl*, Adam thought to himself, *just don't do anything stupid.* As he walked toward his registration area he glanced over at Jarvis and caught his eye. It took a moment for the older man to recognize him, and then with a quick nod of acknowledgment, Luka Reznikov made his way down the hallway to the conference room.

*   *   *

Jarvis smiled. Adam had transformed himself. For a brief moment he was certain that everything was going to work out; the kid was truly amazing.

He hadn't recognized Adam at first. His appearance in no way resembled the young man from the yacht and it had already been a long day. Jarvis had reported to the Security Department at 6 am and once he finished the extensive orientation he'd gotten straight to work. After the initial registration, he would be assigned to the Main Conference. Most dignitaries had their own security so he and more than 50 others were responsible for the facility's overall comings and goings. They were also to ensure that everyone displayed the proper identification whenever on the site. Each name tag contained a minute computer chip that would help validate its authenticity and let security know if its wearer was in the right location. It was a brilliant set up and would be very hard to circumvent.

He glanced over at his daughter and frowned. He knew that he really should get her out of there now, but it would bring them too much attention. Besides she wouldn't go willingly and her position at the Conference made her valuable to the operation.

Jarvis had only caught a glimpse of Shane Stevens and he'd felt the hair at the back of his neck stand on end. Shane had always been soft spoken but behind that demeanour Jarvis knew he could be someone to reckon with. What had happened to his friend? Why would he agree to get involved with the Van Hussen Group? There were so many questions. All would be known soon enough. Currently however, all Jarvis was certain of was the sick feeling he had in his stomach whenever he considered the possibilities.

* * *

Registration had been a breeze for Adam. He'd flashed his smile and flirted just a little. It was all very calculated as it had been earlier at the airport. Decoding had confirmed the wanted reactions to his charm; it made manipulating those around him so much easier. There was no guess work. It also gave insight into who could be the most helpful providing information and who were the right people to give the alibis he would need throughout the week. He made a mental note of faces and names, categorizing them according to their usefulness. There was a brief orientation and he was given an information package.

Adam had a lot to do before the "Meet and Greet" so he didn't waste any time getting to his room. On his way he counted footsteps, observed alcoves and timed how long it took the elevator to go between floors. He was not alone in the elevator and could glean from the ambient thought of the two dark suited men next to him that they were American Secret Service and assigned to protect their Ambassador. He watched unobserved as one slid a security card into a slot on the elevator button panel in order to access the top floor.

The 8th floor was exactly as the floor plan had laid out except for a small cluster of chairs in front of a huge window by the elevator. It looked over the front entrance of the Convention Centre and Adam could see the volume of people arriving was starting to wane. He looked at his watch. He had two and a half hours before he had to be in the main ballroom.

His room was small but functional and Adam quickly searched it thoroughly before opening his suitcase. He took out a small laptop placing it on the desk. I'd been one of the things on his shopping list from the previous day. Before turning it on Adam plugged a small device into one of the computer's UBS ports; it would make his activities untraceable and hide his location. He removed his scarf and jacket, tossing them on the bed and then went to splash water on his face allowing it to relax and become Adam once again. He felt good; he was in his element. He removed his shoes and socks allowing the plush carpet to caress his feet. Adam pulled out his cell phone and read the text Aberdeen had sent; it contained the names of his targets and confirmed their room numbers. *Good Girl.* Placing the phone onto the desk, he rubbed his hands together then sat down. It was time for Adam to get down to business.

Hacking into the Conference data base took him approximately 3 minutes. For the next two hours he systematically went through every aspect of the Conference, who was there and their roles. He paid special attention to Kristof Hoffman, the meetings in which he was involved and those who were attending with him.

*   *   *

The ballroom had been transformed into an elegant dining room. Dozens of tables filled the space, each formally set for the gourmet meal that was to come. Name tags marked each setting and soft music played in the background. Adam was early and before entering he carefully snapped a rose from the flower arrangement near the door and tucked it into his lapel. His suit was well tailored and he was ready to be noticed. Adam had done his homework and made sure that Luka Reznikov's dossier was iron clad and he'd checked to see if any of the other Russian nationals were familiar with the part of Estonia Reznikov reportedly came from. It seemed unlikely. He had to ensure that when they checked his background there would be no gaps and if all things went as planned someone would be definitely checking.

Adam's ticket placed him at table 12 with Hoffman and other 3 other economists; each would be joined by an assistant. None of the targets would be present which served Adam well. He needed to focus on Hoffman without having to expend the energy and concentration on masking his thoughts from other receivers. First impressions were crucial and the lid on Adam's Pandora's Box would not be tested by Shane or Jonathan during the dinner. The young Russian's shoulders relaxed at the realization. As he surveyed the room, others began to trickle in. Waiters placed pitchers of ice water on the tables and a tangible enthusiasm began to fill the room. He stood back and watched, aware that every public area of the Convention Centre had cameras.

Luka waited until the first group arrived at his table before he took his seat. The older woman, her hair pulled tightly back against her head sat across from him. The chains attached to the arms of her glasses jingled slightly as Luka reached for her hand.

"Hello, I am Luke Reznikov it is a pleasure to make your acquaintance." He had introduced himself in English. She took his hand and nodded crisply.

"This is Greek Finance Minister Ada Cosse," her assistant replied. The woman looked at Luka and smiled although the expression on her face did not change. She was tired and the weight of the world pushed on her shoulders. Adam could see her thoughts and for a brief moment felt the extreme pressure. He closed his eyes needing to refocus. Decoding often provided him with information from others he would prefer not to know. It was a struggle to remain focussed with so much. *It's like looking through a window,* Adam recalled Aberdeen's voice, *look past the smudges.* He took his seat and looked over at Cosse's Assistant. She was young, homely and very self conscious.

"And what is your name?" Luka asked flashing his smile. He spoke in Greek.

"Her name does not matter," Minister Cosse interjected harshly. The girl turned away humiliated and Adam couldn't help but feel sorry for her. He knew the older woman was being protective but the girl did not. From the corner of his eye he spotted Hoffman, beside him a distinguished looking man in his mid 30s. Aberdeen gently guided them to the right table and as they approached Adam stood.

"Hello Herr Hoffman," Adam greeted in German, "I am Luka Reznikov and I have been assigned as your interpreter for the duration of the Conference." He paused allowing the German to introduce his companion.

"Hello," the economist answered. "This is Heinrich Maier my Personal Assistant." Adam shook Heinrich's hand and uneasiness crept up his shoulders.

"I look forward to working with you," he said.

"As do I," Heinrich answered. He was already assessing Adam.

"And who may I ask is this lovely lady?" Adam smiled as he took Aberdeen's hand and gently pressed it to his lips. "I trust you have been taking good care of these gentlemen?" He was careful not lay on too thick a Russian accent, after all Luka spoke perfect Greek and German it would only make sense that his English was clear as well.

Aberdeen smiled back; she was amused and amazed at the same time. This was a side of Adam she hadn't seen before. If she hadn't already known it was him she would have taken him for a stranger and been rather charmed. There was no trace of the unapproachable and dangerous man she'd met only a week before. Adam looked so different; his face had changed and the way he moved was not the same. She withdrew her hand. "I do what I can," Alison answered turning to the German Economist, "If there is anything you need Herr Hoffman please let me know." She looked at Adam, **"I'm glad you're here."** Turning to the woman already seated at the table Aberdeen nodded. "You also Minister Cosse, if there is anything, I am here to help." She smiled again. **"I've seen them"** she transmitted. **"I think it's the girl we are going to have to worry about."** Then she was gone.

The evening proceeded well. The others had arrived and everyone at Adam's table was friendly but after the initial introductions few were talkative. Adam flirted a little with the women, being charming and thoughtful all the while aware that he was being watched closely by Hoffman. Heinrich discussed the German's schedule with Luka, who took a notebook from his pocket to write down the details. It was just for show, Adam remembered everything. His interaction was entirely designed to induce a casual friendship with the assistant and to impress Hoffman. Decoding allowed Adam to see that Heinrich was intent on getting a good peg on this young Russian and that he was very suspicious. It was also obvious that there was no love lost between the man and his boss at least from Henry's point of view.

Adam told a few jokes, talked about how cold it was in Estonia and how he'd managed to get his education due to a generous uncle with deep pockets. Heinrich returned the conversation and all the while Hoffman watched. There was something a little off with Hoffman's assistant but Adam couldn't quite figure it out. He was hiding something. Throughout the evening Luka Reznikov helped the others communicate, switching back and forth between languages as the need arose.

A few speeches from the Conference organizers followed dinner, giving everyone instructions and summarizing the planned events. Luka kept Hoffman up to speed making sure he understood the important parts. Afterwards there was a time of mingling and cocktails. Many participants left the Ballroom. Most of Adam's table excused themselves, but Hoffman remained carefully watching his interpreter. Luka Reznikov acknowledged each party as they left, shaking hands and flashing his smile.

"I'm sure to see you again Minister Cosse," Luka noted as he took her hand gently touching it to his lips. "Not to worry, the world is all in this mess together and together it will manage." He had spoken quietly in Greek and as he released her hand Adam winked quickly at her Assistant. "Have a good evening Ladies." As she turned away Ada Cosse stiffly returned his smile and thanked him with her eyes.

Adam turned his attention to Hoffman. "If there is not anything else Herr Hoffman I will take my leave," he said extending his hand.

"Actually young Reznikov, I would like you to speak with you privately," Hoffman replied but after a brief moment he changed his mind, "but it has been a long day. It can wait." The German shook Adam's hand still trying to assess him.

"I am at your disposal," Adam replied. "My room number is 823." He reached into his pocket for his card. He jotted down his cell number and handed it to the older man. "You've no doubt read my dossier and know how I can be of help. My whole purpose for being here is to assist you and your team. I'm also hoping to make some contacts for future employment; Estonia is cold in the winter." Adam smiled again and nodded to Heinrich. "Goodnight Henry tomorrow is another day." It was obvious that Hoffman's assistant was not an easy man.

CHAPTER 7

HEADING TOWARD THE MAIN lobby Adam checked his watch; 9:37 pm. He loosened his tie and unbuttoned his collar. He knew he was being watched; he'd spotted Shane Stevens at the Lobby entrance seated in one of the chair clusters. He was pretending to read the newspaper. Things were moving very quickly. Adam's encounter with Hoffman had gone well; he was interested in Luka, perhaps for more than just at the Conference. Adam scanned the Lobby; *a small group at the elevator, two young women behind the desk, three security and his father sitting at the chairs.*

Adam shook his head. *I've got to get this over with.* He ran through several different scenarios in his head, settled on one then asked one of the women behind the desk for a newspaper. He thanked her, rolled it up under his arm and flashed a big grin. Turning toward the elevator he looked directly at the man he'd dreaded meeting. Adam placed a look of recognition on his face and masked his thoughts.

"Sebastian," he said loud enough in English to get Shane's attention. "It's been so long," he continued excitedly as his approached the cluster of chairs. "This is the last place on earth I was expecting to see you." He shook the other man's hand. "Where was it last we met, Athens? What are you doing here; you seem a bit out of your element."

"I . . . I . . ." his father sputtered as he stood. It gave Adam satisfaction to see him at lost for words. "I think you've made a mistake."

"You're not Sebastian?" Luka asked surprised. He could read Shane's indecision and before the other man could recover, Adam shook his hand again, easily reached into the tall man's back pocket and took his wallet. He noted the name on his ID card attached to his breast pocket. "Please forgive me Mr. Daniels but you look so much like my friend." Adam quickly slipped the wallet into his own pocket and prepared to leave. Shane was obviously shaken; he'd been caught off guard. "Have a good night Sir."

Adam turned and went directly to the men's room across from the elevator. He could feel the eyes watching him from behind. Once in a stall he examined the contents of the wallet. Inside was an American driver's license under the name Hugh Daniels, a credit card and money. There was also a business card. Hugh Daniels, Security Specialist: Houston, Texas. Printed across the bottom were an address, telephone number and web site. A small blank notebook was carefully tucked into a small pocket. He ripped the first page out and put it in his pocket.

Adam returned everything to its proper place and looked again at his watch. 9:49 pm. Before leaving the bathroom he mentally recalled where the lobby cameras were located. Hugh Daniels was still watching. Adam grinned as his pushed the elevator button. A young couple approached. Casually looking around he stopped and focussed his attention on the wallet he'd carefully dropped, prompting the two to follow his gaze. Adam shared a look with the well dressed young man and could decode that he would take the lost item to the front desk. *Perfect*, Adam thought to himself as the elevator door opened. Once inside he watched as the couple retrieved the wallet and headed toward the desk. Mr. Daniels was going to feel very foolish when he returned to his room to find a message from the hotel explaining that someone had found his wallet. The thought of it made Adam smile.

A quick online search proved Adams suspicions; Hugh Daniels' business card was untraceable. The web site did not exist and the telephone number went directly to computerized voice mail held by Daniels with the billing forwarded to a Post Office box in Houston. After rubbing the blank notebook page Adam found something more interesting; a local address and phone number. It belonged to a warehouse in the industrial area of Edinburgh and the Van Hussens were known for meeting in large out of the way places. Adam traced the accompanying number to a small transportation company down by the docks. He quickly included all of what he'd found in an email and sent it off to Flynn. Adam would let Jarvis' people do the leg work; they seemed to know how to get to the bottom of things.

With that taken care of, Adam quickly changed from his suit to something more casual. He put gel in his hair and donned his forest green scarf, draping it with a calculated carelessness across his shoulders. He clipped his ID to the collar of his sweater, grabbed his disposable cell phone and headed out to do what young people do when travelling abroad. He knew he'd be watched; he was counting on it. Adam had only so much time to gain the trust of the people who knew the truth. He'd asked for at least three days to try things his way; Jarvis had given him two. It they could avoid grabbing the targets Adam felt they had a better chance of staying out of the Van Hussen radar; taking them forcefully wasn't his first choice.

The bar was filled with assorted conference goers most were from the translator pool. During registration it was agreed that it would be a good place to meet and blow off some steam after a long day of travelling. The party was in full swing. Adam quickly assessed the premises, calculated how many people filled the area and which table would benefit him the most. It was a small establishment with only a dozen tables and eight tall stools at the bar. The walls were clad with pictures of the Scottish countryside and music played quietly in the background. From the corner of his eye he spotted Aberdeen with a couple of her co workers. They were laughing and enjoying the mood of the place. She looked at him and then quickly glanced over his shoulder. Adam was well aware of the two men that had followed him. He carefully stole a look; one of them was his brother.

As he walked over to the bar and ordered a pint Adam felt the tension in his shoulders intensify. The stress was a part of his new reality. *Just one more thing to deal with,* he pondered as he surveyed the ambient thought in the room. Luka caught the eye of a familiar French translator and smiled as the man waved him over. The noise in the room was a low murmur but with the added visual information bombarding Adam, he was getting a headache. It was a lot to process especially with his brother waiting to decode his every thought. He put his ID tag in his pocket and took Erikson's glasses from inside his jacket. There were enough people in the bar that wearing them for a short time wouldn't be a problem besides Adam could mask his directed thought enough that his brother wouldn't think there was anything out of the ordinary. Ambient thought cluttered the room. If ever there were a time he would need them this was it.

The evening continued. Luka sat with his new friends, shared stories, flirted with the bar maids and watched the others drink a lot of beer. He was careful to appear controlled and secretly observed the two men watching him. They were not facing him but had a great view of Luka's reflection in the mirror behind the bar. As the bar emptied Adam removed his glasses. Franz Weber, AKA Jonathan Stevens, was nothing like Adam. The older brother was more laid back and distracted. His cavalier attitude implied weak character. He'd spent more time paying attention to the beautiful blonde bartender than watching Luka Reznikov. He wasn't impressed with his current assignment and felt there were more important things that needed his attention.

In contrast, his partner was all about business. He was young, but it was hard to tell just how young and he looked familiar. Mentally recalling the faces of those attending the conference Adam came up with a name. Andrew Delorne, one of the two security assigned to Jannick Gabel, Israel's Finance Minister. If the young man was a member of the MOSSAD his demeanour made perfect sense. They were some of the best trained Special

Forces in the world, but there was something else about him that Adam couldn't quite put his finger on. Sitting, shoulders back with a drink that he hadn't touched, the young man watched everything and Adam could tell the he took his job very seriously.

Adam had spent the evening extracting information from the four men at his table. The more they drank the easier it was to get them to talk about the people they were working with. None had a clue what Adam was up to. As he easily manipulated the others, Adam also carefully fed his brother visual messages that would lead him to believe that Luka Reznikov was distracted by his meeting with Hoffman and that he was very curious as to why the German Economist wanted to meet with him. He allowed himself to daydream a little about what it would be like to work for a powerful man like Hoffman.

Aberdeen watched him. Adam sat straight with his shoulders back but down in his chair, legs crossed. With his neatly trimmed beard and styled hair he looked so casual. She marvelled at how different this man was from the Adam she knew from the yacht. He spoke very little but with each word he directed the conversation saying just the right thing to get the others to speak amongst themselves about what he wanted. Each time the waitress served his table, she would smile at him and once as she delivered drinks, made a point leaning forward allowing her hair to brush against his hand. The woman made extended eye contact. Adam casually flashed his own smile. He easily garnered the attention of women. Aberdeen observed with amazement as even his visualized thoughts portrayed the man he'd become. Adam drank very little and only for appearances.

She'd also been watching the two men at the bar. The brother looked enough like Adam that it unnerved her. He confused Aberdeen; his thoughts distracted and disjointed. Franz Weber observed Adam carefully but didn't invest much time in forming an opinion. He seemed distracted and looked like he felt he was wasting his time. His companion was the other extreme and remained totally focused on exactly what Adam was up to.

It had gotten late and his companions were getting loud. Adam looked at his watch; 12:03 am. He glanced over at Aberdeen's table and noticed she and her friends were getting ready to leave. As the young women passed the translators' table one of his companions stood too quickly in order to get their attention. He knocked the table spilling several drinks. Everyone at the table stood to avoid the mess.

"Ladies don't leave yet," the Italian slurred, "let us buy you a drink. The night is still young." The young women paused and although they all smiled it was obvious none were interested.

"No thanks," Aberdeen replied, playing the role. "We've all got to work tomorrow." She looked at Adam. "I met you earlier at the 'Meet and Greet' didn't I?" she asked him.

"Yes," Adam replied with a big smile, "and you're right we all have to work tomorrow. We all should get back." He flashed another smile and turned his attention to his table mates. "Let these lovely ladies continue on their way comrades." He winked at the other girls and then put his hands firmly on the shoulders of the two men closest to him and directed them to the bar. "We'll settle up our tab and then call it a night my friends." All were agreeable and the ladies made a hasty exit.

Approaching the bar Adam caught the eye of the blonde bartender and turned on his charm. Luka Reznikov smiled at her. She blushed deeply and returned the smile. "Thank you for everything," he said looking deep into her eyes his head slightly cocked to the side. "I hope my friends haven't been too much of a bother."

"Not at all," she replied. "I hope you come back again. I'm here every night but Sunday." Adam crookedly smiled at her again and ushered his friends out the door. The two men at the bar watched quietly and before he followed the others Adam saw his brother smirk. The visual information coming from the two of them allowed Adam some satisfaction. They would give a good report but Adam didn't know to whom. It would probably be the Van Hussens but he was still not convinced that they were the ones that had backed Bergstein.

After a noisy elevator ride and the struggle to deposit his friends at their hotel room doors, Adam went to his own room. He was physically and mentally exhausted. He sat on the bed wiggling his toes, letting the plush carpet caress his feet. The soft smell of lilacs filled his memory and he put his head in his hands. Adam's stomach tightened and the tension in his shoulders pulled at his neck. A small pressure began to build behind his eyes. In the past he had always been able to distance himself from the entanglement of emotion; perhaps the Agency had done him a favour after all.

After taking a few moments to regain perspective Adam went to the blinking red light on his phone that had welcomed him to his room and checked his messages. It was Hoffman's assistant wanting to meet before the next day's events commenced; 9 am in Meeting room 7, specifically assigned to the German delegation attending the Conference. Breakfast would be supplied. Adam took a long drink from the bottle of water off his night stand. He assessed the progress he'd made in the last 12 hours and rubbed his eyes. By the end of the morning meeting Adam should know if he'd be able to find the truth without resorting to Jarvis' plan.

As the 24 year old put his head on his pillow he knew it would be a restless night. They all were. The nightmares were getting worse. Closing his eyes Adam ran through his plans for the next day. He hoped to meet the girl; she might be the key. Emotionally drained he rolled onto his side and prepared to face the disturbing images that waited.

His heart was heavy in his chest and he knew there was no way out. The Compound was surrounded and it was getting harder to breath. Thick smoke was filling his room as it poured in from under the door. It made his eyes burn. The familiar sound of a helicopter pounded in his ears. He stepped on the bed and reached up to the window sill. He stood on his tip toes in order to see the landing pad through the small window. The smoke thickened. He could see his mother and father as they held onto each other, an armed guard pushing them toward helicopter. Even if he could break the glass the window would be too small for him to climb out.

"Help them Adam," he heard Munroe plead.

Adam saw another man, his brother, pulling a young woman by the arm as he too headed for the helicopter. She struggled and to his horror Adam realized who it was.

* * *

He sat straight up in his bed. "Aberdeen," Adam said to himself. He was covered in sweat. Taking a deep breath he waited for his heart to stop pounding; it didn't. The bright red numbers on the clock read 4:13 pm. He was certain that if he closed his eyes again the nightmare would continue. Adam headed for the shower. The hot stream of water cascading down his body numbed his senses and he began to count backwards in German from 100. It took until 67 for him to calm down. Since the implant had shut down, most of the feelings Adam had been dealing with were shame and regret. They'd been difficult, almost overwhelming. He was now discovering just how paralyzing fear could be.

For a brief moment his thoughts turned to Jarvis. Adam imagined that this was just a small glimpse of what the older man was dealing with. The intensity of the feelings physically hurt and Adam didn't have the luxury of easing into the Pandora's box that had been opened. The lack of sleep, emotional overload and constant visual bombardment were taking their toll. As he dried himself off with shaking hands, Adam glanced in the mirror. He didn't like what looked back at him.

Adam went over the previous day's events one more time before he decided that what was really needed was a good workout. He still felt as though he was missing something but he was at loss as to what it was. The nightmare had unnerved him but in the back on his mind there was a nagging sensation that he'd learned to trust and depend on over the years. Adam knew whatever it was, was important and obvious enough for his sub conscious to send signals but he just couldn't figure it out. He would get a good workout in the hotel gym and try to regain perspective before his meeting with Hoffman.

Conference Day One Wednesday

Adam absolutely hated the treadmill but as he pushed his body he began to feel like himself. His muscles worked as he focussed to keep his breathing even. It was a familiar feeling and predictable. As he continued to push himself, the tension in his shoulders was replaced with the anticipated burning in his lungs. Even early in the morning there was always at least one other committed soul starting the day the same way. Although aware of the other man, he made a point of ignoring him. Adam's brain needed to turn off and focus only on the rhythm of his stride and the beat of his heart. All became normal, simple and as it had been before he'd even heard of GS.

* * *

The ballroom was already teeming with people. Aberdeen and her co workers were busy directing assorted translators to their stations within the Conference hall. The sound system had to be checked and the ear piece at each seat needed testing to make sure the feed was originating from the right translator. It would be a disaster if the delegates received the wrong translations during the General Assembly speeches. Success was all in the details and even though Aberdeen was focussed on the job at hand she paused when she saw her father.

He had always seemed so relaxed and carefree at least until Shane Stevens found his way back into their lives. The two men had been best friends and done everything together. The anger and confusion Jarvis had expressed when the intel first told them that Shane had gotten involved with the Van Hussens scared her. For years her father had worried about what happened to those that were taken; he'd searched for them tirelessly and then suddenly felt so uncertain and betrayed. Shane had been a type of hero figure to them all. He was the one who had stood up to Bergstein in order to save them. Recently Jarvis had tried to come to terms with the whole situation by believing there had to be an explanation that would not tarnish his ideal of his friend. Aberdeen hoped he was right. She smiled as her father looked over at her, he in turn, smiled back.

*   *   *

The run had helped to refresh Adam and even though he was still operating on very little sleep and too much stress he felt better. He was dressed in dark pants, white shirt and dark sports jacket. The young Russian looked ready to start his very busy day. Adam timed how long it took the elevator to descend to the main floor. People were on the move and the small space was filled to capacity. It was still over an hour before the first International session began but there were a lot of preparations before the opening address. He looked at his watch 8:47 am.

Hoffman had interesting timing. He must have known that Adam was to report to the ballroom by 9:30. It didn't leave much time. The German meeting room was at the rear of the hotel amidst a cluster of other small rooms. As he approached, Adam had an uneasy feeling. On either side of the door stood the two men that had followed him to the night before. Adam feigned surprise and confusion sending those thoughts forward for his brother to decode. He needed them to think they held the better hand. Jonathan was more poised and stood tall although Adam could see his amused thoughts; smug and arrogant. Neither spoke to Adam but their glare purposely communicated caution.

"So we meet again," Jon said opening the door.

It intrigued him that they were so open about having followed him. Adam could interpret it only one way. They were making a statement; whatever game was to be played it would be played by their rules. Again that nagging feeling surfaced and Adam looked carefully at the young Israeli security guard. It finally became clear what he'd been missing. He'd seen the face before; long ago. It was older now but there was no mistake. Adam stepped into an empty room and took a seat; the door closed behind him.

*   *   *

It'd been a long day of training. Hand to hand combat was exhausting but it was one of Adam's favourite parts of being stuck at the Compound. It allowed him to take out his frustrations without being reprimanded by Talbot. At 12 years old, the boy was still not big enough to overcome his opponents but he felt himself getting stronger each day and better able to anticipate what would be coming at him next. He knew that Talbot would be waiting. He would sit the boy down in the screening room and go over his performance bit by bit until Adam could recognize why he'd failed to best his opponent. Talbot was hard on him but the boy knew why. When older Adam would have an important job and he needed to be ready. A lot of lives would depend on it.

Just before reaching the Studio, Adam heard the helicopter and noticed a commotion near the landing pad. He stepped behind the corner of the building where he could get a good look without being seen. Several large, burly men and the Director waited for the craft to land and its blades to stop spinning. There was motion inside the helicopter, a struggle perhaps. As the engine quieted and the doors opened Adam could hear a man yelling. The two burly men went forward and pulled out a desperate man who struggled to get away.

"Leave him alone," the man screamed. "He's only a boy!" As he continued to flail the Director approached and stabbed him with a needle. Almost instantly the movement stopped and the unconscious man was carried into the Compound. Director Ackerman waited for a woman and a small boy of no more than 8 years old to exit the helicopter. She held his hand. Deep sobs escaped from the boy and after only a few steps he dropped to the ground almost causing the woman to lose her balance.

"It obviously didn't go well," observed the Director as he reached down and scooped up the child. They walked toward the main building.

"It doesn't always go smoothly," the woman replied straightening her skirt. "Its much easier when we can drug them so they aren't traumatized. Unfortunately the father tried to make a run for it and

the boy woke up before we could get to them. Another dose would have been dangerous."

"Not to worry he is young enough that in a few months it won't matter," the Director replied. "His test scores show that he will be perfect for 'Epsilon.' We're now ahead of schedule. If all goes well, adding him to the program should speed up our timeline by at least two years." As she held the door the woman turned just enough for Adam to get a clear view of her face. He recognized it from his time on the outside. She was the teacher that had taken such an interest in him just before he had gotten so sick.

* * *

Adam had sensed no recognition from the young Agency operative. They'd only seen each other a few times and met only once. Ironically the meeting had been at a training session when they had briefly sparred with each other. The boy had been 14 years old and more than 6 years had passed. His name was Caleb. Adam knew of only one other child that had been brought to the Compound and she had been there for only a short time. Things had not gone well for her.

Adam sat considering the ramifications of this new development. Did this change things? Was he in danger of losing his cover? What was Epsilon? As Adam glanced at his watch, Heinrich Maier, Hoffman's assistant, entered flanked by the two men who'd been stationed by the door. He looked angry.

"What's going on Henry?" Luka inquired rising to his feet. "Have I done something wrong?" He spoke German. "Look I don't want any trouble."

"Let's quit playing games," The German replied speaking perfect English and pushing Luka back in his chair. He had no accent. "You have an agenda, a very calculated agenda and there are sensitive issues afoot."

Adam carefully looked at the three men, masking his visual transmissions but setting his concentration on Caleb. It was obvious to him now why the young man's thoughts were so disciplined. Adam could easily recognize the operative's discomfort and dislike for Heinrich. Caleb was biding his time until . . . until what?

"I didn't realize you were a pick pocket," Heinrich continued. "Our man insisted he hadn't been near the main elevator where you conveniently dropped his wallet for others to find." Heinrich smiled as the three men looked down at the nervous Russian. "What were you looking for?" There was a threat to his voice.

Luka Reznikov looked around like a caged animal searching for a way of escape. He found none. "I don't know what you're talking about." He rubbed his eyes.

"We know it was you," Heinrich insisted. "Why else did you approach our man in the lobby?"

"I thought he was someone else," Luka replied his voice quivering only slightly. "You've got the wrong guy. All I know is I'm tired of being an underpaid academic that has no prospects of getting out from behind the desk I've been sitting at for the last three years. I'm better than that and I'm not going to wait around any longer to get catch a break. It'll never come." He ran his hands through his hair then covered his face with his hands. Looking up at the others he continued. "This Conference is my chance. Back home I've already lost my girlfriend and my apartment." Luka sighed heavily and looked down at the floor defeated. "What do you want from me? I'm just trying to do my job and get noticed."

"You are a foolish amateur and you have no idea who you are dealing with," Hoffman's assistant concluded walking over to a table covered with breakfast food. He poured a large glass of water and glanced at his watch. "You have ten minutes to get yourself together before you need to report." Approaching Luka he handed the broken man the glass. "Remember we are watching you. This meeting *never* happened." Adam realized that Hoffman was not involved in any of this and if Luka didn't keep his mouth shut and stay focused on the Conference he'd come across these three again with a more serious outcome.

Luka took the water but his eyes remained downcast trying to save as much face as possible. He glanced up only long enough to decode his brother's thoughts.

* * *

Flynn and Munroe had spent hours trying to trace Hugh Daniels with not much success. The Houston post office box had been opened for three years and was regularly emptied of junk mail by a legal firm that received a monthly payment of $200 by money order in the mail; no return address. The firm also paid the bill associated with the address. Hugh Daniels hired them the day he opened the post office box and the service contract had his signature on it. It was a dead end.

They'd had more success with the transportation company. Hacking into to its computer had been easy. MacFarlane Scott Transport was a small shipping company that had recently been importing large crates from a Denmark based medical supply company. They'd been delivering packages to the local address Adam had found in Daniels' wallet. It was a warehouse located in a quiet part of the industrial district but it was evident that the amount of freight being delivered and the size of the building made it unlikely that a clandestine Van Hussen meeting was to take place at that location. The shipments included medical pharmaceuticals. There was also a shipment coming out of Florida containing several dozen compact rebreathers used for shallow coastal dives.

"This is not good, Ken," Flynn determined as he scanned through MacFarlane Scott's import summaries for the last year. "There are several shipments here marked as unknown and one that contained 10 hazmat suits. These guys are up to something and it can't be good. We've got to let others know about this."

"Flynn . . . , the Shane we knew would not be a part of something like this," reflected Munroe. "maybe he doesn't know what he's gotten involved with."

"Or maybe he's changed," replied Flynn. "Twenty five years is a long time."

*   *   *

Things couldn't have gone better under the circumstances. After the three men had left the room Adam splashed water on his face and continued to perform for the cameras. Caleb hadn't recognized him and Jonathan reacted exactly how Adam had expected. He'd been certain that Hoffmann would find Luka Reznikov's resume impressive enough to give him a second look but there was something a lot more serious going on. He had no idea what and he didn't understand was how Caleb's cover hadn't been blown. Was it possible that the young agent's thoughts hadn't tipped off the others? Things had taken an interesting turn. Adam had known taking the wallet was a calculated risk but he hadn't counted on the Agency being involved. It'd paid off, gotten Luka on the Jonathan's radar. If Flynn came up empty handed it didn't matter. None of it really mattered; at this point the question had become whether or not they should abort the mission altogether. The Agency's involvement changed everything.

Adam headed toward the gathering area for his department. He was the last to arrive and after a brief orientation everyone left for their assigned rooms. Each room had eight translation cubicles which consisted of a chair, a pen and paper on a small table and audio equipment. The large earphones at each station blocked out all outside noise and received the transmission to be translated from the Conference Hall. Each had a microphone connected to the one or more delegates needing translations in the station's assigned language. Adam was to transmit German to Hoffman and three others. It was hard work and took intense concentration. Translations would be done on the fly. He was one of only three others that were familiar with all eight languages that would be used throughout the day. There'd be few breaks and only an hour lunch. Adam set two bottles of water on the small table, took a seat and settled in.

The next few hours were a blur. The fact that 2 of the 3 morning speakers each spoke for over an hour didn't help. The afternoon would hopefully be a little more interesting.

Luka stood as the last morning speaker left the podium. His eyes were burning and his shoulders tight. By-passing the huddle of translators gathering in the lobby he went directly to the buffet spread in the Ballroom. He grabbed another bottle of water and a sandwich then set off in search of either Jarvis or Aberdeen. A team meeting was in order and the sooner the better. He went down the hallway and as his rounded the corner came face to face with his father next to him was the girl.

"So we meet again," the older man mused.

To Adam it seemed as though the man standing in front of him had gained size since their last encounter. Shane Stevens stood a full 5 inches taller than his son and even without his height would have made an imposing figure. He was well build and the smattering of grey along his temples only hinted at his age. Jarvis had characterized him as a gentle giant. Looking up at his fiery eyes Adam would've disagreed. The girl to his left was strikingly beautiful despite her attempts to hide it. Her long blonde hair was pulled tightly back and she stood with shoulders back, graceful and dignified. Adam took a step back and looked at the pair. He narrowed his eyes and concentrated on their visual signals.

"**This guy isn't a threat,**" the blonde assured, "**we have bigger problems to worry about.**" They were in a rush.

"**True,**" answered Stevens, "**but we need to find out what he knows.**" Grabbing Adam by the arm, Shane made an about face and pulled the young man down the hallway, through a door and into the stairwell. The girl followed. Adam was unceremoniously deposited on the floor.

"See those cameras," Shane said with a wry look on his face; he motioned toward them with a quick glance. "Don't think they'll keep me from teaching you a lesson. He pulled Adam to his feet. "You don't know who you are dealing with." It was a threat. Adam was careful to mask his thoughts; he was afraid but interestingly enough so was his father, the girl too. Their emotions were clear. They were in the middle of something big and Luka Reznikov was a wild card that had to be dealt with. Adam took a deep breath. This was the last thing he needed and wasn't sure what to do next.

Caleb's appearance had thrown him for a loop. If the Agency discovered Luka's true identity things would get very messy. He would not go back. Adam had been a prize operative but he now held no loyalty toward them. He thought of Talbot and felt anger well up from deep inside.

"I don't know what you people are talking about," exploded Adam. "I thought you were Sebastian." He leaned against the wall of the stairwell, glaring and waited for a reply.

"You didn't take the wallet?" Adam studied the girl as she spoke. She was wound very tight and just below the surface it was obvious that she felt like she was in over her head. She had sad eyes but whatever was going on had terrified her. Suddenly Adam knew exactly what to do. He took another deep breath and changed his countenance.

"Look, I don't know what's going on," Luka said quietly looking down at his shoes, shaking his head. "I just want to make a good impression with Hoffman." He stood tall, defiant. "Where I grew up you take every opportunity; this Conference is my chance." Adam visualized a crowded ghetto and imagined how it was to be a small boy hungry and alone. He allowed a sense of hopelessness to envelope him. He played on the girl's own sense of helplessness. With his jaw set and shoulders back Luka looked up with desperate eyes; filled with a life full of struggle and disappointment but his body language didn't match his thoughts; he appeared calm and in control.

Adam watched as the others shared a look. They'd bought it. **"Danni,"** Shane concluded, **"He knows nothing."** He stepped forward towering over the younger man. He grabbed Luka by the shoulders and pushed him pinning the young man against the wall. "You'd better stay clear of us," he threatened narrowing his eyes. "I've got more important things to deal with and if you get in the way I'll put an end to you. Do you understand?" Luka looked up at him holding his breath. He nodded.

The pair left suddenly, leaving Adam alone in the stairwell feeling quite small. He leaned against the wall bending at the knees, allowing himself to slide against it until he was sitting on the floor. He took a few minutes to regain his composure; the emotions that surfaced were overwhelming, besides it looked good on camera.

* * *

When Jarvis received Flynn's text he knew something was wrong but didn't have the freedom to check it right away and then he spotted Adam. He looked terrible. The young man paused as he entered the lobby scanning the area quickly. His shoulder hurt from the encounter in the stairwell. On the surface Luka Reznikov still looked confident with a casual swag to his step but it was obvious that he hadn't been sleeping and an intense day had taken its toll. Translating at these conferences was stressful and took a lot out of people. With a newspaper tucked under his arm Adam looked at his watch and then took a drink from the half empty water bottle he'd pulled from his jacket pocket. He seemed distracted but at the same time purposeful. He was looking for someone and as their eyes met Jarvis realized that it was him. Adam approached the security desk leading to the elevators and quickly examined each face in the lobby; there were not many, the afternoon session had ended but the entire translation team had attended a 60 minute debriefing afterward.

"**We have a problem,**" Adam communicated, confident that no one else could decode his thoughts. "**The Agency is here. We need to meet.**"

Jarvis' partner asked to see Adam's ID before he allowed the young man to continue toward the elevator. Adam took the newspaper from under his arm, placed it on the desk and then he fumbled with his ID.

"**Take the newspaper,**" he suggested, unclipping the ID card from his lapel and handing it to the other guard. "Its been a long day already," Luka quipped, "I'm glad I got out here before the big push." The trio could already hear the murmur of many voices coming down the hall.

"Do you mind?" Jarvis asked as he reached for the paper.

"Not at all," Luka replied taking back his ID and smiling at the man handing it to him. "Have a good day gentleman." He watched Jarvis take the newspaper and place it in his bag. Adam then headed toward the elevator hoping to avoid the crowd. He succeeded; the doors slid open the moment he touched the button and Adam retreated inside.

Jarvis looked at his watch. There was an hour left in his shift and although he knew that what was in both the text and newspaper could change everything he would have to wait. The bulk of the translators were trickling into the lobby on their way to get ready for dinner. There would be no time to get away; the dinner rush was about to begin.

*　*　*

Adam sat on the floor of his room waiting for his dinner. He'd decided on room service, endeavouring to avoid bringing more attention on himself. His absence in the ballroom would be noted by those watching but it seemed to be the safest course of action. There were too many variables for Adam to know what to do next. He didn't like the lack of control facing him. Besides he was hungry and wanted to know what Jarvis thought of the situation. As he sat, bent kneed, head in his hands, Adam began to think.

The Agency must be trying to infiltrate the Van Hussens and it looks like Caleb succeeded in getting somewhat on the inside. Heinrich's involvement in the morning's confrontation with Luka shows that something more than just the Conference is going on. Stevens and the girl are also hiding something; something that terrifies Danielle; something that made them fearful of Luka and what he may have discovered. Do they know who Caleb is?

The girl, Adam thought, *Danni.* She was afraid and out of her element but the photos had proved she'd been involved with the Van Hussens for some time. What was putting her on edge? What were "the more important things" they had to worry about and why hadn't they discovered Caleb's involvement with Agency? It really kept coming back to Caleb. How did this all work?

A knock rapped on the door. *That would be dinner,* Adam thought. *Maybe some food will make me feel better.* He carefully peeked through the peep hole before opening the door to make sure it was food waiting on the other side. It was and it smelled delicious. The waiter wheeled the tray into the room and dutifully lifted the plate cover so Adam could see what was inside; roast beef. He smiled and reached into his pocket.

"A lovely young woman at the front desk asked me to deliver this," the waiter said with a wink and a smile. It was a white envelope with Luka's name on it. Below the beautiful handwriting was the perfect lipstick imprint of a kiss. Accepting the tip Adam placed in his hand the waiter said "Thank you Sir," and he left the room.

Adam took the envelope off the cart. It was from Aberdeen; he knew even before he opened it. Her hand writing was how he imagined it; a flourish of curves perfectly formed. Adam couldn't help smiling as he pictured her pressing her lips gently against the envelope. He shook his head. Every one of Adam's adult relationships had been purposeful and calculated; he'd never become attached to anyone but somehow a small band of amateurs had gotten under his skin.

Adam ripped open the envelope and read the note inside.

Luka

> *I was disappointed when I realized you had ordered dinner in your room. I was hoping we would have the chance to get to know each other better. I don't mean to be too forward, us American's are known for that, but I would like to get together after my shift this evening. I get off at 8:00. I know a lovely local pub in the neighbourhood.*

> *Hope to hear from you,*
> *Alison*

Adam looked at his watch; 6:37. His time of reflection on the floor had lasted longer than he'd thought. Jarvis had obviously gotten Adam's note and was calling a meeting. He was clever. A quiet rendezvous with a girl wouldn't cause too much concern for those watching Luka. Adam picked up the phone and called downstairs.

"Front desk, how may I help you?" a pleasant voice answered.

"May I speak to Alison Mitchell?" Luka asked his Russian accent thick with anticipation.

There was a slight pause at the other end of the line. "One moment please." Alison's co-worker waved the phone at her friend. She smiled and laughed as she held back the receiver. "Guess which handsome interpreter with the sexy Russian accent wants to talk to you?" she teased. Alison smiled and grabbed the receiver.

"Front desk, Alison Mitchell speaking." Aberdeen announced. Her face had gone red. She'd tried to keep her meeting with Adam a secret or at least a secret from her new friend. She knew that an in depth interrogation was headed her way as soon as she hung up and surprisingly she felt her heart rate increase as she waited for the voice on the other end of the phone.

"Hello pretty American lady," Luka greeted, "I am being very pleased to receive your letter." He sounded amused and was laying it on thick.

"I hope I wasn't being too forward," replied Alison blushing even more as her friend listened.

Luka chuckled quietly. "Not at all, I am enjoying that you are not so busy as to not notice my admiration." He was indeed enjoying the little ruse. "Shall we again make our acquaintance this evening?"

"I would like that." Aberdeen also chuckled quietly. Luka was so charming; so unlike Adam. Her brain had a hard time reconciling that they were the same person. "Shall we meet in the lobby at 8:30?"

"Most certainly," Luka agreed. "The minutes shall pass slowly until then."

Aberdeen put down the phone and turned toward her friend. Jewel Danz was vibrating with anticipation. "Do tell all," she insisted, "and start from the beginning."

"Really Jewels its not that big of a deal," Aberdeen blushed, getting caught up in the moment. "It's just a couple of drinks." But of course it was a big deal just not quite the one her friend had in mind. Something big was going on or her father would not have taken the risk of calling a meeting.

*   *   *

Adam was thrilled that his dinner was still hot; he'd been so much looking forward to it. The implant had stolen so many things from him and he was starting to discover some of what he'd missed. Things like music, chocolate and a really good cup of coffee. The difficulties that came along with being human were offset by these simple pleasures. As Adam savoured each bite, the Van Hussen Group, the Conference, his father; all of things pulling at him faded away. Satisfied, Adam sighed deeply folding his linen napkin and placing it on his plate.

Well Adam, he thought to himself, *time to get to work.* He looked at his watch; it was just before 7 o'clock. The former operative still had enough time to hack into the Agency computer before it was time to get ready for Luka's date with Alison Mitchell. His first order of business would be to find out about Epsilon. During his time at the Compound, Adam had heard rumours about the top secret program but needed to get something more concrete to bring with him to the meeting. There were some very serious decisions to be made and Adam wanted them to be informed decisions.

*   *   *

Jewel had been pestering Alison since she'd gotten the phone call from Luka and now, as the elevator descended to the main floor, Aberdeen took a moment to catch her breath. She'd never gone through such an intense pre-date ritual and never wanted to again. The care her friend had taken in making sure Alison looked just right for the young handsome Russian had been almost ridiculous. Aberdeen liked to be real; if someone didn't like her for who she was and how she dressed too bad. She'd been romantically involved a couple of times but had never put in so much effort. Jewel Danz had befriended Alison Mitchell but may have not connected as well with Aberdeen Jarvis.

Luka waited in the lobby dressed for an intimate night out. His black pants and white shirt were topped by black evening jacket. His collar remained open and he looked casual yet ready to attend the most formal of events. He'd trimmed his beard and was ready to woo the young woman he expected to spend the evening with. He sat across the room facing the elevator, in full view of the cameras. His gaze was directed at the magazine opened in front of him but his thoughts were focussed on the information he'd extracted from the Agency's database. He hoped Jarvis' people were able to find out more but with so little time he had his doubts. What he'd discovered was incomplete but it led him to only one conclusion; the only thing that made sense.

He looked up from his magazine and his heart skipped a beat. She was truly breathtaking. Her long dark hair was carefully piled atop her head with a few gentle wisps left down to frame her face. A black dress hugged tight against her, short enough to show off her legs but long enough to maintain a graceful decorum. She smiled as their eyes met. Adam took a deep breath before rising to his feet and reaching for her hand. There was no need for him to pretend; he was enamoured by her beauty.

"You are exceptional," Luka concluded as he lifted her hand gently to his lips. "I've never seen anyone as lovely." She unnerved him but he maintained eye contact; he couldn't help himself.

"Thank you," Aberdeen blushed, fighting to keep her chin up and not look away in embarrassment. Then she looked deep into his eyes. They were so blue and she could see right through them; beyond the wall he'd erected between himself and the rest of the world. She felt Adam wince but he didn't look away; his transparency allowed her to see. Time stopped for a moment, but then the moment was gone and the wall reappeared. Luka smiled weakly and released her hand.

"I ordered a car," Alison said shaking off the encounter. "Its a warm night, we could wait outside," she suggested.

"Let's," Luka replied. "I'm prepared to make sure the pretty lady doesn't get cold." He took her hand again and they left the hotel. Those watching were satisfied and turned their attention to other more pressing matters.

The car was waiting for them. The driver stepped forward to open the back door for the couple. The man under the chauffeur's hat winked at Aberdeen as she passed and nodded crisply toward her companion. Before Adam entered the car he removed his jacket. He'd sensed Aberdeen's discomfort with her dress and he gently placed it over her shoulders. With the passengers safely in the backseat, Flynn drove away from the hotel and all the watching eyes. He wove through several backstreets until he was confident they were not being followed. The two in the back remained quiet. Both were unsure as to how to react to their brief exchange. By the time they pulled up in front of a small restaurant it was a quarter past nine.

"We've arrived," Flynn announced. "Everyone should already be here." He looked back at his passengers, aware that something had happened between them. "Is everything okay with you two?"

"Yes," Adam answered as he opened the car door and stepped out onto the curb. He put his hand out to Aberdeen and helped her from the car. She smiled at him avoiding his eyes. He looked like the Adam from the yacht; his face closed and jaw set. Pulling his jacket tightly around her shoulders she headed quickly toward the door, Adam following close behind. As they approached he stepped ahead and opened the door allowing Aberdeen to enter first and then Flynn.

CHAPTER 8

THE RESTAURANT WAS EMPTY except for kitchen staff and the waitress who met the new comers at the door. She ushered them into the back room where the others were waiting. Munroe, Jarvis and Erikson were all there. So was Johnson, the other GS agent Adam had met at the Compound. They sat around a table. Adam looked at each face. They looked grave. It was obvious there was more going on than he'd thought.

"Now that we're all here," Munroe stated, "the number and address Adam found in Shane's wallet led to some very disturbing news. Over the last 9 months shipments of a serious nature have been delivered to a warehouse located in a secluded area of Edinburgh's industrial district. The deliveries include hazmat suits, rebreathers and unknown pharmaceuticals; all which lead us to believe that the Conference is at risk of a chemical or biological attack."

The room was silent as everyone tried to absorb what had been said. Aberdeen looked at her father with horror in her eyes. Adam considered the information, trying to fit it into what he already knew. He'd recognized that he'd stepped into something big but this was truly disturbing. Heinrich was definitely a part of what was planned; it explained his suspicion and demeanour but the Van Hussen Group had spent many years setting up a network of powerful people and it made no sense that they would behind such an attack. It was also unlikely the Agency would carry out such an operation. Their methods might be questionable but the type of political chaos it would cause went against their mandate. Many world leaders and more than 500 people were involved in the Conference not to mention the hotel staff. There had to be another player; one who would benefit from such a horrific event.

Flynn cleared his throat and ended the silence. "As soon as we discovered the possibility of an attack I got a hold of our contact at Interpol to let him know what we'd found. Without taking the time to breathe he told me to get my people as far away from the Conference as possible but to do so without bringing attention to ourselves. He also warned us to keep what we knew quiet."

"It gets worse," Johnson declared. "Our satellite office in London has been raided," he shook his head. "Flynn called wanting me to do at little sniffing around; see if I could find out who was behind the shipments. Within 20 minutes the door in London was broken down. All of my calls are routed through that alternate location." He was visibly upset. "All I did was make one call to MacFarlane Scott pretending to be a potential customer. I asked if they shipped dangerous cargo. The call must have been traced to London. Whoever broke in found a generic office; no one was there." Another quiet pause came over the room.

"The company could have been set up specifically for whoever was receiving the shipments," Munroe suggested. "They could have select customers and no advertising so any unknown caller asking questions would be traced and red flagged." He paused for a moment thinking things through.

"If these guys were that on the ball," Flynn interjected, "they would have had a better firewall on their database. It was too easy to hack into." Munroe agreed.

Adam also dismissed the possibility; there was another explanation but he needed some time to work it through. The Agency could easily have the phone bugged. He looked up at Jarvis. Adam shook his head working through all the possibilities.

"Do we have any idea who raided the office?" Jarvis asked.

"I had the neighbouring business questioned," Johnson answered. "The owner saw a black car parked in front of the building." He looked around the room. "Whoever it was went in, rifled through everything and left. There was nothing for them to find."

"So they must have already had people in London," Aberdeen noted.

"It could have been the Van Hussens." Munroe added. "They have people everywhere."

"I know who it was," Adam announced with certainty. He spoke quietly. Both his elbows were on the table, the palms of his hands against his temples. With eyes downcast toward the table's flat surface, his mind raced. Everyone looked at the young man who was hunched forward in his chair avoiding eye contact. He had to pick his words carefully. "Its the Agency. They are on site and they know what is going on and are there to keep it from happening." He paused considering what that meant. "I have full confidence in their ability to stop any impending attack. Whoever is behind it can't make a move without them knowing. They're on the inside, deep on the inside."

"Even if that is the case," Dr. Erikson said protectively. "Going back is out of the question. Its too dangerous. There's no guarantee things won't get messy. Interpol wants us out; we need to get out and stay out."

"What about the others?" Munroe asked in desperation." He looked at Jarvis. "You were so close. This might be our last chance."

"Ken," Flynn said as he rose from his chair approaching his friend. He placed his hand on Munroe's shoulder. "Ken . . ." Flynn repeated trying to calm him down.

"No," Munroe insisted looking around the room. "We can't just walk away and even more so now with everything going on."

"Ken," Flynn took him by shoulders and looked into his eyes. **"We don't even know how they are involved in all this. Things have gotten out of control. As things stand we need to back off."** Everyone was silent.

"I don't," Adam announced. They were two small words spoken quietly and with conviction. Before anyone could respond he stood, took out his phone and dialed a number.

"Adam . . ." Aberdeen exclaimed. His look stopped her from continuing.

"Marcus," He said into the phone, "Its Franco, reroute this call from a New York exchange." He paused. "The number is 0845-555-3618." Again he paused, waiting for the Hotel to pick up. "I need to speak to Alison Mitchell, room 254 please." A pronounced New York accent flowed easily from his lips. Adam's gaze remained on Aberdeen but all it held was a warning; he'd blocked everything else. The others around the table exchanged glances. The phone rang three times before Jewel picked up. "Is Alison there? No . . . . well its very important that she get this message as soon as possible. I have tried her cell but she's not answering. There's been a family emergency and she needs to return home. Please get her to call her brother, Mark." There was another pause. "Yes, yes . . . Thank you very much." Adam shut off his phone. Almost immediately Aberdeen's rang. She responded appropriately, telling her friend she'd call right away but when she hung up she was livid.

"You can't possibly be thinking of going back to the Conference?" she asked obviously upset.

"I am and I will," Adam replied, "and so will you but for only just long enough to make your departure credible." He was stoic and detached and turned to face Jarvis. "You need to leave as well and there's something I need you to do. We need to talk."

"This isn't just you're battle Adam," the doctor reminded him.

"It is for now," the young man answered, "and for now I will do it my way." His voice was deadly serious and filled with intensity. "Jarvis, I need ten minutes of your time and then Alison needs to get back to the hotel. She is booked on the first flight back to the States."

Jarvis was a good man. He didn't bat an eyelash when Adam explained what he'd discovered about Epsilon or what those findings implicated. Both men agreed that telling the others before things could be confirmed was not a good idea. Jarvis agreed to help but it would take time. There were three days left of the Conference but no guarantee that things wouldn't come to a head before then. With their plans in place the two men prepared to rejoin the others. Adam paused, took Jarvis by the arm and looked into his eyes. The older man saw fear.

"**Now I need you to promise** *me* **something.**" The young man set his jaw and took a deep breath. He could deal with the danger of the attack; the risk of injury or death but one thing terrified him. It had filled his nights with tortured dreams and was always in the back of his mind. "The implant . . . the Agency . . . don't let them take me back there." Adam's voice shook. "**I never want to be that man again.**" He narrowed his eyes. "**I would rather die.**"

Jarvis looked down at the hand gripping his arm and placed his own on top of it. "Adam you don't have to do this," he said. "We'll find another way."

"**Promise me, Jarvis.**"

"**I promise,**" he answered.

*   *   *

On the way back to the hotel Adam knew Aberdeen was angry but it didn't matter. He'd done what he had to do in order to make sure she would be safe and that was what mattered. Neither knew what to say.

"The the car will be waiting for you at 8:30 tomorrow morning Lass," Flynn said trying to break the silence and ease the tension. "From there we'll head back to the yacht." His passengers did not respond and no one spoke during the rest of the ride back to the hotel.

After exiting the car at the hotel Adam again reached for Aberdeen's hand, helping her onto the curb. As their eyes met Aberdeen quickly looked away; she'd been crying. The front passenger window rolled down and Adam leaned forward to acknowledge the driver.

"**I'll let you know as soon as there is movement out at the warehouse,**" Flynn assured. "Be careful Lad," he said. "**We'll help you however we can.**"

Adam nodded curtly and as the car drove away he turned to Aberdeen. Even covered by his jacket he could tell she was shivering. He put his arm around her to shield her from the rain that started to fall softly on the city. He ushered her toward the hotel entrance but she hesitated.

Aberdeen knew that nothing she could say would change his mind. She felt like a little girl tossed here and there by the things happening around her. Circumstances beyond her control were once again taking over as they had been doing her whole life. This time things were different though. Never before had she felt so helpless. She searched for the right words but could find none. She mustered up her courage and looked up into his face. Her eyes deepened; her confusion and frustration remaining just below the surface.

"Adam, I don't know what to do," she admitted. **"I don't want to lose you."**

Looking at her, Adam battled to keep his own struggles hidden. He forced himself to remain closed but softened his eyes. **"I'm not yours to lose Aberdeen,"** he answered gently. **"A few weeks ago you didn't even know I existed. You've got to let this go. Regardless of what happens in the next few days I still won't be the person you want me to be."** His own words saddened him. Would he ever be the man he wanted himself to be? He knew couldn't go back and change the past; the things he'd done; the people he'd hurt or destroyed, but he could save the others from a similar fate. One line he'd read about Epsilon kept coming back to him. *'Operatives who are to have direct contact must have no knowledge of the Agency's prior involvement with the program.'* As hard as he tried not to, Adam kept coming to the same conclusion.

"I just don't want you to get yourself killed." Aberdeen insisted.

"Don't worry," he assured her, **"this is what I do and I'm very good at it. It's who I am."**

"You're wrong Adam," she said softly. "It's not who you are; it's who you were." She sidled closer to him and he let her.

"We need to get you inside pretty American lady." The Russian accent returned and his face changed. "The weather is being not happy to have us out here." Adam needed to distance himself from what Aberdeen had said. He walked her toward the hotel entrance. "You have a long day of travel ahead of you Alison."

Aberdeen let him change the subject. She'd seen beyond his wall earlier and knew that his strong exterior had to hold. It was crazy and she didn't understand. There was something going on that Adam hadn't told anyone but her father. She was already horrified by what she knew but this unknown put her even more on edge.

The warm air in the lobby welcomed them and as Adam placed his hand on the middle of her back guiding her toward the elevator. Aberdeen looked at the faces of the people milling around. It was almost 11:15 and people were still going about their lives. They had no idea what kind of danger they were in. Without knowing she began to shiver again. Luka looked down at her and smiled, trying to reassure her. It didn't work.

Aberdeen knew as she stood beside Adam in the elevator that she was already alone. She could tell his mind was racing; pouring over details she knew nothing about. It was truly amazing. But he was only one man and she wasn't sure if things went bad he'd think of himself and get out alive. Aberdeen closed her eyes and imagined herself back on the yacht. '*Failure is not an option,*' he'd said. Adam had also told her that if he didn't think the plan would work he'd come up with another one. The plan had changed; she just hoped his safety was part of it.

They stopped in front of room 254 and could hear the TV. Jewel was waiting for her roommate to return. Aberdeen turned to face the man whose presence unnerved her so much; the man she was afraid she'd never see again.

"What do I tell her?" Aberdeen shook her head not expecting an answer. **"How do I look in her eyes knowing I'm leaving because its not safe?"** She took off his jacket, leaned against the wall and looked at Adam desperately. **"And I'm leaving her behind."**

"Play the role. Tell her your mother is in the hospital," he replied taking his jacket from her. "Be Alison and nothing more."

There was a pause as she studied his face. All trace of Luka was gone.

"Promise me I'll see you again." Aberdeen quietly insisted. **"Promise me if things start to go bad you'll get out before its too late."** She took his hand and held it tight. Adam stepped forward putting his chin on the top of her head. He held her close. He smelled her hair and felt her heart pounding in her chest. He cradled her face in his hands then gently kissed her forehead. He stayed there for a moment and then reached down and jiggled the door handle to let Jewel know Alison had returned. He stepped back and smiled.

"I need to go now," Adam replied as the door to Alison's room burst open.

"Oh Alison, I'm so sorry," Jewel exploded, "I hope things aren't too serious. I didn't know what to think after your brother called. Is everything okay?" She hugged her friend, oblivious of what she'd interrupted and before Aberdeen had the chance to say goodbye, Adam was gone.

* * *

After Jarvis watched his daughter leave the restaurant he called the hotel to let them know he wouldn't be in the following day. Then he and Johnson went to the airport. He'd made sure the helicopter would be ready once they reached Boston. He looked at his watch and then over at his partner.

Dale Johnson was the only person outside the inner group that had been entrusted with the knowledge of their abilities. He accepted the science and the need to find the others without knowing all the details. Jarvis had found him 5 years ago and had added his name to the list of contacts to be cultivated. Then one day while watching Johnson question a mission given to him by the CIA, Jarvis had taken the opportunity to recruit him.

"We don't have much time Dale," he said to his partner. "I hope we can pull this off."

"We are taking a big risk going back," Johnson replied, "I hope it's worth whatever it is you need."

"It is."

* * *

Adam was not happy with himself. He'd let his guard down and she'd gotten to him. He headed back to his room trying to figure out exactly how he'd let it happen. That girl made him crazy. He was conflicted. In one breath he wanted to get as far away from Aberdeen as possible; in the next he wanted to hold her close. It was maddening and dangerous. As Adam opened the door to his room he froze. Someone had been through his things. Before proceeding he thoroughly scanned the room hoping to see the residual light signatures of those who'd been in his room. Whoever it was had been alone. Adam followed the smatterings of colour, careful not to seem obvious in case they had installed a camera. Satisfied they hadn't, he went over the room carefully. The slice in the carpet under the bed hadn't been noticed and his papers remained hidden.

The ex-operative removed his shoe and snapped back its heel retrieving his jamming device from inside. He plugged it into his laptop and opened the lid. After a few keystrokes he determined they had copied his hard drive and history but would have found nothing of consequence. His secondary firewall remained intact.

Confident that he hadn't been compromised, Adam went to the jacket he'd worn during his date and pulled a small thread on the inside of the lining making a small opening. He retrieved the two passports and small wallet he'd hidden inside then went under his bed and slid them under the carpet. Satisfied he headed for the shower.

Totally exhausted Adam climbed into bed hoping the nightmares would leave him alone for the night. Stress, disturbing dreams and uncertainty, all were new to him. He closed his eyes and saw Aberdeen's face. He'd made a mistake earlier behaving in a way that reinforced the girl's connection with him. It was trouble and he knew it. It was getting harder to push her away especially when he knew he was giving mixed messages; messages he seemed unable and somewhat unwilling to control. Thankfully, she would be gone in the morning and then he could regain his ability to focus.

Adam needed to sleep; the next day would be another busy one at the Conference. Luka was assigned directly to Hoffman as the German attended a brain storming session with other assorted economists from around the world. Adam hoped he could avoid trouble by just allowing Luka to do his job. He had to wait to see what Jarvis would find and then figure out how to approach . . . his father.

Conference Day Two Thursday

Adam arose early and went to the gym. He'd had a reasonable sleep and felt stronger. He finished his workout at 7:30 and felt ready to face the long day ahead. After showering and dressing he went to the lobby to make sure Aberdeen made it away safely. He waited in one of the chairs at the far side of the lobby, away from the elevator. He watched as she exited the elevator with her luggage, checked out at the desk and walked toward the door. Jewel was by her side and as Aberdeen reached the door she put down bags in order to give her friend a hug. She paused before she left; looking for Adam, but only for a moment then she turned and was gone. Adam sat for a moment imagining the smell of her long dark hair. He closed his eyes and took a deep breath to shake it off.

The morning session went much as Adam expected; a half dozen arrogant people who thought their own solutions were the only ones with merit and the few people around them trying to keep the peace and help them come to some sort of consensus. Adam was careful to let Luka do his job and not ruffle any feathers. His main focus was to discover the players in the unfolding drama.

The ability to see people's thoughts was invaluable and now that he had a better idea of what he was looking for, Adam was able to determine that out of the eight security he'd come across two of them belonged to the Agency. He'd also spotted Caleb and the girl heading to one of the other brainstorming sessions but there was no sign of his father or brother.

Adam was invited to lunch by Hoffman. The older man suggested it would be a good time for them to have that talk he'd mentioned at the 'Meet and Greet.' Throughout the meal Heinrich Maier did his best to make Luka uncomfortable and Adam decoded that he wasn't happy that Hoffman had taken a shining to Luka.

"Well young man," Hoffman spoke in German. "You certainly are very gifted with languages. I think my office could greatly benefit by having your skills available." Lunch had been delivered to meeting room 7 where the German delegation had assembled to eat. Adam was aware that both Shane, who was wearing his glasses and Jonathan Stevens were seated at a table nearby. The economist continued, "We have a lot of dealings with countries within the Euro Zone and as you know being able to communicate is paramount to success."

"I am always open to new adventures," Luka replied trying not to sound too excited. He looked over at Heinrich and purposely faltered. "Right now I need to concentrate on the Conference. If I get through these next few days I can get through anything." It was a loaded remark, designed to see how Heinrich would react. It became clear to Adam that Hoffman's assistant did not think that his boss or Luka would be around long enough to cement a working relationship beyond the Conference. Heinrich looked away almost grinning, but Adam narrowed his gaze and searched the others man's visual transmissions. *Day 4,* Adam thought to himself, *they intend to make their move during the morning session of day 4; the day after tomorrow.* The Agency would probably wait to execute their takedown until those responsible had most things in place. Jarvis had less than two days to get back to Adam. Time indeed was running short.

"Excuse me, Herr Hoffman," Luka said, "I have an errant to run before the afternoon session begins. I will see you in the Ballroom a little later." As he rose from the table Adam nodded curtly at Heinrich and headed for the exit. Shane Stevens watched him carefully as he left the room; it was obvious that he'd sensed something wrong with Luka's demeanour. Adam hoped he wouldn't have to show his hand prematurely. He needed to be certain his suspicions were right. What Jarvis discovered would determine Adam's next move.

* * *

Shane Steven's was tired. He never imagined things would turn out this way. Not only had he all but lost his son, he'd also found himself in the middle of something that was so totally beyond what he could wrap his head around. The Agency had been good to them. It had liberated them from Bergstein and helped them through the difficult time of transitioning back into the real world or at least part of it. They'd put both Jonathan and Danielle in their academy near Newark, suggesting it would be a good way to get them back on track after what Bergstein had put them through. They were young, not quite teenagers; their cartal glands were just starting to mature. Thankfully the people funding Bergstein hadn't been able to use the children's enhancement for whatever plan they'd conceived.

The Agency continued to provide both 1st generation survivors with the drugs necessary to hold off the effects of the enhancement and tried to make things right after many years of confinement. Bergstein had kept them drugged in order to keep control and for Shane most of those 12 long years were a blurry nightmare. He'd been helpless when he'd watched from the helicopter as the Swiss clinic burned and helpless as Bergstein's men pulled his beautiful Elena from his arms. The Agency gave Shane and Sophia time to readjust but they were prohibited from contacting their families until the Agency was able to provide safeguards that would keep existence of the enhancements from going public. Shane was told it was in the survivors' best interest. The Agency's involvement must also remain secret. Years passed and Sophia became anxious to move on so she took her daughter out of the Academy and moved on with her life.

All seemed to be going well. With no family to go back to Shane remained close to the Academy, restarting his life knowing his son was well cared for. As time wore on however, the Agency began to call upon his special abilities. It was just for little things at first and then with more frequency and with greater expectation. The way it had unfolded left Shane with suspicions and unanswered questions; questions that he would insist on being answered once the threat on the Conference was over.

Shane adjusted his glasses and looked at his son seated across from him. It was hard to hide things from him but as Jon had gotten deeper into the Agency's clutches he'd become less open minded. It was as though they had taken away the boy's sense of reasoning. He took their word for everything and they were very careful to insulate him from anything that would make him question it. Shane had expressed his concerns once but the young man had discounted his argument.

"I understand why you have trouble trusting anyone after what's happened," Jon had said, **"but you have to move on. We should to be loyal; look what they've saved us from."** His son had looked at him as though looking at a fool. **"Besides Dad, they are the good guys."**

It was not long after that Caleb arrived; a young 18 year old, utterly devoted to the Agency. Although older, Jon was partnered with him and little by little, Shane lost his son. Now as he sat looking across the table at him, Shane knew he had to find out what was going on. For too long he'd felt like he was back at the clinic, being manipulated and deceived. The fact he couldn't decode any deception wasn't good enough anymore. Something was definitely wrong.

Jon had become enamoured with it all and took an active position with an undercover operation dealing with the Van Hussen Group. It was he who had first discovered dissension in the ranks; strong enough opposition to destroy all those who got in their way with no consideration of collateral damage. Little by little he was able to eek his way in and gain the trust of those who were planning to take over the organization. The Edinburgh Conference had provided the perfect opportunity. The Agency was able to convince both Shane and Danielle to become involved due to the extreme ramifications of what was in the works. He hadn't seen the young woman in over a year and what she'd told him of what had happened since they'd last talked only made him more suspicious.

"You've been wearing those glasses almost constantly," Jon commented as he took another bite from his sandwich.

"Its the headaches," Shane lied. "I'm having trouble with visual overload." He didn't want his son to know that he was trying to hide his own thoughts. It was not the time for a confrontation; there were more important things in play and until the threat on the Conference had ended Shane would have to keep his concerns to himself.

"When this is over you should get checked out," his son replied concerned. "Maybe you need an adjustment to your inhibitors. Danni said Sophia's been having trouble with her doses for years. Promise me you will go when this is all done."

"I promise."

*　*　*

CHAPTER 9

THE RISK PAID OFF, at least partially. Jarvis had known Jonah Ackerman long before he'd become the Compound's director. He was one of the few that had moved up through the ranks and become truly useful. The relationship had been cultivated over many the years. The other man never knew who Jarvis was and when or where he would show up next. Their shadowy interactions began when Ackerman was a young Agency operative. Every once in a while, Jarvis would put in an appearance and provide information that was crucial to a mission's success. Jarvis had a notebook full of individuals that he assisted over the years. Some were with the CIA, others with Interpol or other organizations; anyone that he thought would be useful. At times he even saved their lives or at least that's what they thought. He was always anonymous and left them with the impression that he was always watching. He'd garnered much influence but rarely asked for anything. Of the eight long term connections Jarvis had cultivated, the one with Ackerman had been the hardest to maintain, but had turned out to be the most fruitful.

It was under those circumstances that Smith had approached Ackerman in order to acquire Adam. He'd finally introduced the Director to Global Security, a secret international body that oversaw the world's well being and protected those on the front lines fighting for the cause. They answered to no one and had eyes everywhere. He easily convinced Ackerman that the GS recruitment of one of the Agency's most effective operatives was in everyone's best interests. Decoding had given Jarvis the ability to know what people needed to hear in order to get them to do what he wanted.

At huge risk Global Security once again gained access to the Compound. During his last visit Jarvis had determined that his well cultivated reputation had remained intact but getting Adam out had taken weeks of planning and carefully placed misinformation. Today he would have to improvise and he didn't have time to play games. He'd called ahead and urgently requesting an appointment with Ackerman. Once he mentioned the Edinburgh Conference, the Director made himself immediately available.

Jarvis had taken a few minutes to confer with Adam during the Conference lunch break; he needed to appear informed. He'd never met anyone like the young man. Jarvis had come across many people who were in the global espionage game; he'd made it a point of having people all over the world he could call on. It was a network of individuals who knew nothing of one another. Adam was different and it was more than just his adaptation; he was brilliant and able to see things no one else could, not even Aberdeen. He gave Jarvis hope but he also gave him reason to worry. The 24 year old's iron exterior was tenuous and fragile. Jarvis had seen the confusion and uncertainty during their last meeting. Inside he was an emotional wreck. It was only by sheer will and necessity that Adam hadn't crumbled. At the end of everything the young man would have to face himself and Jarvis wasn't sure how that would unfold.

"Yes Janet, what is it?" The Director asked as he pushed the button on the intercom.

"There are two men to see you, Sir," the voice coming from the speaker informed him, "a Mr. Smith and a Mr. Johnson from Global Security." Ackerman didn't wait for his visitors to be sent in; he met them at the door ushering them himself.

"What's going on?" Ackerman asked as he closed his office door and motioned to the others to take a seat. "This is highly unusual, Edinburgh is not my jurisdiction."

"We had a problem," Jarvis replied. "Although we were able to meditate the breech, some of your people in Edinburgh were briefly compromised." He could read the confusion on Ackerman's face. "It has to do with Epsilon." The confusion turned to disbelief and panic. Jarvis stopped for a moment to read the jumbled thoughts coming from behind the desk. Everything became clear. Adam had been right and it changed everything. Jarvis fought to hold back his anger before he continued. "The Compound is under investigation," His voice was ominous. "What we find will determine whether I shut down the whole operation down." It was a calculated threat. Ackerman was blindsided by the news and rose to his feet.

"Sit down Mr. Director," Johnson quietly but forcefully demanded. He'd stepped forward ready to physically intervene.

"Tell us about the implant Jonah." Jarvis continued. "Whose idea was it?" It was obvious that Ackerman had no idea what Smith was asking. "Who sanctioned the kid's implant. The device shut down and the boy went sideways. He recognized one of your guys at the Conference and remembered that he was connected to Epsilon. If I hadn't neutralized Adam we'd be dealing with more of a political nightmare than we already have." Jarvis narrowed his eyes. "He was supposed to be a part of my team and as it turns out I lost three good men trying to keep him from causing a global incident."

Ackerman sat dumbfounded. He considered very carefully what to say. "The implant program was discontinued 10 years ago and the procedure was banned. It had a poor survival rate and most of those who made it through were cognitively compromised. We had a few altered operatives in place but they were deactivated long ago."

The Director flipped open his computer and began to type. Jarvis refined his gaze concentrating on visually retrieving the other man's security codes and clearance. "Talbot," Ackerman said aloud. "What has the little snake been up to?" He glanced through Adam's file and found no record of an implant. "I'll take care of this Smith. I don't know how he got away with it. There will be a full investigation and I will be getting on the phone with my people in Scotland to let them know there has been a problem."

"Scotland is intact Jonah," Jarvis responded, "my people are watching. They've got enough to worry about right now. This mess with Adam has left me short of man power but be assured we are in place to provide aid if necessary." He paused for a moment looking at Johnson and then back at Ackerman. "I want to talk with Talbot before you confront him." It wasn't a request.

"Absolutely," the Director replied, "and if there is anything I can do to help let me know." Whenever he had dealings with Smith it made him feel better, like someone was looking out for him. Hopefully Talbot would come clean and the Compound wouldn't be under suspicion. Ackerman rose and shook Smith's hand before the two visitors left his office.

*　*　*

Talbot felt the panic rise to his chest. He'd seen the two GS men on the security cameras. They'd gone straight to the Director's office. He knew they were trouble; his trouble. Adam had been gone for 10 days and as each day had passed Talbot was able to convince himself a little more that it was over; that what he'd done would not come back to bite him. He sat back in his chair and looked around his office knowing there was no way out. He'd had a good run; a good life. He reached inside his top drawer and felt the cold hard metal of his gun but knew he was too much of a coward to end his own misery.

And it was misery. He'd sat in the same chair 10 days before but then he'd taken the gun out and laid it down on the desk in front of him. He'd lifted it to his temple several times before coming to the conclusion that he just didn't have what it took to pull the trigger. Eight years ago the implant seemed the only way to salvage years of work and help the boy be the kind of operative he was destined to be. Talbot needed to regain control or Adam would have been terminated. It had been through his masterpiece that the Handler had found his success. As he looked back through the years heaviness came over Talbot that almost crushed him. They wanted the world to be a safe place but were not willing to give him the tools to get the job done. He'd taken matters into his own hands with great success. No one could argue how effective Adam had been in the field. His face became flush and sweat began to bead on his forehead. He wondered how long he would have to sit and wait before they would burst in. He didn't have to wait long.

Jarvis walked past the receptionist, went down the hall and calmly opened Talbot's door; his partner close behind. Calvin Talbot sat behind his desk sweating and but expressionless. Johnson closed the door and flicked the switch that turned off the cameras. He would start asking the questions allowing Jarvis time to decode exactly what was going on in their target's head. They'd been a team for a long time; he knew how it all worked.

"Mr. Talbot I assume you know why we are here?" Johnson asked as he walked up to the desk and leaned toward the man sitting behind it. Talbot said nothing. He didn't want to give any information until he knew just how much they knew. Jarvis could decode each scenario that went through Talbot's mind: maybe Adam lost control and ran off, maybe he fell over dead during a mission and GS were unable to recover his body, maybe he disappeared. Panic increased with each possibility until the man behind the desk started to hyperventilate.

"Do you know what your stupidity has done to Epsilon?" Jarvis said softly; almost whispering. Johnson stepped aside allowing his partner to take over. Both men watched Talbot try to reconcile how Adam and Epsilon may have been connected. He knew Adam was not involved with the program. If he had been, the Director would have taken him at the beginning. The Agency handler began to run through everything he knew about it. Jarvis could decode bits and pieces but could make no real sense of all disjointed images. He narrowed his gaze.

"Its over Talbot," Jarvis stated calmly; again his voice ominous.

"Who are you?" Talbot desperately demanded rising to is feet. Without warning Jarvis took two full strides forward and pushed the desk straight back. It's force drove Talbot back making contact at hip level. He landed awkwardly on his chair which propelled backward only stopping as it hit the wall. Jarvis stood looking down at him. "What does Adam have to do with Epsilon?" Talbot asked weakly.

"Who sanctioned the implant?" Talbot didn't reply. He was shaking and a small red spot began to form near his left hip. Jarvis put his weight behind the desk, shoving it closer to the terrified man. "Who sanctioned the implant?" Jarvis stated calmly, his voice deep and thick with warning. Talbot flinched. "If you don't answer you're going to wish you had used that gun you've got hiding in your drawer." Jarvis stared at him and tried to understand how he had ever risen in the ranks of the Agency. The master manipulator had become a quivering coward.

"No one," Talbot replied as he continued to hyperventilate. He was getting light headed so he closed his eyes and slowed his breathing. Pain began to cloud his senses. "It was the only way I could control him. He'd begun to question everything. The Agency needed him.'

He was confused that Smith knew about his gun. He wondered how long they'd been watching him and what else they might know. Images of what he'd been doing since Adam left flashed through his mind and Jarvis was able to pick out a few of Talbot's recent encounters. It was obvious that the Agency would not approve.

"You've been a very bad boy Calvin," Jarvis observed, "and the Agency is not happy with you." Jarvis took Talbot's laptop that was sitting askew on his desk and spun it around. He inserted a device much like the one Adam had into a USB port and typed in Ackerman's password. He then opened the Epsilon file. Everything he needed was there. He looked at Johnson and nodded. The other man switched him places and began to copy the needed files onto a thumb drive.

Jarvis stared at Talbot. "Its people like you who make this world a dangerous place," he said. "Even though you know what you are doing is wrong you convince yourself that doing it for the right reasons makes it okay. It doesn't." The man quivering in front of him was no different than Anthony Bergstein. Jarvis had spent much of the last 25 years searching for the ones that were taken and it had led him here. Along the way he'd made choices he wasn't proud of and crossed the line more than once but he'd also told *himself* it was for the right reasons. It made his stomach turn realizing what the past had also turned him into but there was no turning back now. He was certain that it was going to get a whole lot messier. He needed to get back to Scotland. Adam could not be left to face everything alone. He had to tell the others about what he'd discovered and they needed to figure out what their next move was going to be.

*   *   *

Aberdeen was going crazy. No one would tell her where her father had gone. She paced up and down the observation deck too angry and worried to join the others for lunch. Flynn had assured her that Jarvis was no longer at the Conference but on other business.

"What other business?" she said aloud. The young woman was seething. "I'm not a child; I have just as much to lose as everyone else." Flynn had also assured her there had been no movement at the warehouse so Adam was in no immediate danger. *No immediate danger,* she laughed. *Who are they trying to kid?* She was still reeling from her experience with Adam the night before. She'd caught a small glimpse of what lay beyond the guarded outer wall of who he wanted people to see, but she could not be sure it had been genuine. Aberdeen was more confused than ever. He hadn't said goodbye or seen her off. Maybe she'd read his signals wrong or maybe it had all just been part of the act.

She stopped short, trying to decide her course of action. Biting her lower lip she quickly braided her hair and tucked it into the back of her blouse. "I need to do something," she muttered smoothing out her sweater and heading back into the warm of the yacht's cabin.

*   *   *

At the afternoon session all the different brainstorming groups came together to discuss what they thought was the most pressing issues facing global economic stability and growth. The ballroom was filled with passionate, defensive people trying to jockey for position and influence. It was grueling for Adam. He saw the problems as black and white. He knew that with objective reasoning and forward thinking real solutions could be found and positive outcomes for everyone could be reached, but most were still playing the blame game. It continued much the same way until the final speech.

Kristof Hoffman approached the podium with dignity and authority. After the crowd quieted he remained silent for a few moments looking at the faces seated before him. Back at his station Adam listened through his earphones and translated the impassioned message. Hoffman addressed the conference, speaking of equality and unity. The German spoke for over an hour summarizing his ideas on how to solve the debt crisis but reminding those in the greatest trouble that past standards of living could not be sustained.

During this riveting speech there was activity in others parts of the hotel that was going unnoticed. A large shipment of supplies was delivered to the laundry and housekeeping department. Inside half of the large boxes marked detergent was the second to last shipment of the materials needed to fulfill the attack. They'd arrived on schedule. The entire second shift was made up of conspirators and they were able to transport the substance to where it could be easily accessed when the time was right.

"Everything is in place sir," a large man dressed in a hotel usher's uniform spoke into the phone. "We're right on schedule." He looked at his watch; 4:45pm. "We are a go in 42 hours 15 minutes." Everything would be put in place in plenty of time and the countdown to Saturday 11:00 am began. All the big players would be gathered together for one last quick meeting before the General Assembly had their final session. Among those present would be Ada Cosse, Kristof Hoffman and the American finance minister, 18 other important officials would also be representing the most powerful countries in the world, most of them belonging to the Van Hussen Group.

41 hours 30 minutes until the attack.

Adam put down his headphones and took a drink of water. The last few hours had been a test of his ability to multitask. Hoffman's speech had been brilliant and easy to translate but about halfway through it Adam had noticed a small burst of activity at the Security desk. He was trying to stay alert and aware and still allow Luka to get his job done. He'd been unable to focus enough of his attention to the desk earlier, so he made his way to towards it hoping to find out what had happened. Things had settled down but he could tell that something was up.

He quickly assessed the men behind the desk. "Have you gentlemen seen a tall man with a moustache pass by here?" he asked. "He was wearing a green jacket and was in a big hurry." Adam chuckled. "It was like he needed to get somewhere before the world ended."

"No one like you described had passed by this desk," one of the guards replied. "Sorry." The young guard in the back rubbed his brow and nervously inhaled. Adam focussed on him narrowing his gaze. His hunch paid off. The order had come down: Saturday at 11 am; the end of the world. Decoding made things so easy. A small group of receivers would give any organization a huge advantage especially if it remained secret.

Adam thanked the guards and headed up to his room. He looked at his watch: 5:37 pm and then set his stopwatch to countdown how much time remained before the attack. His head hurt. There were too many variables for him to deal with easily.

He needed to find out when the Agency would make their move. If things unfolded before he had a chance to talk with his father it could be too late. They may disappear. Hopefully Jarvis had been able to get the needed information and would get back to him before the night was through. Time was running out.

Back in his room Adam took off his socks and shoes. He sat at his desk enjoying the feel of the warm carpet cradling his toes. Removing the heel of his shoe, the tired young man retrieved the USB device and pushed it into his laptop. Immediately an email notification popped up. It was from Jarvis; he'd sent the entire Epsilon file. Adam phoned down to room service and settled in for a long read.

Conference Day three Friday
27 hours 32 minutes until the attack. (7:28am)

Jarvis arrived at the airport early in the morning. Along with sending Adam the Epsilon file, He'd set up a meeting for 8:30am. Adam would leave for a run sometime around 8 am in order to make the 5 kilometers to a small park near the hotel. The drive from the airport would take about 35 minutes if all went as planned.

*   *   *

Sleep eluded Adam yet again. He'd had the dream but this time it was different.

Thick smoke was filling his room as it poured in from under the door and it made his eyes burn. He needed to get out he had to save her but the door was locked. He pounded on it in vain. The familiar sound of a helicopter pounded in his ears. He stepped on the bed and reached up to the window sill. He stood on his tip toes in order to see the landing pad through the small window. The smoke got thicker. He began to cough. Even if he could break the glass the window was too small for him to climb out.

"Help me Adam," she screamed. It was Aberdeen and pulling her toward the helicopter was a man Adam had seen many times before; Talbot.

"Don't worry young lady," he said to her, "I'll have you fixed up in no time at all. After the operation things will be a lot simpler . . . for both of us." She struggled against his grasp terrified.

"Let go of me," Aberdeen pleaded. "Adam where are you? You promised," she screamed again. From inside the helicopter a tall man who looked strikingly like Jarvis reached out to take her. His eyes were blank and his face expressionless. Helpless Adam watched her ushered into the helicopter.

*   *   *

Sleep was out of reach. The nightmare terrified him because of its underlying possibilities and the sleeplessness gave Adam's mind a chance to race. The Epsilon file had given up secrets that the Agency had kept for more than 25 years. If anything, they'd planned for the long term. The scope of the program was three fold; experimentation, cultivation and reproduction. It really wasn't about his father and the others; it was all about Bergstein's genetic mutation. The 1st and 2nd generation had served their purpose and would soon become expendable. Use of their abilities would be of great benefit until phase three kicked in but the Agency would not allow them to become a liability. If necessary the kill orders had already been given.

It was phase three that disturbed Adam the most. He wiggled his toes in the plush carpet one more time before putting on his socks and running shoes. The run would help clear his mind and hopefully energize him. He knew that adrenaline was all that was keeping him going. At some point he was going to crash. *A few more days,* he thought looking around his room to make sure everything was in place. Then putting on a small backpack, he headed out.

It was just before 7:30 am when Adam began his run. He'd studied the route and calculated the morning traffic patterns. Five kilometers would not be enough so he took to the back streets. A cool breeze flowed through the city and the clouds threatened to burst open. It didn't matter; if it rained it would help distract Adam. His mind was racing with all the "what ifs" of the next few days. He worked and reworked different scenarios leaving nothing to chance. Dr. Erikson would be mortified; they all would be.

At last Adam was able to concentrate on the pounding sound of his heart beating in his chest. It was therapeutic. He focussed on keeping his stride a constant 1:3 ratio with his heart rate. He became aware of every step and every beat. His breathing slowed; Adam was in the zone. It was as though the world around him moved at half speed. His senses picked up everything; the squeal of a tire, a woman opening a window, the leaves gently rolling along the curb side. This was Adam's favourite place. It always had been. It was where the cares of the world did not exist. It was all about the next step, the next landmark and the next mile.

Jarvis was waiting. He sat on the green park bench; the metal, cold through his clothing. Behind him running along the length of the pathway, a decorative metal wall kept park goers off the landscaped flower beds. Vibrant colours peeked from between thick green foliage. A drinking fountain stood next to an imposing lamp post just across the cobble stoned path where Jarvis sat; next to it another bench.

He felt old and very small. He'd thought that once they'd found the others things would be finished. He'd been so wrong. The sound of shoes falling caught his attention and he glanced over his newspaper and then at his watch; 8:29 am right on time.

Adam had to admit he felt better; he knew he would. Taking off his pack and placing it on the bench he turned and took a long drink from the water fountain. **"I'm glad you made it back safely,"** he communicated looking over at the man who was exactly where he said he would be. **"I don't know how you were able to pull it off. I've underestimated you."**

"Somehow I don't think that is entirely true." Jarvis replied. **"Maybe one day we will be able to sit down and compare notes. You read the file?"**

Adam began to use the bench to cool down. Placing one leg up, he stretched one hamstring and then the other. **"Yes."** He paused. **"The attack is scheduled for 11am tomorrow; the Agency will be on the move sometime before then. We have no way of knowing exactly when. My best guess will be just as all the elements are coming together. They'll want to eliminate any future threat."**

"Agreed," replied the man looking over the newspaper. **"The sooner we are able to approach Shane the better. We have no idea when the Agency will pull them. I should be the one to tell him. I think my past relationship will leave him with no doubts."** Jarvis took a deep breath. **"We don't have time to answer questions. He needs to understand how much danger they're in."**

"Agreed," Adam switched stretches and then took a light wind breaker from his small back. He was starting to get chilled. **"What are you going to tell the others?"**

"I've sent the file to Flynn and told them to stay put until we contact them. I also left instructions for him to try and locate the second clinic making sure he was aware that the Agency would be watching for anything suspicious."

"Stay close," Adam told him. **"I will set up a meeting with Shane as soon as possible, then text you. Be alone and be careful."** Adam looked directly at Jarvis and crisply nodded before grabbing his pack from the bench and jogging back down the path. It was 8:36 am.

The run back was direct and quick. By the time Adam arrived back at the hotel he was covered in sweat and beginning to shake. He quickly stopped at the gym where he replaced his electrolytes and then went directly to his room to shower and get ready for the day's Conference meetings. He needed to eat so Adam headed for the German meeting room to make the most of their daily buffet breakfast.

Heinrich Maier glared at Adam as he entered the room. Hoffman's assistant looked somewhat dishevelled, as though he hadn't slept well. The anxiety of being involved with such a cold blooded attack was obviously getting to him. He tried to act natural but inside he was a bundle of nerves. Adam ignored him. The attack was the Agency's problem; they would take care of it. He just wanted to know when they would make their move.

Adam would attend a strategy meeting with Hoffman at 10:30 am. It was now 9:25 am and he scanned the room as his filled his plate. Shane Stevens sat next to an older man in a security uniform. He was obviously with the Agency. Adam considered his next move. There was no time to look for opportunity so Adam had to make one. He swallowed and inhaled. *Why does this have to be so hard?* Adam made a bold move and sat across from his father.

"**We need to talk,**" Adam didn't look directly at him, "**but not here.**" He waited for a reply, decoding the reaction to his transmission. Shane remained calm, outwardly ignoring the young man, but inwardly surprised and confused.

"**Who are you?**" came the reply.

Adam chose his words carefully. "**I know about Anthony Bergstein, the clinic and about Elena. Can you get away?**"

Her name caught his Shane's attention and he involuntarily coughed. He reached for his coffee and took a slow calculated drink in order to regain his composure. "That went down the wrong way," he said aloud clearing his throat several times. He calmly scanned the room.

"**When and where?**" Shane asked.

"**15 minutes; outside the front entrance to the left; just beyond the cameras.**" Adam sipped his coffee.

Both men continued to eat their breakfast. Shane chatted casually with the man next to him for a few minutes continuing to intermittently cough and sputter. Adam finished his meal quickly, nodding at the two men as he left the table. He went directly to the nearest restroom, into a stall and texted Jarvis.

Shane coughed and sputtered again. He moved his chair back from the table continuing to clear his throat.

"Are you okay?" asked his companion.

"I've got to walk this off," Shane replied sputtering. "Maybe some fresh air will help." He got up from the table still clearing his throat. "I'll be back shortly."

His companion looked at his watch. "You've got about a half an hour. I'll meet you back here." With a quick nod Shane Stevens excused himself still trying to clear his throat; he headed for the front entrance of the hotel being careful that he was not being watched or followed. Not one to get flustered, he remained calm going over everything he knew about Luka Reznikov. He had to be 2nd generation but where did he come from? Shane had always thought there weren't any others . . . What was going on?

* * *

Jarvis' heart raced. He hadn't talked with his friend in 25 years. They'd been close; best friends even before arriving at Bergstein's clinic. Shane came from a little town in Canada. He'd grown up in the prairies on a ranch owned by his father. Discontented he'd left for Europe wanting to see what the world. They'd met in Madrid and forged an instant friendship; two 20 year old kids looking for adventure. Shane was tall, handsome and suave. He could talk to anyone and was absolutely fearless. In contrast, Jarvis was quiet and thoughtful, trying to keep them both out of trouble.

The car was parked in a lot a block from the hotel. He waited just out of camera range. He stepped forward as Shane approached. "**Shane,**" he transmitted. "**Don't react, just walk.**" Shane was stunned, recognizing his old friend immediately. He fell into step beside him, his head a storm of questions. As they approached the car he stopped to look at his friend.

Daniel . . . ?" Shane replied his thoughts raging, "**I** . . . ?"

"**I'm sorry. There's no time to explain,**" Jarvis replied, opening the front passenger door of the car. "**Get in.**" He went around the car and got in behind the wheel. "**The Agency is not what you think it is. Your usefulness to them is running out.**" Jarvis put his hand on his friend's shoulder and took a deep breath.

I've been looking for you for 25 years." He shook his head. "I wish we had more time but we don't.

"What's going on Daniel?" asked the dumbfounded man.

"The Agency was the one funding Bergstein. They didn't rescue you from him: they relocated you once the children were ready. They used the goodwill they'd cultivated from that lie to manipulate you. Everything the Agency has done has been a well executed plan." Jarvis stopped long enough for his comments to be absorbed.

"How could that be?" Shane asked, "None of us picked anything up." He was struggling, trying to make sense of what his friend was telling him. "At some point someone would've let something slip. How could the Agency hide this?"

"It was very careful that your direct contact was only with those that had no prior knowledge of their involvement," Jarvis replied. "Very few know of what is really going on and none of it is sanctioned by the government."

Shane had a sense of dread. He'd been suspicious of the Agency for some time but could not have imaged what he was being told. "What do they want?"

"Once Jon and Danielle proved to be enhanced they set their eyes on the 2nd generation but for whatever reasons they were unable to produce anymore offspring." Jarvis took a deep breath. He too was having a hard time coming to terms with the depth of what was going on. "They switched their focus to the third generation. Shane ran his hands through his hair, struggling with Jarvis' words.

"What exactly are you saying Daniel?" he asked, afraid he already knew the answer.

"Altering our genetic code was the hard part, producing 3rd generation offspring in the lab was easy." Jarvis replied. "What I'm saying is there's another clinic and its filled with children. They used Danielle and Jonathan's DNA to produce more children."

*   *   *

The man in the white lab coat looked down at the lifeless child lying on the operating table. He was angry and frustrated. He'd been so sure he'd gotten it right. Ambrose would not be happy but what did he expect; they were asking the impossible. He'd tried to tell them. These children were invaluable. Risking their lives to gain a few short years seemed haphazard.

The outcome was the same; deterioration of the lower brain. Accelerating the cartal gland's development had not allowed the child's natural defenses enough time to offset the breakdown and death occurred within hours of the treatment session. The deadline would pass without success. The intensity and frequency of therapy needed to be decreased and the introduction of inhibiting neurotransmitters considered.

Tomorrow they would start again. As he took off his latex gloves the man made a mental note to change the oscillation rate of the light flashes during the initial treatments. He took a deep breath and tried to prepare himself for a confrontation with Ambrose.

CHAPTER 10

A SATELLITE IMAGE CAME up on the meeting room screen as Flynn quickly rechecked the printout in front of him then zoomed into a large group of brick buildings surrounded by high fences and hedges. He played with the resolution and then transferred to another satellite in order to get a crisper image. Every detail was crucial. Aberdeen and Dale Johnson entered just as Munroe reached over to the printer to retrieve a group of awaiting papers.

"This clinic is off the radar," Johnson stated. "I've scoured the Agency budget and there is no way to trace any monies going in and any knowledge of Epsilon seems to be limited to the Compound with only a select few knowing of Bergstein's work and even fewer, the scope of his experiments."

"I checked and the personnel files of the others don't include any record of Epsilon, their enhancement or their time with Bergstein." Aberdeen continued. "They're all labeled as civilian employees, except for Jonathan who is an active operative."

"Secrecy seems to be paramount," Johnson added.

"So we are certain none of this is sanctioned by the government?" asked Flynn.

"Definitely. We aren't even sure any of this is sanctioned by the Agency," Dale Johnson replied. "My guy at head office is unable to confirm Epsilon or the existence of a clinic."

"Was he careful?" asked Flynn. "We don't want them to know we are onto them."

"Not to worry," Johnson replied, "He went in through the back door."

"I found her," Munroe said quietly. He looked up from the pages stacked in front of him. "They've got her in a special care home in Dallas." Everyone was silent. Sophia would be their first priority. She was in great danger. The Agency had already red flagged her and there was evidence that they would soon stop giving her the drugs needed to stay off brain deterioration.

"Ok," Flynn responded, "let's switch gears. Aberdeen, tell the doctor and get him up here." He looked over at Johnson. "Dale, get a hold of your people stateside; we are going to need their help." Both left the room, leaving the two old friends alone together. Munroe sat staring at the pages in front of him, a heaviness of uncertainty weighing him down.

"What will I say to her?" he said not really wanting or expecting an answer. Flynn didn't look at his friend. He was lost in his own thoughts deep in the past, thinking of the one he'd lost forever and wishing things were different.

*   *   *

24 Hours 55 Minutes until the attack (10:05 am)

Shane Stevens was visibly shaken when he returned. Adam didn't know exactly what was said but it was obvious the older man understood. Adam's goal was still to help get those who were taken and then get out, but it had gotten a whole lot more complicated. The Agency had to be stopped.

His phone vibrated. *Jarvis,* Adam thought as he answered the phone. "Hello," he said walking toward a chair placed at the back of the lobby.

"The Agency will make their move at 10am tomorrow," replied Jarvis. "Shane knows everything and will deal with the others although he is worried about Jonathan. He thinks the Agency has him and its too risky to get him out now. His loyalty might put the others at risk." Jarvis paused. "Shane's had concerns about the Agency for awhile."

Adam took a seat and scanned the lobby. People were getting ready for the morning's session. "They need to get out without tipping the Agency too much. If it finds out what we know . . ." he said.

"I know." Jarvis replied, "The second clinic will be unreachable. Focussed chaos during the last stages of the Conference operation may be the perfect opportunity to make a move. He will get back to you with the details.

"Any news from Flynn?" inquired Adam.

"Not yet," Jarvis responded, "but I'm on my way to the yacht now. I'll call you after I talk to the others."

"Hold off on that," Adam looked at his watch again. "The morning session is about to start. I'll call you during the break." Adam paused and took a deep breath. "Jarvis?"

"Yes?"

"Did you tell him who I am?"

"After everything was said and done you never came up," Jarvis answered, he heard the anxiety in Adam's voice. "Besides neither of you need that right now. Call me when you can."

"Expect it around noon. Make sure the others don't get ahead of themselves; it could be disastrous." Adam hung up. He sat back in the chair and looked at his watch. 10:12 am—less than 24 hours until the Agency made their move. Adam only had a few minutes before it was time to report for the morning session. He debated with himself as to his course of action.

The only good thing about all of it was the Agency now thought Adam was dead. It gave him a small sense of security. He needed to know what Flynn had found and had to make sure his departure from the Conference wouldn't be premature. Adam didn't want to jeopardize the Agency's chance of stopping the attack in anyway. Luka was a wild card; if he disappeared it might take some of the focus off the task at hand. There were a few things he needed to decide. Once the others got away things would start happening fast within Epsilon. What string of events would their departure begin? How would the second clinic be affected? Epsilon was a covert project, how many people knew of its existence? It became clear to Adam what needed to happen; he needed to talk to Flynn and he needed to find his father.

*   *   *

Jarvis said nothing when he arrived at the yacht. After a hug from his daughter he watched the activity in the meeting room. Flynn explained their plan to recover Sophia. It was brilliant and would no doubt succeed but he remained quiet until he'd finally seen and heard enough.

"I want everyone to stop," Jarvis said quietly. "You've all forgotten something." He took a moment to look at each face stopping at last on Munroe. "Every move we make will have a domino effect on everything else. What do you think Epsilon will do if when they discover Sophia is gone? They'll look for her, the others will be put in more danger and the second clinic will be unreachable. The Agency has too much to lose." Everyone was at a loss for words. "I understand the urgency but we must look at the whole picture. We can't show our hand too soon. Shane told me a few things that will make a difference. We need to think the whole thing through." He paused for a moment. "We must do this all in such a way that will put an end to the Agency's interest in Epsilon. Their file on Bergstein and the results of his experiments must be closed. If it isn't we'll always be running."

No one spoke for a long time; their respect for Jarvis and the truth in his words gave them reason to pause. It was Munroe who broke the silence and as he spoke his eyes burned. The two people he thought he may never see again were so close yet still out of reach. As much as he didn't want to admit it Jarvis was right. "Visual decoding is obviously too valuable to them to just let go. They've invested a lot of resources and time doesn't seem to have been a barrier. We either need to silence the few who know about it or make them think the project has failed."

"Dale," Jarvis said. "What have your people found out about Epsilon, the Bergstein experiments and the second clinic?"

"They are still working on it," Johnson answered as he looked down at his tablet, "but it looks as though knowledge of what Epsilon is limited to the Compound and its small satellite group. There are also 2 Agency operatives directly assigned to it under a different code name. We only know this because we tracked Caleb. Shane and Danielle are considered civilian security specialists and are called in on special assignment. There is no record of their abilities. It's the same with Jonathan. He became active 5 years ago but there is no mention of the enhancement. Epsilon is not classified top secret, it doesn't have to be. There is no government record of the program at all. We are trying to access general Agency records now. Jonas Ackerman seems to be the only one with full access to the entire project. His clearance is the only one that can access the file, but it isn't likely that he is the guy at the top. He does make several references to someone code named 'Julian' and it looks like he may be the one calling the shots."

"Do we have any idea who 'Julian' is? asked Jarvis.

"No."

"What about the second clinic?" Dr. Erikson inquired.

Flynn cleared his throat. "The second clinic is actually a small private school just outside of Akron Ohio; the St. Thomas Academy. It looks like the children have been integrated into the student population.

"We should be able to find some other evidence of it in Agency's files," Johnson interjected. "If it is being masked as another training compound it should be easy to track down."

Jarvis considered their options. If not for decoding Ackerman's reaction to Jarvis' mention of Epsilon, the clinic would have remained secret. If the information they needed couldn't be found through conventional methods they would have use other means. He shook his head trying not to imagine a world where decoding was used for political and military purposes. They had to get to the second clinic and stop the Agency from following through with Epsilon.

"Dale get your guys to set up surveillance on the school as soon as possible. Flynn, you and Johnson need to head to Akron. We need to find out as much we can before we make a move and decoding may be the easiest way. They must use outside workers on some level; make contact and glean as much as you can and if possible get inside." He paused for a moment looking at his daughter then turning to face Munroe. "You, Aberdeen, the Doctor and I will reassess the Dallas plan to get Sophia out." Jarvis looked at his watch. "Adam will be calling in about 30 minutes hopefully he'll give us a better idea what's happening at his end and we can compare notes."

* * *

The morning session had gone long and Adam had seen no sign of Shane Stevens or the others. At the lunch break he went straight to his room to call Jarvis. Holding his jaw to change from Adam to Luka was taking its toll and as he relaxed his face he took a deep breath. It was almost over. He searched his room again looking for a listening device. He couldn't afford to take any changes. Adam then took out his phone and called Jarvis.

"Hello Adam."

"Fill me in Jarvis," Adam replied. "I don't have much time." Jarvis told of the school in Akron.

"The clinic is at the St. Thomas Academy. It's a private school in Akron. Flynn and Johnson are on their way there now. We haven't had any success finding any more information about it at this end, other than what Ackerman let slip." Adam could hear Jarvis fumble through some paper. "Hopefully Dale and his people can figure out who is coming and going and Flynn can pick something up from one of the workers there." The older man paused for a moment. "Its the best we can do for now until we can give the school our undivided attention. Anything from Shane yet?"

"No," replied Adam. "I haven't seen him or the others since before the morning session."

"He was pretty shaken up when he left," Jarvis said. He went onto explain that a plan was in place to get Sophia out. "Ken, Aberdeen and the Doctor will be leaving for Dallas later in the day. We've got a plan but we'll need to coordinate times. If we move too soon it may put the others in jeopardy."

"Do you think Munroe will be able to handle?" Adam asked.

"He wouldn't be going if I didn't," responded Jarvis.

There were two crisp knocks on Adam's door. "Someone's at my door," he said quickly, "I'll call you back."

Adam turned off his phone and approached the door carefully carefully from the side, sliding along the wall. He wasn't expecting company. He waited for another knock.

"Who is it?" Luka answered ready to pounce if necessary.

"Room Service," replied Shane's voice. Adam quickly looked through the peep hole to make sure it was him and then opened the door. Shane entered dressed as a hotel waiter pushing a cart full of food.

"Thank goodness," Adam said aloud, "I'm starving." He clanked the plates a little. **"I've been looking for you."**

"It took me a bit to recover," Shane shook his head. **"This is all so incredible I don't think its really sunk in yet."** He sat in the chair across from Adam sitting on the bed.

"Have you spoken to the others yet?" Adam asked.

"No, Jon is most certainly lost to the Agency; they've already made him think I'm paranoid. He won't believe me and no doubt he'd go straight to them with everything." Shane rubbed his eyes. He felt old. He knew the young man across from him could see his weakness but short of putting on his glasses there was nothing he could do about it. **"Telling Danni would not be a good idea either. She is already totally over her head and when the time comes she will follow me without question. We can explain everything after we're out. The big problem is her mother. They have her under lock and key."**

"Not to worry," Adam assured, **"Jarvis will take care of Sophia. When can you make your move?"**

"Danielle and I are to be on a plane at 9 pm tomorrow to head back to the States." Shane replied. "There's a layover in London and we'll be alone but no doubt watched. If we can get away at Heathrow it might give us enough time to disappear before the Agency expects to pick us up at the airport in Boston.

"What airline," Adam asked, "and how long is the layover?"

"United, flying out of Heathrow at 11:30 pm," answered his father. "That leaves about an hour in London."

"Okay let's leave it at that for now," the young man suggested. "Plan to get out in London. Leave the details to us and don't worry about Sophia, the others will take care of it." Adam looked at his watch. "I need to get back to the Conference soon," he said rising to his feet and heading toward the door. The other man didn't move.

"Luka," Shane looked deeply into Adam's eyes, both confused and terrified, "who are you? Are there others?"

"You were right earlier when you said Danielle is in over her head but the truth is we all are," responded Adam. "When everyone is out and safe there will be plenty of time to explain everything." Shane got up and followed him to the door. "Are you going to be okay?" Adam asked.

"I have to be, don't I?" Shane replied.

Adam's head pounded. With every beat of his heart pain erupted at his temples. He slowed his breathing and regained control. He'd tried to block his father's emotions but it was impossible. Shane Stevens was terrified and confused. Adam opened the door for the man towering next to him. "We all do."

Once alone Adam inhaled deeply, calming his nerves. He made two calls before heading back down to the Conference. The first was to Jarvis. He summarized Shane's visit and explained what needed to happen at Heathrow.

"Their plane will land in Boston at 6:45, Sunday morning," Adam told him. "Munroe and the others have to get Sophia out before the Agency is tipped off that something is going on. They don't need extra agents sniffing around in Dallas." Jarvis agreed.

Adam's second call was crucial to making sure the Agency remained unaware that Shane and the girl would slip away until after their plane was on the ground in Boston.

"Pizza," the voice of the other end of the phone answered.

*   *   *

21 hours 23 minutes until the attack (1:37 pm)

Jon leaned against the wall smirking. There was no guess work involved. The dissidents had taken him in and considered him one of their numbers. It was so easy to tell people what they needed to hear when you knew what they were thinking. Peoples' own thoughts often betrayed them. The Agency was ready and no one would escape their net. The young decoder watched as two men arrived pushing a small trolley. The large laundry room doors opened as one of them pushed the large round button on the wall.

Only two more deliveries and everything will be in place for the attack, Jonathan thought to himself, *or at least that's what is believed.* He smirked again. The hotel decor had allowed all the important elements to be hidden where needed. Large brightly coloured floor vases were placed in the halls at 30 foot intervals giving an opulent air to the corridors but providing excellent hiding places. Pre-conference renovations had afforded the opportunity to have several pots with false bottoms strategically placed throughout the ground floor. Inside were canisters filled with a gas that would destroy the respiratory system of anyone who inhaled it. Security had been purposely predictable, making sweeping checks early in the morning and at night. The disgruntled Van Hussens were confident that everything would be ready to go and that by 11:15 the following morning a new era of global influence would begin. The Agency however had other ideas. Each canister had been disabled and the cache of weapons being amassed filled with blanks.

Only Heinrich Maier and a few others knew all the details; it was better that way. Those involved with the execution of the plan had their job to do and need not worry about anything or anyone else. Jon and the other receivers had gleaned much of what they knew from Maier but contact with the front line players had shown the little things. Things like exactly who would be where and when. If not for decoding the Agency would have needed to move in much sooner and there was no doubt that dangerous men would have escaped.

As Jonathan waited for the men to exit the laundry room he reflected on how much more effective the Agency would be if his father got on board. Danielle didn't have the backbone for such things but his father would be a great addition to the Agency arsenal. They were the good guys but Jon wasn't sure if his dad believed it. The things that had happened in Bergstein's clinic coloured everything about Shane. It seemed that every day he was becoming more paranoid and uncooperative and then there were the headaches. Jonathan was concerned with how frequent they were becoming.

At the other end of the hotel Danielle sat quietly in the lobby watching the comings and goings. She knew something was terribly wrong. Shane had seemingly disappeared only to return looking ill. He was on edge and had again taken to wearing his glasses. The headaches must be getting worse just like they had with her mother before the Agency sent her to Dallas. Danielle felt a sense of dread beyond the stress of the imminent attack. She shook her head knowing how important is was to stay focussed on the task at hand but it was difficult.

The Agency was asking a lot of her. In the last three days, 2 more conspirators had been identified through decoding; bringing their numbers to 14. As the attack neared there may be others so she needed to remain vigilant.

So there she sat studying those that came and went, surveying the ambient thought drifting about the lobby. It was hard and tedious work; people's thoughts were so random and scattered. One moment someone could be thinking of whether or not he charged his cell phone, the next about an upcoming appointment and then suddenly switch to thoughts of uncertainty and panic. Multiply it all by the dozens of people passing through the lobby and it all became a maze of confusion to absorb and decode. It was difficult but Danielle was good at it; better than the others. It was why the Agency kept calling her back, compelling her to get involved in a world that she wanted no part of. She'd moved to Dallas to be close to her mother and gone back to school, trying to break all ties with them but there was always another emergency. She'd determined that this was the last time but so had the last time and the time before that.

*   *   *

Adam looked at his watch for what seemed like the millionth time. He was exhausted and losing focus. Adam knew he had to stay at the Conference until it ended but he was wishing he could just go and find a quiet place to escape. He was torn. He wanted to block everyone out and just let Luka do his job. Getting lost in his character would be so much easier. The attack wasn't his problem; Adam was sure the Agency had everything under control. He wanted to stay out of it but couldn't help himself. He needed to know how things were unfolding. It was easy to detect the elevated emotions in the hotel. They were coming from all sides. The dissidents were not the only ones on edge; the Agency was everywhere. It had become obvious to Adam which hotel workers and security were aware of what was going to go down but almost everyone was oblivious and the delegates knew nothing.

As the speaker's final words continued to drone on Adam surveyed the others sitting around the room. They too, were biding their time until they could stretch their legs and get out of the stuffy room in which they'd all been confined. It was a small space filled to capacity with those that had unluckily chosen to explore the global economic model the English delegation was putting forward. Kristof Hoffman sat next to Adam intermittently asking him for clarification but even he had long since lost interest. When the session ended people began to rise and head for the exit.

"Luka," Hoffman began, "I want you to join me for dinner. I have a proposition for you."

"It would be an honour," Adam replied although he'd intended to spend the evening in his room. He wanted to familiarize himself with Akron and see what he could find out about the St. Thomas Academy. It was not going to be easy to get the children away from the Agency.

18 hours and 32 minutes until the attack (4:28 pm)

As Adam finally headed to the lobby he saw the girl quietly sitting out of the way with a book in her lap. She was scanning the area, totally focussed and fascinating to watch. Adam leaned against the wall and took out his phone. Placing it to his ear he continued to watch Danielle. Her guard was down and he could decode her sadness and frustration. He could also observe her reaction to everything she saw. Suddenly something caught her attention and she narrowed her eyes; Adam followed her gaze. Entering the lobby was Heinrich Maier; he looked professional and controlled but his thoughts betrayed him. He was seething as he walked toward the elevator. Adam looked back at Danielle. She was on her feet with her phone to her ear.

"Something's up with Maier," Adam saw her mouth into the phone. Then the girl turned, walked quickly to the security desk at the entrance. Moments later Jonathan arrived through the hotel worker's entrance and headed straight for the elevator. He pushed the button and then looked over at Danielle.

"**What happened?**" he asked her.

"**I don't know Jon,**" the girl replied, "**but he's angry and up to something.**"

"**Don't worry,**" he nodded to her, "**I've got this.**" Then the elevator doors opened and he was gone.

Adam looked again at Danielle. Her hand was shaking as she ran it through her hair. She was terrified although she hid it well. Her thoughts were clear. She wanted this to end; she wanted out. Watching the girl struggle made Adam angry. The Agency was using these people as disposable pawns. The depth of its calculated indifference had never been so clear. It had to be stopped; they had to be stopped. Adam took a deep breath and looked at his watch. He was expected at dinner in less than an hour.

*   *   *

Aberdeen sat across from the man she'd always known as Uncle Ken. His eyes were closed but she knew he wasn't asleep. Doctor Erikson was to her left in the window seat looking down at the canopy of clouds that hid the ocean far below. The small private jet would land in Dallas in just over 4 hours. Aberdeen was confident that the plan to get Sophia out would work and marvelled at this group of people she'd thought she known so well. The one who surprised her most was her father. In the last few weeks she'd seen a side of him that was foreign. She'd known of his search for the others but had not understood how much it'd consumed him. She wondered where it would all lead. She thought of the children at the school and shook her head in disbelief. Closing her eyes, Aberdeen leaned back onto the head rest and tried to put it all out of her mind. She set it on happier times but to no avail. No matter how hard she tried her thoughts kept going back to one thing; were her father and Adam safe?

*   *   *

Kristof Hoffman sat by himself at a table for two. Adam paused long enough to assess his countenance. This was a man who was accustomed to respect and power. There was no doubt he'd gotten his position within the Van Hussens for a reason. Heinrich Maier's hatred of him was rivalled only by a healthy sense of fear. Adam had seen it cascading in amongst the venom directed toward Hoffman. The scope of the coming attack was extreme but felt to be justified in the minds of those who were willing to kill so many. Adam wondered what the German had done to elicit such strong feelings. All of Luka's dealings with the man had been amiable almost grandfatherly but there had always been something forceful and dark underneath the surface. Adam pasted on Luka's grin and approached.

"Hello there my young friend," the older man greeted motioning for Luka to take a seat.

"Good evening Herr Hoffman," Luka replied. "We will be dining alone tonight? Where is Heinrich?"

"We have come to a parting of ways," answered Hoffman. "That is what I want to talk to you about." He paused as the waiter poured water into their glasses and took their order. Once they were alone again he continued. "I have been watching you young Luka and am very impressed. Your talents would be of great benefit to me and my work." The German smiled. "The truth be told I don't always come across well and could use your help with unruffling feathers. I mean to replace Heinrich and I think you should be the one to do so."

Adam did not answer right away. He took a drink of water and carefully considered what to do next. He determined that Luka would jump at such an opportunity, but he took his time in answering so he could decode Hoffman's position. Before Adam could answer the other man continued.

"I will be leaving the Conference first thing in the morning for London and would like you to accompany me to an important meeting there." Hoffman hesitated for a moment. "If you agree I will let the Conference organizers know so they can release you from your responsibilities at tomorrow morning's closing general assembly." Again he paused; weighing Luka's reaction to his offer.

Adam detected no knowledge of the upcoming attack from the German and it became clear why Maier had been so angry. The man he hated so much would escape the fate planned for the Van Hussen leadership and with his survival, jeopardize any hope Maier had of making his own power play. Before Adam could give Hoffman an answer the older man spoke again.

"You would be paid well and have the opportunity to travel around the world." He wanted Luka to commit.

The young Russian smiled and leaned back in his chair. "I am honoured that you would consider me, Herr Hoffman," stated Luka, "but I need a clear idea of your expectations and for how long I would have to commit."

"Minor details, I'm sure we can come to a mutual agreement," answered the German. "Let's focus on tomorrow's meeting in London and we can discuss the rest afterward. No pressure, if we cannot work out an acceptable contract we will go our separate ways from there."

"Agreed," replied Luka. "After that snoozer of a presentation this afternoon I think I've had enough of the Conference anyway."

Adam bided his time through the rest of the meal, being charming and entertaining. The two discussed the London meeting while they dined. When he finally left it was after 8:00 pm. Departure before the Agency's intervention would simplify things but Adam was certain that Maier would not allow Hoffman to leave the city alive. If Adam did accompany the German economist to the airport the likelihood of arriving without incident would be slim. It didn't matter. He would deal with whatever came his way.

Once upstairs, Adam removed his socks and shoes. He sat on the carpeted floor in the middle of his room and considered everything that had happened since he'd left the Compound two weeks prior. He went over every personality, every resource at his disposal and every bit of information. Extrapolating from his present circumstance Adam formulated several dozen scenarios based on different outcomes of the plans that had already been put into motion. He calculated each possibility and determined its likelihood of success. Confident of his projections, the exhausted young man glanced at his watch; 10:37 pm. He was to meet Hoffman in the lobby at 8 am and still had much to do.

* * *

It had been another sleepless night. The dream had evolved into more disturbing images and left Adam feeling more determined than ever. The Agency had to be stopped. He'd gotten up early and gone to the gym in an attempt to run off the anger pounding within his chest. By 7 o'clock he was ready to depart, having removed all evidence of Luka from every surface in his room. He needed to remain calm and work through the protocol that had kept him alive and undetected in the past. Falling back on what the Agency had drilled into him for so many years was the only way Adam would make it through what needed to be done.

Kristoff Hoffman and his body guard exited the elevator just as Luka had finished checking out. Adam could see the tension in the air and as the German approached the front desk the Conference organizer arrived to bid him farewell.

"I hope the Conference met your approval Herr Hoffman," he said, "and that you are not leaving early due to some inadequacy of our staff at the hotel."

"Everything was as expected," the economist replied, "but important business calls. You have my regards as does your staff." With a quick nod to the girl behind the desk, Hoffman turned and walked toward the large glass doors leading out to the street. Adam and the body guard followed. Waiting at the curb was a dark limousine with the driver ready to open the door. Adam looked at him for a long moment trying to read his intentions and determine if he posed a threat; he didn't. His thoughts were divided between the task at hand and the young woman that awaited his return at his small flat. Once his passengers were comfortably seated, the driver slid behind the wheel and pulled away from the hotel.

Adam sat next to Hoffman in the spacious leather backseat. The body guard faced them. Adam could decode that the big, burly man had not had a good night and was looking forward to napping on the plane. He was on his guard but not at his best. Adam knew that the farther the car got from the city the more danger they would be in. There was no doubt that Maier would not allow Hoffman to get on a plane. Adam took a minute to revisit several scenarios and decided his course of action. As he listened to Hoffman summarize the details of the upcoming meeting, he kept his eyes on the man seated across from him and then with one swift movement Adam's elbow made contact with Hoffman's jaw just below his right ear. It was perfectly placed and delivered. The German would be incapacitated for several hours. Neither man saw what happened and Hoffman collapsed, unable to breathe.

"Herr Hoffman," Luka exclaimed in a panic. "Herr Hoffman are you alright?" The economist's eyes stared back in terror. Springing into action the bodyguard went to him. Adam moved giving them space. "Driver," he insisted, "take us to the hospital!" The next 6 minutes passed slowly. Unable to breathe, Hoffman lost consciousness and the large man trying to care for him started mouth to mouth resuscitation. The driver called forward to the hospital so when they arrived medical staff were waiting and quickly took the unresponsive man into the building on a gurney. In the confusion that followed Adam easily retrieved his bag from the car and disappeared.

He walked the two blocks to the bus station quickly and with purpose. He'd removed his jacket and scarf and replaced them with a dark hoodie. Once at the station he took his satchel from his bag and put his suitcase into a locker. With nothing of value or consequence left inside he would abandon it there. Within 10 minutes Adam was on a bus that would arrive in Glasgow in less than an hour and a half. His flight to Gatwick would leave at 11:30.

CHAPTER 11

THE AGENCY HAD BECOME very proficient at setting up shadow operations within legitimate institutions and organizations. It was the only way to hide their true nature from those who could see through deceit. Sophia's care givers were good people who'd been lied to in order to keep her unquestioning. Not even Danielle had been able to detect what was really going on.

Aberdeen straightened her pink housekeeping uniform and smiled at the handsome young doctor. It was 11:30 am at the Dallas Diagnosis and Treatment Center. She would be doing her rounds in the residence ward, checking in on the nine live-in patients currently under treatment. Sophia was the only long term resident. Aberdeen had paid attention to every detail of the plan to get her out. She reached into her pocket and felt for the syringe that Doctor Erikson had given her. It would all but stop Sophia's heart and needed to be administered 30 minutes before the next shift change. Aberdeen looked at her watch; its timer was set to vibrate in 4 hours and 13 minutes. That would allow her enough time to get to Sophia and administer the drug. It was going to be along day but the others she'd met that were in housekeeping were both friendly and helpful.

When Aberdeen entered the common room, the voice on the TV caught her attention. "Breaking News from the World Economic Conference in Edinburgh," the news anchor announced. "It seems that on the final day of the Conference, international security agencies in partnership with the venue's organizers have successfully played out a well timed and effective antiterrorist simulation. Few of the delegates were aware of the modern day war game and admitted that everything happened so fast they didn't know what was going on until it was over. The closing events continued on as scheduled and the exercise is being touted as a great success by all the agencies involved."

"It is important that international security is ready for worst case scenarios," a representative of INTERPOL added. "By staging such exercises it will give us all a heads up as to what needs to be done in order to protect all citizens from those trying to destroy democracy and freedom." The man paused, "I assure you that at no time was anyone truly in danger and what we have learned today has made us better able to protect not only the public but those who have chosen to serve it."

Aberdeen smirked to herself as she emptied the garbage and wiped down the tables. She was not nearly as naive as she had been even a week ago. The craziness in Edinburgh was over but the knot in her stomach wouldn't go away until she knew everyone had made it out safely.

*   *   *

St. Thomas Academy was a beautiful structure well protected and gated off from the public. It was heralded as a prestigious private elementary school catering to the children of diplomats and politicians from kindergarten to grade 6. Flynn and Johnson were able to trace much of the student population to their families and were in the process of trying to determine which children were part of the third generation. Hacking into the school computer system had helped and they knew from the Epsilon file that there were 14 subjects all under the age of 11 but identifying them was proving to be difficult. 32 children fell within the age parameters and 38 of the 67 students lived at the Academy; the others arrived at the school in the morning and left at the end of each day's instruction.

Flynn had managed to get hired on by the landscaping company that kept the grounds at the school but getting any type of access to the inner workings of St. Thomas would take time. He found it difficult to interact with the faculty but had made friendly contact with some of the kitchen staff and a janitor. He'd seen some children on the playground; they were happy and well cared for. They hadn't learned much but it was a start.

* * *

Adam watched the Edinburgh breaking news report at the Glasgow airport while awaiting his flight. The Agency had mitigated the situation perfectly, contacting the media before the attack had become public knowledge and thereby able to spin the story. During the 1/2 hour flight he finished reading the report Jarvis had forwarded to him. One name caught his attention, 'Julian.' It caused Adam to rethink everything.

He'd met him only once but had seen him several times at the Compound before their encounter. Julian had set up a meeting through an encrypted text while Adam was in the field. He recruited the young operative to terminate a high profile political candidate in London. Adam was told to tell no one of the assignment. Julian was a shadowy figure. He had influence, access to Agency resources and Adam could only imagine what else. Calvin Talbot had no idea he existed and Ackerman pretended he didn't. Foreign political assassinations were banned by all legitimate governments and not even the Agency was willing to elicit such actions from its operatives. It made sense. Neither Bergstein's experiments nor Epsilon could be governmentally sanctioned programs. They flew in the face of UN sponsored Human Rights and Freedoms. If anyone ever discovered their scope "crimes against humanity" charges would be enforced.

As the plane descended for landing in Gatwick, Adam closed his computer. Jarvis would meet him at Heathrow later that evening to make sure Shane and Danielle got away safely and then unbeknownst to the others Adam would take a few days to clean up some loose ends.

Adam booked himself into a hotel near Heathrow. He had nearly 11 hours before meeting Jarvis. In the bathroom he shaved and cut his hair; Luka was gone as was the man who had gotten on the plane in Glasgow. Adam needed to refocus. His nerves were shot and he wasn't sure how he was going to face his father again. Sooner or later the truth would come out and Adam wasn't looking forward to questions about his mother. He knew what the others hadn't had the courage to say. Without medication Elena had long since succumbed to the side effects of the experiment. Adam took a deep breath, laid on the bed and closed his eyes.

He slept until his alarm went off 5 hours later and cleared his head with a shower. He then sat on the bed scanning through pictures of Washington big wigs hoping to find Julian's face in the mix and be able to put a real name to it. At 7 o'clock his hunger forced him to call room service and just as a knock sounded on the door with his food, he spotted what he'd been looking for. Trying to remain invisible in the background of a government press conference was Julian. Adam smiled as he went to the door. It was only a matter of time until he would track him down.

*   *   *

Shane and Danielle checked out of the hotel together. Jon was there to see them off and as the young man hugged his father goodbye, Shane knew it might be the last time he'd see his son. His glasses filtered ambient thought and emotion but he still struggled keeping his directed thoughts positive and light.

"I'll see you in a few weeks," Jon said. "We've got to clean up the remnants of this mess and then I'll be able to take a break before my next assignment." He embraced Danielle and whispered in her ear. "Please make sure the old guy has the headaches looked at and we'll all have dinner as soon as I can get away." She held him tight. It'd been so good to see him even under such stressful circumstances. Danielle smiled. They'd been so close growing up. He'd been her rock and she his. Her mom would be so glad to see everyone. Maybe it would raise her spirits.

During the first minutes of the journey Shane didn't say much. He sat in the aisle seat and kept his eyes closed trying to decide how to explain everything to Danielle. He'd battled with himself many times over the last two days, concerned with how the young woman would react.

"Danni," he began. She turned from the window to meet his gaze. **"The Agency is not who they seem."** Shane used his glasses to filter his thought; his inability to do so without them had always been a frustrating. **"They've been lying to us for years and if we don't get out now they'll never stop."** He looked away. "I have reason to believe we're no longer safe." He turned back and touched her hand. **"Do you trust me?"**

"Yes."

"We have friends at Heathrow."

*   *   *

"Jarvis . . ." Adam directed toward the man leaning against the wall near arrivals. The airport was teaming will travelers and Jarvis looked right past him several times before making eye contact.

"I didn't recognize you," he answered. Adam's appearance had again changed radically. He looked smaller and older. He sported a grey tinged moustache and goatee with dark clothes capped with a black toque. **"Their plane is just landing,"** stated Jarvis.

"Over at the first group of chairs, third seat, reading a newspaper." Jarvis looked over at the man sitting there; he was obviously with the Agency. **"I'll distract our friend,"** Adam said, **"while you direct the others to the washrooms."**

Shane spotted Jarvis immediately. His old friend stood casually by the men's room talking on his cell phone. He made eye contact and directed them to go to the washroom for further instruction. At first Danielle thought nothing unusual of Jarvis' communication. During their dealings with the Agency it had become necessary for a select few to learn to communicate through sight although none were able to receive.

"**It's good to see you again old friend,**" Shane replied. His travelling companion paused, reaching into her bag, giving herself time to scan the people filled space opened before her. It was easy to pick out the Agency sitting at the chairs and she briefly studied Jarvis before turning to Shane.

"**Who is he?**" she inquired.

"**I told you, we have friends. His name is Daniel Jarvis.**"

As Danielle stood in front of the mirror washing her hands a young woman placed a black carryon bag next to her on the floor. There were several other people at the sinks. "Change into these clothes," the woman whispered. "Leave what you are now wearing, your passport and all your ID inside. Take the smaller bag; it has your new passport and travel itinerary." The woman took a brush from her purse and began to run it through her hair. "Go directly through International Security; your flight leaves in 45 minutes."

Danielle took the bag and went into the farthest stall. She quickly switched clothes and retrieved the small bag. Money, a passport and other ID were inside along with a 1st class ticket to Denver, Colorado. She put it in her purse taking out her own wallet and dropping it into the black carry on. Danielle was scared but determined. She was Agency trained. She placed the bag next to the young woman waiting at the sink.

"You'll be travelling alone and someone will meet you once you land in Denver," The woman picked up the bag and turned toward the back stall. "Tuck your hair into your hat; walk with purpose and good luck."

With her hair tucked in, Danielle exited the washroom and scanned the waiting area. A man of Shane's build sat wearing his clothes. He was no doubt waiting for the woman from the washroom. An older man dressed in black spoke loudly into a cell phone causing many of the waiting travelers to look his way. Danielle forced herself toward International Security.

*   *   *

Sophia's room was pleasant and looked out into the back garden. Aberdeen could decode how weak and confused she was and surmised that whatever the medical staff was giving Sophia through the tube coming from her arm, it was keeping her sedated. Code RED was called 12 minutes after Aberdeen administered the contents of the syringe into Sophia's IV. Aberdeen waited in the hallway with others from housekeeping as the chaos in the private room continued. The nurses and doctor tried their best to revive the weakened woman but to no avail. They called time of death at March 23rd 5:37pm.

Perfect timing, thought Aberdeen, *with the time change Shane and Danielle's plane will have just taken off.*

There was a deep sadness coming from the staff and Aberdeen was heartened to know how much the people at the Center cared for Sophia. She'd been there for 8 months and had earned many friends. One man's thoughts however caught Aberdeen's attention. He was an orderly and all he wanted was to quickly get to where he could make a phone call and inform someone of Sophia's unexpected death. Aberdeen waited for him to return. It was just as Dr. Erikson had expected; whoever had been on the other end of the phone would immediately be sending a special coroner. The orderly was to keep everyone from interfering with the body until then. He entered the room, flashed a badge and asked everyone to leave.

Munroe's cell phone rang as he sat in a rental car at the Center's back parking lot. It was Aberdeen and it was time. 8 minutes passed before a black van with Coroner stencilled on the side arrived at the clinic's back entrance. The pylons Munroe had placed, forced the incoming vehicle to park out of the view of the cameras. He and the Doctor each had a syringe.

"We can't allow you to take her body." Munroe whispered in the driver's ear as he plunged a syringe into the man's leg. "She deserves more dignity in death than she had in life." They covered both unconscious men with thick blankets and left them in the van, then retrieved the gurney from the back of the vehicle before entering the building. Dressed the part, it took less than 9 minutes for Munroe and the Doctor to fill the body bag and get Sophia out. Aberdeen drove away in the rental car; the others followed in the Coroner's van.

It was several hours until the two drugged men in the van awoke. They found themselves a long distance from Dallas on a back road; the van's battery gone and their cell phones missing. They had no idea where they were and walking would be their only means of transportation. It would be a full 4 hours before anyone knew with certainty that Sophia had been taken and by then she would be a long way from Dallas.

*   *   *

Jarvis had already left for his plane as Adam watched Danielle's look-a-like sit next to her partner. They sat with their backs to him. He could see the man with the newspaper watching them, and then rise to follow the two as they left for their flight. They breezed through security and boarded their plane without incident. Before leaving the Agency operative made a quick call affirming the pair's departure. Relieved, Adam exhaled deeply; his own flight would be taking off shortly.

*   *   *

Bjorn Erikson came from a family that knew how to make money and although his need to remain hidden over the years had impeded many things, his acquisition of wealth was not one of them. His expansive Denver ranch would provide the perfect hiding place. Sophia would have time to recover and reunions and first time introductions would happen in a safe place. It was well after 11pm when the four travelling from Dallas arrived. They'd taken a small plane from an out of the way airport near Dallas and landed at the ranch. All precautions were taken to ensure their travel couldn't be traced.

Sophia was given a room close to the Doctor's treatment room. The same room where he'd developed the treatment designed to stay off the cerebral complications due to the Bergstein's experiment. Her blood was tested to make sure the side effects were still under control and to determine the time and dose of her next treatment. Munroe stayed by her side while she slept. He was an emotional wreck and he under great stress; almost 25 years had passed since he'd last seen his wife. Doctor Erikson decided to keep her sedated until Danielle arrived. Munroe would have to wait to reunite with his wife until she had regained some of her strength.

Aberdeen curled up in the same bed she'd slept in as a child. Her visits to the ranch had been filled with joy and belonging. It had always been a safe haven. Seeing people's thoughts was a double edged sword. Most things they chose not to say out loud should remain private. There was far too much casual evil in the world floating around to maintain any faith in humanity. The others that gathered here understood that and it had shaped each one. Not even Adam had been immune; he'd also changed profoundly.

Shane, Danielle and Jarvis would all arrive before lunch; Flynn and Adam a little later in the day. Aberdeen struggled with it all. Only a few short months ago everything had been so different and now nothing would ever be the same. She turned on the bedside lamp and reached for her bag. She pulled out a file. It was the same file filled with pictures that her father had shown Adam; pictures of happier times. They all had such promise is their eyes. Aberdeen shook her head. Now, they were burdened with the heaviness of how things were unfolding and whether this small band of people could do anything about it.

*   *   *

Jarvis arrived in Denver first and quickly went to meet Danielle's plane. She recognized him as soon as she entered the terminal and turned away slightly in order to catch her breath. Jarvis approached smiling. Wanting to control over how the truth was revealed he wore his glasses. It would not be an easy tale to tell or to hear.

"Hello Danielle," he greeted, "I've been waiting to meet you for a long time." He gently took her arm and led her over to small group of chairs. It was early in the morning and there were very few people milling around. He waited patiently allowing her time to regain her composure.

"You're from the clinic aren't you?" she asked already knowing the answer. Jarvis nodded. Tears welled in her eyes; she blinked them away. "You died in a fire 25 years ago along with my father."

"There are other survivors and he is among them." Jarvis reached for her hand. It was icy cold. "There hasn't been one day go by since that fire that we haven't searched for those that were taken from us." Jarvis replied with a whisper. Danielle pulled her hand away and inhaled deeply. She turned away trying desperately to absorb his words. She was quiet for a long while.

"My mother . . . ," the young woman began. "I need to get to Dallas . . . I need to . . ."

"Sophia is resting nearby," Jarvis told her. "Once Shane's plane lands I'll take you to her." Again the girl was quiet but she searched his face; tears flowing freely.

"The glasses . . . you're hiding something more from me," she concluded.

Jarvis took a picture from his wallet. It was of Ken and Sophia, taken more than 25 years ago. He handed it to the young woman. "There's plenty of time Danielle," he smiled, "one step at a time."

*　　*　　*

Shane greeted his old friend with a hug. He towered over Jarvis.

"Why didn't you tell me?" Danielle asked. Shane put his hands on her shoulders.

"I didn't know how to Danni," he confessed. He turned to Jarvis, ". . . and Sophia?"

"We've got her," Jarvis replied. "Let's get going she should be waking soon."

On the way to the ranch Shane explained to Danielle some of what Jarvis had shared with him days before at their first meeting. He hid much of his own thoughts behind his glasses, trying to protect her from the little he knew about the second clinic. He explained how Jarvis had been looking for them for so many years and how the Agency was involved with Bergstein from the beginning. They'd manipulated and lied to all of them.

"Does Jon know?" Danielle asked.

"No," replied Shane, "there was no way of telling him without jeopardizing our escape. He is so certain that the Agency are the good guys." He was quiet for a moment. "He already thinks I'm paranoid and I couldn't take the risk of him telling Caleb everything. Besides he had his hands full at the Conference." His voice was heavy with emotion.

"Don't worry my friend," Jarvis assured. "We haven't given up on him." Again Shane was quiet. Then he asked about Luka.

"Luka?" Danielle inquired. "You mean the interpreter at the Conference, the guy from the stairwell?"

"Yes, he's 2nd generation," Shane replied. "Daniel, who is he?"

"You'll know everything soon enough," the other man answered as he pulled in next to the ranch house. He was avoiding the question and his friend knew it. As Jarvis put the car in park Danielle noticed a man waiting at the door. It was her father.

* * *

The weather was comparable to Edinburgh but the trees were in bud. Adam had been to the US capital only once before on assignment. No matter where he'd travelled it had always been while on assignment. He rubbed his eyes and took another sip of coffee. The young man had been scanning through government staff photos for more than two hours with no success. The morning rush had left the little Internet cafe and he considered his next move.

He'd identified three of the men at the press conference in the picture but no one associated with them matched Julian's appearance. Adam closed his eyes and imagined himself back at his only encounter with the mystery man.

Snow was falling as Adam waited near edge of the bridge. It's expanse looked over the Seine and tourists strolled leisurely along enjoying the sights. He was to meet his contact in a bookstore nearby. He spotted the overcoat clad man enter the store; he was late.

The man waited at the back of the shop scanning through books. He'd unbuttoned his coat and loosened his scarf. Adam approached and took a book from the adjacent shelf.

"I prefer reading the classics," the contact said on cue.

"As do I," Adam replied. The man turned and studied him carefully. The young man felt exposed and vulnerable. Bright blue eyes not only assessed him but sent a very clear and dangerous message; this was no game. The figure that stood before him was both ageless and powerful. Adam had caught glimpses of him at the Compound.

"I've been watching you Adam." It caught the young man's attention; he hadn't heard his name in over three years. "I've been waiting patiently for you to become effective and now I can see you're ready." He handed Adam a package. "You will tell no one of me and when I call you will be ready." It was a warning. Adam would never forget those eyes.

Adam paused within the memory and carefully soaked in each detail of Julian's appearance. He made a conscious effort to avoid the man's eyes. Large feet were fitted with expensive shoes. A black overcoat hung below his knees and beneath was a green sweater with large cabling down the front. A green scarf surrounded his neck. The older man was just over 5'10" and a black wool fedora crowned his head hiding his hair. Grey speckled his well groomed eyebrows and three small, round pock marks scared his face to the left of his nose. He had long fingers and just above the thumb of his right hand Adam could see faded numbers inked deeply into the inside of his forearm ". . . 714." Adam instantly recognized the pattern and realized he'd found the clue needed to discover the man's identity. Holocaust survivors were well documented in the US.

*   *   *

CHAPTER 12

DANIELLE TOOK SEVERAL DEEP breaths trying to will herself out of the car. She reflected on how unfair life had been to her parents and how things could have been so different. Jonathan and Danielle had been unaware of many things while growing up. Their childhood had been filled with structure and purpose. The constant assessments and testing were presented as part of normal life and although the children's inability to decode frustrated Dr. Bergstein, the staff at the home kept them from his wraith.

The others did not have it so well. The children didn't know until many years later the events of the first few years after the clinic fire.

"Are you ready Danni?" Shane asked as he opened her door.

She closed her eyes and took another deep breath. **"I'm not sure I ever will be."** As Shane helped her from the car, Danielle looked up at him. "How do I do this?" Taking off his glasses, their eyes met. They smiled at her and were filled with hope.

"We'll all take it moment by moment," he answered. Then the big man hugged her and took her hand. "It's all we can do," he said. They walked hand in hand toward the house. Danielle felt like a little girl. Jarvis stood next to Munroe at the door; he placed his hand on his friend's shoulder in support as they approached.

"Ken," Shane began, "it's been a long time."

"Too long," Munroe replied not taking his eyes off his daughter. "You look like your mother," he said quietly.

His eyes filled with tears; he left himself open wanting no misunderstanding. It was too much and Danielle looked way.

"I need some time," she whispered, ". . . time to process all of this." The young woman closed her eyes and stepped toward the ranch house. She paused for a moment and reached back keeping her eyes turned away. She briefly placed her hand on Munroe's arm in a gesture of acknowledgement. "I'd like to see my mother now please," Danielle asked quietly as she walked through the door.

The ranch house was warm and inviting. Shane followed the girl into the bright interior and instantly recognized Aberdeen from the hotel; they both did.

"Hello Danielle," she smiled. "I'll take you to your mother." Aberdeen guided the young woman down the hall. "This all must be very difficult for you. We haven't told your mother anything yet. We thought it might be easier coming from you, when you think she is strong enough." She paused at the door and waited for a response. There wasn't one, so with another smile she turned back down the hall. "I'll check in on you in a little while, lunch will be in about an hour."

Entering the main sitting room Aberdeen could see that the Doctor had joined the others. They spoke quietly in disbelief of what had transpired over the last few hours. Spotting the young woman Shane rose and stepped toward her.

"How are they?" he asked looking at her with deep concern. Aberdeen had known about this giant of a man her whole life and because of his involvement with the Van Hussen Group had doubted a positive outcome to a reunion. She was happy that her father would not have to reinvent the man he'd spent so many years searching for.

"Sophia is very weak. The drug has worn off but the efforts to revive her at the Health Center caused some injury." Aberdeen replied. "It will take a while before she recovers." She put out her hand to the giant of a man standing in front of her. "My name is Aberdeen Jarvis, **I feel like I've known you my whole life.**" They both turned as Jarvis' phone rang.

"Hello," he answered. Jarvis listened for a moment then looked at Shane. "Yes everyone arrived safely." Again he listened. "When can we expect you?" Another pause. "We'll wait for your call."

"Adam?" Aberdeen asked.

"He has some loose ends to tie up," her father answered. He looked at his friend. "Shane you'd better sit down; there is something more we need to tell you."

* * *

From his small hotel room Adam could see the Potomac River. He looked out over the city. It wasn't a great view but he hadn't expected much for what he'd paid. He could tell Jarvis hadn't been thrilled with his call, but the others were not Adam's first priority. Scattered across the table were a half dozen small electrical devices. He adjusted the miniature transmitters, gathered the other bits and pieces he needed and put them all into a small black back pack.

Adam looked at his watch then went to his laptop to access the city's building and street plan. A blueprint came up on his screen and he carefully went over how he would gain entry. Access could be made through a fifth floor window facing the alley. His target location was on the ninth floor in the corner suite facing the street. The young man took a deep breath and rechecked his bag, retrieved his gloves and toque from the bed. Stuffing them into his coat he donned his back pack and headed to the lobby. In the elevator Adam made a call.

"Federal Building: how may I help you?" the woman's voice on the other end asked.

"I have a package for Joseph Dresner," Adam replied. "It's important he receive it before the end of the day; when will he be leaving his office this evening?"

"One moment please . . . . His final appointment is at 5:30, so I would say about 6:30."

"Thank you." Adam hung up as the elevator doors opened.

* * *

His fingers burned as their tips held tightly to the small crevices of the brick clad building. The alley was deserted and darkness had descended on the city. Hiding from the dim lights Adam stayed in the shadows. He scaled his way bit by bit up to the fifth floor. A cold wind started to blow and a rattle from below caused the young man to pause, clinging quietly until he determined its origin. Satisfied he continued his ascend.

Reaching the access window, he took a small, round glass cutter from his back pocket and made an opening just large enough to reach his hand inside and move the latch. The window slid open easily and Adam pulled himself inside the stairwell. He quickly opened his pack, retrieved a silver tube from inside and used it to fuse the glass back into place. He applied the precise amount of heat to make the mend virtually invisible. Taking a deep breath, he assessed the area. There were cameras at both the door below and the landing above.

From his pack Adam removed one of the small electrical devices and put grey putty on its underside. He quickly calculated the distance and propelled it from a tiny sling shot apparatus he'd kept in his other back pocket. The device attached to the camera and caused it to freeze its recording, sending a still picture of the stairwell to its receiver. Ascending the stairs Adam repeated the process at each landing until he reached the ninth floor. Long pieces of nylon string were connected to each device allowing Adam to retrieve each one with a swift tug as he cleared each camera's line of site.

The apartment door's security was easily overcome and the young man entered cautiously. It seemed spacious for a single occupant and it reminded Adam of Talbot's office. He did a quick survey of the area, memorizing every detail; gleaning information about the man who lived there. Then he settled in to patiently wait for his target.

*　*　*

Danielle watched her for what seemed like forever. Sophia finally stirred. Taking her mother's hand, she smiled and gently caressed her face.

"Hello sleepy head," she whispered. "They said you were asking for me." Sophia smiled back weakly and then looked around the room. Danielle helped her sit up, putting pillows behind her shoulders. The older woman winced feeling the results of the heroic efforts made to save her life. Her ribs hurt and the lingering effects of the strong sedative used to fake her death continued to make her groggy. Danielle poured her mother a glass of water from the pitcher resting on the night stand.

"**Something's happened; where am I?**" Sophia asked. Her eyes were filled with fear as she tried to find something familiar in the room. "**Where have they taken me?**" She ran her hands along her chest in an attempt to discover the origin of the pain.

"**It's ok Mom,**" Danielle reassured her. "**You're in a safe place. Shane is here too. We are finally free from the Agency. They have no control over what happens to us anymore.**" Sophia weighted her daughter's words.

Lunch had been called but Shane stayed back trying to regain his composure. His entire body felt numb yet his head wanted to explode. It was all such a nightmare. Jarvis had told him everything and as his friend's words still echoed in his head, Shane tried not to lose himself. He felt a familiar angry pressure build up from deep within his chest. It was fuelled by the helplessness of not being able to save those he loved.

*   *   *

All attempts to duplicate the initial experiments had failed so Bergstein's goal became producing more children. He suspected that as they grew their abilities would develop. Danielle's birth had been difficult and Sophia hadn't fared well. It caused many complications that wouldn't allow her to conceive again. Bergstein soon realized that Shane and Elena were his only option and made it very clear that the young couple had no say in the matter. If need be he would produce their children in the lab.

They were horrified and helpless. Jon was only five months old and had been taken from them months prior. The idea of their children being used as test subjects for who knew what was unbearable. Elena made Shane promise to take care of the others. She told her husband over and over that it was the only way; the only way to stop the evil. The couple held each other and cried. When they came to take her, Shane knew it would the last time they'd be together; the last time he'd touch her beautiful face. She would get away or die trying. Once she was gone Bergstein raged and Shane took the brunt of his anger. In the end it was all for naught, the monsters had still managed get what they wanted; children. They'd just waited for the next generation to mature.

All this time Shane thought she'd died. He closed his eyes and imagined her beautiful face. The Agency made a point of destroying everything that could have helped find her. Jarvis had exhausted every avenue and Adam remembered very little. Shane felt as if he'd lost her all over again and knew that without treatment there was no chance of her still being alive.

. . . *We have another son* . . . Shane thought . . . *my beautiful Elena, we have another son* . . .

Sophia listened as her daughter went over the events of the Edinburgh Conference. Lunch was delivered by a young woman and although she still felt a little queasy from her earlier ordeal, the recovering woman tried to eat. Danielle avoided any explanation of what had happened and where she'd been taken but it didn't matter. Sophia loved hearing the sound of her daughter's voice and knew eventually all would be revealed. With her head feeling clearer than it had in months, she smiled. If indeed they'd gotten away from the Agency she wouldn't have to pretend anymore and the others had finally discovered the truth; the truth she'd known for quite some time.

* * *

As the door opened Adam remained motionless in the dim light of the small sitting room. He could make out the outline of the stocky man who'd entered and he managed to decode his demeanour in the darkened apartment. Frustration muddled the man's consciousness and fatigue weighed him down. This was not the powerful figure Adam remembered from the bookstore in Paris and he was no longer ageless.

"Hello Julian."

Joseph Dresner froze and inhaled deeply. "Hello Adam." He turned to face the dark shadow casually reclining at the back of the room. "I was told you were dead." He was afraid but his actions betrayed his thoughts. Calmly he sat across from the young intruder. "What do you want?"

"Answers . . ."

"As do I," the old man replied. He tried to get a sense of what he was up against but Adam remained silent, not showing his hand. "I thought you were smarter than this," Dresner continued, "you could have disappeared." Inwardly he panicked, desperate for a clue that would tell him how to proceed. "This is not a game you can win." He took a deep breath. "How did you find me?"

"I'm not playing a game," replied the dark shadow, "and I never lose. You of all people know what I am capable of. You are the one who made me who I am." Again Adam waited, watching Dresner's thoughts unfold as if reading a book. His suspicions were right. It was not the Agency; it was all Dresner: Bergstein, the implant, Epsilon, the school, all of it. Adam considered his next course of action.

"Why?" he asked quietly.

Confused and unsure of exactly how much Adam knew or what he was referring to, Dresner chose his words carefully. "For the greater good," he said sincerely. "If the world goes unchecked, evil men infect others while they do unspeakable things. Bystanders watch and do nothing." His thoughts turned to his childhood and he unconsciously rubbed at the faded inked numbers on his right forearm. He shook his head. "You can't possibly understand."

"What haunts you is not my battle; I'm done and I don't have time for this. Epsilon is finished." Adam looked deeply into Dresner's eyes. "What you've done is also evil. Do you know how many died at the hands of Bergstein? Do you know how many lives were destroyed? Even one is too many. I know about the school and the children." The old man looked stunned. "You see Julian . . . I'm one of them. I can see your thoughts." The young man laughed for effect. "It's rather ironic actually. My mother's name was Elena Stevens." Adam waited until Dresner recognized the name, then took a deep almost cleansing breath. "You thought she'd died years ago but she escaped before Bergstein discovered she was pregnant and by some bizarre act of fate I ended up on your radar. Imagine her nightmare." Adam fought to keep his voice even and emotionless. "Then before my abilities had a chance to mature, Talbot took your advice and gave me the implant which not only controlled me but inhibited their development." Adam took another breath. "Imagine my surprise when the implant shut down." He hesitated taking the time to decode Dresner's thoughts. He decided to push on; apply more pressure.

". . . . and it gets better," he continued. "Not everyone died in the first clinic fire. The survivors spent 25 years looking for Bergstein and the ones he'd taken." Adam paused giving Dresner time to put the pieces together; he didn't. "I thought you were smarter than this Julian. . . . haven't you figured it out?" The old man sat dumbfounded and broken. "Yes, Global Security . . . the ones who duped Ackerman. You must have been furious when he told you I was gone, but it wasn't his fault. Smith could see his thoughts."

Joseph Dresner sat motionless. He was still idealistically deceived, believing that everything he'd done was justified. He was trying to save the world from the next great evil; evil like what could've happened in Edinburgh. He thought he'd survived the camps for a reason and was fulfilling his purpose. Adam knew there would be no way of convincing him otherwise. The young man also knew he had to be stopped.

"The human mind is an incredible thing," Adam stated as matter of fact, "but it is very predictable." He remained quiet for some time watching a bead of sweat run down the length of Dresner's face. The old man's thoughts became jumbled and still Adam waited. "The thing is," he finally said at just the right moment, "we can't help ourselves." He smiled slightly. "So Mr. Dresner where is the lab and which one of your minions shall I visit first?"

* * *

Shane continued to struggle with his new reality as Flynn arrived at the ranch. Without a thought he'd called the big man's name and rushed to his old friend with arms open wide for a bear hug. Shane had no choice but to comply and within moments they were both smiling.

"I was beginning to think this day would never come," Flynn confessed. "Did you all make it safely?"

"Sophia and Danielle are here," Shane replied. "It was too dangerous to get Jon out." He rubbed his face. "Its complicated." A deep sadness spread across his face.

"I was hoping you'd all make it out together." He looked at his friend with concern. **"Not to worry its not over yet. Right now I need to talk to the others. Is Adam here?"**

"No," Shane replied. **"He called Daniel and said there were some loose ends."**

"I'll bet there are," Flynn commented wryly. "Let's find the others," he said heading toward the back of the ranch house. "So you haven't met Adam?"

"I met Luka in Edinburgh," Shane answered.

"Then you haven't met Adam."

Danielle ventured out of her mother's room; Sophia had drifted off to sleep. Only Aberdeen sat quietly in the sitting room. A gentle fire burned in the fire place. It was apparent that wherever the others had gone she'd stayed behind to talk with the new comer.

"Hello," she greeted as she looked up from her book. "I take it Sophia is resting?"

"Yes," Danielle replied. She looked around uncomfortably. "I don't know how to react to any of this." She looked at Aberdeen. "One minute I'm terrified, the next . . . . I don't know."

"I can't imagine how you feel." Aberdeen said. **"I've known about you my whole life but never imagined we would ever find you."** The new comer inhaled deeply and took a seat. She ran her hand through her hair and smiled.

"I'm still struggling with there being others . . ." she confessed. **"It's just been the four of us for so long, knowing we aren't alone is tough."**

"That first time I saw you in Edinburgh I almost jumped out of my skin," Aberdeen laughed. **"I wanted to . . . well . . . it doesn't matter."** She exhaled shaking her head. Reaching over to the file of pictures Jarvis had given her, she slid closer to the Danielle. **"These might help put things into perspective."** She'd made sure the pictures of Ken and Sophia were on the top of the pile and watched their daughter's eyes as she recognized the faces. "When I was a little girl my mother told me about Sophia. They were very close."

"Angela . . . ," Danielle said, "is she here?"

"She's been gone for eight years," answered Aberdeen smiling sadly.

"I'm sorry."

* * *

Adam wore the long black overcoat, wool hat and green scarf he'd brought with him to Joseph Dresner's apartment. He hunched forward making himself small and walked with the same aged gait the old man had struggled with earlier. He kept his back to the cameras and casually took out a newspaper to shield his face once inside the elevator. He didn't want to raise suspicions.

It'd been easy to extract information from Dresner. In the past Adam had resorted to very unpleasant methods, decoding now made them unnecessary. He was relieved; it made staging an accidental death much simpler and there'd been no mess to clean up. He felt no guilt; the end had been swift and he'd had no choice. Walking quietly through the lobby Adam left the building disappearing into the night.

He now knew everything and understood exactly what needed to be done. Adam calculated it would take two days before the body was found. He went straight to the airport. He still had a couple of things to cross off his list before meeting up with the others. Besides he figured it was time to introduce himself to his big brother.

*   *   *

Flynn briefed the others of his findings. The five men sat around the dining room table; blueprints of St. Thomas Academy and a list of its students were spread out before them.

"Nothing in the student files stands out." Flynn informed them. "Taking the right age range and recorded sibling groups into consideration there may be up to 15 families we'll have to physically track down and confirm; many of them out of country. The Agency was very in-depth with background records. Everything seems above board."

"So why can't we identify them through their DNA profiles?" Dr. Erikson asked. "It certainly would leave no doubt." Everyone at the table became silent, trying to emotionally detach from the reality of what they were dealing with.

Jarvis looked at each face. "What do we do once we have them?" he said. "fourteen children . . ." Everyone was thinking the same thing. A heavy burden weighed upon the group.

"Enough," Erikson demanded never the one to give up. "This is no different than finding the others. It's just another necessary step to finishing this. We need to get it together and get moving. We have the resources to deal with them and we'll do what needs to be done." He looked at Jarvis. "Daniel you succeeded in doing what you've been tirelessly working toward for 25 years. But its not over,

switch your energy to the task at hand." The doctor's voice shook
with anger. "Don't let those monsters win. We've been placed in
a position we didn't ask for but we are all those innocent children
have."

No one spoke for a long time.

Jarvis took a deep breath. "Flynn when are you expected back
at the Academy?"

"Thursday morning" he replied. "I work part time 3 days a
week; Thursday, Saturday and Monday, all early in the morning.
My days are finished by 11 am. If need be I can phone in sick, the
boss likes me and I told them I wasn't feeling well before I left this
morning"

"Adam told me he needed two days," Jarvis informed them,
"Hopefully he will get here before you leave. In the mean time let's
get as much intel together as possible. I want background checks
on all the staff at the school. My guess is the entire school is run by
the Agency. Dale Johnson has set up a base in Akron and we need
covers for those of us who will be going."

"Does the girl know about all this?" Flynn asked.

"No," Munroe answered, "and how do we tell her? Of all the
nightmarish things I imagined over the years this wasn't one of
them."

"I'll tell her," Shane said rising to his feet. "The longer we keep
this from her, the harder it will be."

* * *

Jon tirelessly searched for clues. Back at the base near Phoenix
all his free time and energy had gone toward finding his father
and Danielle. He'd gone through every frame of footage he could
find. Luka Reznikov's encounter in the stairwell with his father
flashed across the screen. He'd watched it over and over, looking
for some clue as to what happened to Shane and Danni. There was
no obvious collusion between them and fear could be seen in the
Russian's eyes. Jon hadn't decoded anything from Luka that would
lead him to believe he was anyone other than who he claimed but

the incident with Kristof Hoffman left him with questions. Why had Luka disappeared from the hospital?

"You should give it a rest Jon," Caleb suggested to his friend. He'd finished going over notes from the operative that surveilled the pair at the airport before they'd gotten on their plane to Boston. There was nothing helpful. "You can't recall anything that would help; nothing unusual from your father?

"He wouldn't take off his glasses," Jon replied. "He said he was having headaches and problems with visual overload. He must have been hiding whatever was going on." He rubbed his eyes and shook his head in frustration. "He knew I wouldn't let him go." As he sat going through every detail of the last conversation with his father, he was called into his handler's office.

As usual Jon was handed a pair of filtering glasses before entering. It was normal protocol. The Agency was very particular of its secrets and careful to protect them from Jon and the others. The glasses were part of procedure, very few knew why because very few knew about their abilities. His heart pounded as he took a seat. George Deacon, his handler, sat behind the desk; two other men sat to Jon's right. "Did you find them?" the young decoder asked wishing he could see their thoughts.

"Not yet," the man behind the desk replied, "but the investigation has been reclassified. From here on in you will leave it to these men." George Deacon leaned forward putting his elbows on his desk. "Do you understand?" Trying to get his frustration under control Jonathan Stevens said nothing. His breathing became shallow and he clenched his jaw.

"Do you understand?"

". . . Yes."

"Good," Deacon continued. "Now, tell these men everything you know about the disappearance."

"May I speak openly?" the young operative asked, his training taking over.

"They know about the enhancements; tell them everything."

Later back in his room Jonathan Stevens tried to calm down. He trusted that the Agency would find them but he felt helpless.

He was glad to have Caleb with him; it helped. Over the last few years they hadn't been on assignment together. Edinburgh was the first time he'd seem his friend in almost a year.

"The Agency will find them," Caleb assured the young operative. A cell phone buzzed and Jon reached into his pocket. It was a text message.

"Indigo"

He looked at Caleb and then entered his encrypted pass code to receive the full message. "I've got to take this," he said as he read the entire message. He rose to his feet and grabbed his jacket. "I'll be in touch."

*   *   *

Shane and Danielle first looked through the pictures of life at the clinic before the fire. He hadn't seen Elena's smiling face in so long, he transfixed on it. Aberdeen quietly left so Danielle sat close to him giving him strength. With a deep breath he turned to her, took her hands in his and gazed deeply into her eyes.

"I'm sorry," Shane began, "but there's something you need to know and I don't know how to tell you." He didn't speak but rather showed her everything, his eyes glossy with emotion and regret. When Shane finally looked away weakened by her realization of the truth, he felt guilty that Bergstein's efforts had transferred from him and Elena to the next generation.

For a long while Danielle remained motionless except for her tears. She then pulled her hands away from him to wipe her eyes. "Is that everything?" she asked becoming resolute. "There are no more surprises; nothing more to this nightmare?"

"That's everything we know," he answered.

". . . and you trust these people?" She looked around the room and then at the pictures scattered on the coffee table before them. "You're sure of all this?"

"Yes."

"How do we tell my mother?"

"She already knows more that we thought," Aberdeen said coming down the hallway from Sophia's room, "and I don't think we should keep any of this from her much longer."

"You're right," Danielle agreed. She hesitated for a brief moment. "Aberdeen, would you please go find my father and ask him to join us"

* * *

Adam's heart raced as his brother approached. He had to make sure Julian's twisted plan would end. The young man had battled with himself over how to handle Jonathan but for the first time he was unable to manage all the variables and come up with a definitive course of action. His emotions made it impossible. He'd wanted to avoid this introduction, remain neutral but realized the truth was his only option and whatever happened, happened.

Only a handful of people were seated in the small bistro. Adam sat at a small wooden table with two chairs near the far wall, well away from the other patrons. Jonathan quickly scanned the area before approaching; he was on his guard. Adam remained silent and motionless as his brother took the seat across from him. There was no recognition in the newcomer's eyes. Adam looked nothing like the young Russian from the Conference.

"You're well trained," said Luka's voice. Jonathan froze, staring at Adam, quickly trying to decode any information he could from the man in front of him. He came up against a wall, but Adam for a brief moment saw everything: frustration, worry, anger and confusion. Then suddenly Jon rose to his feet, reached across the table and grabbed the younger man by the throat. Adam forced himself not to react.

"Who the hell are you and where's my father?"

"I think it best you sit down," he warned. His attacker was taken totally off guard, his eyes narrowed and his grip eased from around Adam's throat.

"Is everything okay over there?" the woman at the coffee machine asked nervously. A phone was in her hand. "Should I call the police?" Adam looked at the man holding his throat. Jon let go and took his seat.

"Just a little misunderstanding," he said not taking his eyes off Adam. **"Where is he?"**

"Safe," Adam replied, **"as are Danielle and her mother."** He struggled to keep his own thoughts clear and hidden. He wanted to remain detached; his head pounded and eyes burned. **"My name is Adam; I'm your brother."**

* * *

". . . and Ken's here?" Sophia asked again. "He's really here? She held a photo of the two of them that her daughter had found in the file from earlier. She looked out the window at the dimming light of the evening. Shane went to the door while Danielle continued to hold her mother's hand.

"Are you ready?" he asked looking back at Sophia. She nodded. "I'll leave you all to get reacquainted then." Munroe appeared as Shane opened the door, touching the nervous man's shoulder he left the three of them.

Shane entered the sitting room. Dr. Erikson had turned in for the night but the others waited to find out how Sophia was doing. She'd told Shane that she'd discovered the Agency was up to something long ago and to keep her quiet they'd started to give her a drug cocktail that not only confused her but made her sick. They sent her away to keep their secret from the others. Shane sat down.

"Tell me about Adam," he said. "Tell me what he's like."

It was a long night for everyone. Ken and Sophia talked for hours and Danielle joined the others to give them privacy. It was hard; so many years had passed. Jarvis and Flynn told Shane Adam's story or at least what they knew of it. They talked of Angela, the night of the fire and of Elena. The two young women listened quietly. It was well past midnight when everyone settled in for the night but no one had a restful sleep.

After breakfast they reviewed the information they had about the St. Thomas Academy. Feeling stronger Sophia joined them and kept a watchful eye on her daughter who remained quiet. Just after 11:30 Jarvis' phone rang; it was Adam.

* * *

Jarvis and Shane waited for Adam's plane to land. It was behind schedule and Shane couldn't help but pace. Finally when the passengers filed into the terminal it was Jon that caught his attention. He stepped forward and gave his son a giant bear hug.

"I'm glad to see you. I didn't know you were coming." He stepped back and grimaced. **"I'm sorry I didn't tell you.**

"You didn't have much choice," Jon replied. **"I'm sorry I didn't believe you."** Both men looked back at the young man Jarvis had approached. He looked nothing like Luka. "Do you know everything?" Jon asked.

"I know enough."

"Don't expect too much from him Dad," he told his father. "He's . . ."

"I know." Shane looked over at the young stranger. He put his hand on Jon's shoulder. "How long do you have?"

"Until they call with an assignment," answered Jon. "They think I'm in Europe. It should be a while. Adam's very clever. My hander jumped at the chance to get me out of the way until the Agency found you."

Back at the ranch house, Adam tried to stay in the background during the emotional introductions and reunion. He nodded politely but remained silent. He watched as his brother reunited with a tearful Danielle.

"I'm glad you're alright." Aberdeen smiled, gently touching his arm. She bit her lip. **"This must be hard for you."** She studied his face but was unable to read him.

Her touch got his attention. It was in trouble. Adam thought he'd gotten a handle of how to deal with the girl; he was wrong. Her hair flowed gently around her neck and one small wisp curled against her face. He wanted to brush it away. His heart pounded as her eyes searched his face.

"I'm fine," he lied, hoping his voice wouldn't crack. "How is Munroe with all this?" he asked changing the subject.

"It's been hard, so many years have passed," she replied frustrated at his response.

They both turned and watched the others. Adam wondered if she could hear his heart pounding in his chest. He waited a while longer before he got Jarvis' attention. Everyone needed to get focused. There was a lot to talk about and a lot to do in a very short time.

*   *   *

The dream had changed.

His heart was heavy in his chest and Adam hurried down the smoke filled hallway opening each door. It was getting harder to breath and he was running out of time. Where was she? He could hear her terrified screams.

"Adam . . . Adam help me!" It came from behind each door as he approached and disappeared as he looked inside each classroom filled with empty desks. The familiar sound of a helicopter pounded in his ears. The smoke got thicker and his eyes burned. Opening the last door at the end of the hall Adam was hit by down draft coming from the chopper blades. Aberdeen looked at him tearfully from inside as it took off. To his left he heard a car door slam. A large white passenger van pulled away and Adam could see dozens of small heads through the windows. When the dust cleared Jarvis stood alone on the curb.

"Adam," Jarvis accused, "you promised you'd save her!"

"Adam," a woman's voice from behind asked, "where are the children?"

It was just getting light and Adam's attempt at sleep was over. He needed to run and the ranch provided all the space needed. Outside it was a warm, with morning with dew glittering on each blade of grass as the sun touched it. The fresh air filled his lungs and cleared his mind. He'd run on the tractor trail bordering the fence line. As he stretched and warmed up the ranch house door opened.

"I see we have at least one thing in common," Jon quipped. He put two bottles of water on the stairs and he too began to stretch. He looked at his watch. "I've got an hour before I check in with Deacon."

"I run alone," Adam replied.

"Not today you don't," his brother informed him. Adam furrowed his brow and set out at a brisk pace. Jon matched him step for step and as they settled into a steady rhythm Adam began to relax. He concentrated on the pounding sound of his heart; aware of every step and every heartbeat. His breathing slowed as did his pace; his brother mirrored him. Adam focused on the cadence of their stride perfectly in tune. His senses sharpened and he was free. It was all about this moment and Jon was part of it. Everything else melted away.

Both men were covered in sweat when they arrived back at the ranch house. Jon threw his brother a bottle of water and then took a long drink. "What was she like?" he asked quietly thinking of his mother.

"I can't remember," Adam lied as he stepped past him back into the house. There was a lot to do before their relocation to Akron. Failure was not an option and factoring in all the variables was getting harder. Especially the one wild card he couldn't get a handle on; himself.

CHAPTER 13

1 Week Later

THE EPSILON LAB WAS hidden inside what appeared to be a storage unit enclosure near Omaha, Nebraska. Jon and Adam had been watching the building for several days. Jarvis dressed in black, hid in the shadows awaiting their signal. As Jon cut the power, Adam carefully approached the building before the backup generator powered on. He placed a jamming device against the metal outer wall. It killed all wireless transmissions to and from the cameras before the lights came back on.

With a quick wave he motioned to the others. All three men spread out quickly neutralizing the outer perimeter guards. Adam took a key card from his motionless target and slipped it into the slot next to the nearby door. The others joined him and with a quick nod Jarvis went inside to the left, Jon to right. Adam continued straight down the hallway until he came to the inner door. Within moments his brother arrived with another key card. The two stepped into the inner room.

As they entered a quiet alarm continued to announce that the main power had failed. Two men dressed in white lab coats stood to face the intruders. Adam took three swift strides forward and jammed the heel of his hand under the jaw of one and then brought his elbow around connecting with the man's temple. Incapacitated, the target crumpled to the floor. Adam turned in time to see Jon take down the other.

The freezer was at the back wall. Quickly the two brothers took the small containers from inside, smashing them onto the floor. There would be no more children. They then made sure nothing would survive the upcoming blast, pushing over several shelves and emptying the contents of a dozen or so drawers and cupboards.

"4 minutes 36 seconds," Jarvis announced as he looked in the door and then quickly headed back out of the building. After one last look around the two brothers each picked up one of the fallen men and quickly ran down the passageway leading to the outer door. As they exited Jarvis was dragging the last of the three perimeter guards behind a small out building. They followed depositing their unconscious cargo next to the others.

"We should have killed them," Adam stated dryly, "dead men don't talk."

"These men have families," Jarvis replied," and will have nothing important to say." The three turned and sprinted into the darkness. Within moments of arriving at their van an explosion rocked the building. Although almost a block away the blast lit the night sky.

Adam would have preferred to delay the attack on the lab, but allowing its activities to continue was not acceptable. There was reason to believe that the lab would begin reproducing more progeny before long. Alerting Epsilon before getting the children out was not ideal. It would put them on guard and make things difficult. They'd taken a very dangerous but necessary risk.

Jarvis took out his phone and punched in a group of numbers. ITS DONE, he typed.

* * *

Joseph Dresner had been compelled to give Adam a list of people involved with Epsilon. The three main players would know about the destruction of the lab. The first, Enoch Borden, the Dean of the St. Thomas Academy had retired to his rooms at the school.

Flynn waited from behind the hedge, a listening device pointed toward the upper window. Dale Johnson had flown to Washington to watch the second and now sat in a van parked outside Colonel Russell Harris' residence. He'd tapped the man's phone and now waited for the call about the lab. The third man on the list, Thomas Blithe was driving home. He'd exhausted all leads and was beginning to think that Shane Stevens, Danielle and Sophia Munroe had dropped off the face of the earth. His eye glasses had been switched two days prior and the microphone in hidden the replacement had allowed his progress to be tracked. When Adam had shown Blithe's picture to the others, Jonathan had recognized him as one of the two men from George Deacon's office.

How these men reacted would provide the last bit of information needed to determine the next steps toward liberating the children and finally closing the file on Epsilon. Since Dresner's death there'd been posturing from those now under surveillance.

The others like Jonah Ackerman seemed oblivious. They would shut down Epsilon if directed. To them it was just another Agency program; one of many. There was no indication that any of them even knew Julian's true identity. The real scope of what had transpired was known by very few; only three: Russell Harris, Military Advisor; Thomas Blithe, CIA; and Enoch Borden, Dean at the St. Thomas Academy. Julian had been careful. Most of his influence was not based on collusion but fear. Adam had sensed it that day they'd met in Paris. Joseph Dresner had the ability to get people to do what he wanted without question.

*   *   *

Jarvis parked the van under an old over pass and the three exited. Adam quickly wiped it down leaving no trace of who may have been inside while Jon went to one of the two waiting cars and opened the trunk. He took the bag from inside and proceeded to change from his dark clothes into the ones he in which he would be travelling. The others went to the second car and proceeded to do the same.

"I'll see you in Akron," Jon said. Jarvis approached and shook his hand.

"Be careful," the older man replied. **"This will not have gone unnoticed."**

Jon smiled, **"I know."** He looked over at his brother and then back to Jarvis. "I wish things were different," he said sadly.

"We all do," Jarvis added.

Again Jon looked at his brother. He expected nothing from him. They'd barely talked in the last week and never on a personal level. The only real contact was their daily morning run. At their first meeting Adam had clearly stated the terms of their relationship. It was to be temporary and professional. As he approached, Jon could see the younger man's demeanour change, for a brief moment he caught a glimpse of something softer, something real but Adam set his jaw, took a deep breath and the moment was gone.

"I'll see you in Akron," the older brother put forward.

"Talk to Danielle when you get there," Adam replied, **"we need to know if she is going to be able to handle this, if not we go to plan B."**

Jon nodded. He turned his head hearing sirens in the distance. "We've got to get moving," he said aloud. He inhaled deeply, studying his brother's face.

Adam's resolve was weakening. *Get yourself together*, he thought to himself. "Yes we do." He stepped back. Working together had been exhilarating, almost bonding in some way, but his concern was with what the next few days had in store. He watched his brother get in the car and nod before driving away.

"You don't make it easy Adam," Jarvis concluded as he slid behind the steering wheel and started the car, "for anyone . . . including yourself." He looked over at the young man whose head rested against the passenger seat. Adam's eyes were closed. Jarvis shook his head in frustration, put the car in gear and headed for the airport.

* * *

Aberdeen had paced all evening and finally found herself sitting alone quietly in the kitchen of the old house on the outskirts of Akron. She felt better. Her father had reported in. He'd given no details, but none were needed. It would take them at least seven hours to get back and as frustrated as she was with Adam she still felt an excitement knowing he was on his way.

He'd all but ignored her since arriving at the ranch with his brother. Actually he'd all but ignored everyone. Luka had been so engaging but Adam was trying hard to isolate himself and keep from connecting or getting attached. It was tough on everyone but especially his father. She wished there was some way to get through to him. Aberdeen knew that behind Adam's wall he was hurt and lost.

"You're thinking about Adam aren't you?" Danielle asked as she entered the kitchen and sat next to the young woman. She looked tired and washed out.

Aberdeen smiled. "**What are you doing reading my thoughts?**" They both laughed quietly. "I just wish we could get through to him."

I've seen the way you look at him," Danielle said gently, ". . . and the way he looks at you."

"That's funny," Aberdeen replied. "He's barely spoken a word to me." She bit her lip and tucked her long hair into her sweater.

"I've seen him watch you," Danielle smiled. Aberdeen considered her carefully.

"**Are you okay?**" she asked. "**Are you going to be able to do this?**" She couldn't imagine what her new friend was going through.

"**I just can't fathom all those children . . . my children.**" Tears welled in her eyes. "**. . . and Jon . . . he's my best friend . . . like a brother.**" Danielle covered her face with her hands. "**He's the closest person in the world to me and I can hardly look at him . . . fourteen children . . . our children.**"

"They belong to all of us Danielle," Aberdeen tried to reassure her. "We're all in this together."

* * *

Adam sat back with his eyes closed. His plane would be landing in Barberton soon; he'd drive the rest of the way to Akron. It would take less than an hour. Jarvis and Jon had both taken direct flights but on different airlines. He would arrive at the rental house early in the morning leaving little time for sleep and to Adam's relief, little time for nightmares.

He'd had never faced the kind of unknown he now faced. He could logically extrapolate every scenario, factoring in all the variables including how others would react. Statistically his projections had always been within the 95th percentile and when the outcome deviated from the expected, the "if this: then that" had already been considered and preplanned. Adam had gone over all the possible outcomes of their decision to destroy the lab. He hoped they hadn't shown their hand too soon and Epsilon didn't decide to move the children. If they did, everyone was ready if they had to move in fast.

* * *

Shane was getting ready to rally the troops. Both Flynn and Dale Johnson had called in. Everyone else except Sophia and the Doctor had made their way to Akron and were all still sleeping. The last questions were now answered. The pecking order was now firmly established and Russell Harris had come out on the top of the heap. The call about the lab explosion had come to him first and it was he who contacted the others, giving them instructions. Enoch Borden was to circle the wagons at the school and increase security. The children would stay where they were for now. Thomas Blithe would be on the next plane to Omaha to interview the survivors from the lab. Shane looked at his watch and decided to give everyone a few more hours sleep.

When Aberdeen awoke the house was quiet but the smell of coffee came from the kitchen. Sitting at the table was Jon; Adam's file open in front of him. He looked up.

"I knew he was with the Agency, but this . . ." He flipped through several pictures of different men Adam had been over the years. "I met Luka . . . but Adam . . . well . . . he's not Luka." He was incredulous and shook his head trying to accept it all.

Aberdeen poured herself some coffee and joined Jon at the table. She watched him skim through the reports. He was nothing like his brother. His face was open and the reality of everything that was happening hung on him.

"Jon." He looked up. "You do know about the implant?"

"Yes," he replied. "Daniel and I had a long talk . . . about everything." Jon closed the file and turned to her, softening his eyes. She saw the connection with Danielle that was being threatened by the existence of children neither of them were prepared for. She'd been the only constant in his life for many years; his rock, and now he didn't know to do.

"Just talk to her Jon," suggested Aberdeen.

"I wouldn't know what to say," he confessed. "There's been a distance between us since I became active with the Agency." Jon shook his head. "We were so close; like brother and sister . . . and now this . . ."

The crisp knock on Adam's bedroom door woke him from a dead sleep. It was just before noon. 8 hours had passed since he'd laid his head on his pillow and still feeling groggy he rubbed his eyes. Another knock jarred his senses.

"I'll be out in a minute," he answered.

Everyone gathered at the table to eat.

"I take it you didn't sleep on the plane lad," Flynn grinned from his chair as Adam entered.

"So," the young man said. He took the empty seat next to Munroe. "Tell me how they reacted to the lab explosion?"

"If things were pressing we'd have waken you up hours ago," Jarvis replied. "First we eat, then we talk." Friendly banter ensued and Adam glanced around the table, compliant. He was hungry and everything smelled so good.

* * *

It looked like a typical mission briefing room. Pictures of the three main players were pinned to one wall; each had a bio tacked next to it. A blueprint of St. Thomas' spread across another wall and Flynn's laptop projected images onto the third. A large wheeled white board stood in the middle of the room, covered with pertinent information and questions yet to be answered. The large table surrounded with chairs awaited the group. Adam was impressed; everything seemed be covered. He sat back and listened. By the end of the day everything was laid out. It would have to be done from the inside.

"But how do we close the door on Epsilon?" Jarvis asked. Everyone knew the answer but no one wanted to say it aloud.

"There's got to be another way," he insisted looking at Adam. "Even it's for the right reasons its still wrong."

"They don't play by your rules Jarvis," Adam responded. He'd watched the group try to come to terms with what needed to be done. "Do you think any of them agonized over what they did to all of you?" His voice was deep and foreboding. "Or what they've done to those children? They feel perfectly justified." Adam's eyes blazed as he stood and felt a well of emotion. "They don't care about them. They're just pawns. Every time I close my eyes I'm tortured by what these people are capable of . . . I was there. I was one of them." He paused; eyes burning. "You've read my file Jarvis . . . well . . . I lived it and more. The things I did . . ." Adam shook his head as if trying to erase the memories. "They made me a part of their world and I know how they think; what they're willing to do," his body shook. "Unlike you, they have no moral boundaries and they need to be stopped."

Everyone was silent; they all looked at Adam. He was dangerous and for the first time transparent. His rage quietly filled the room. It was thick and tangible. They could see the pain, the loss and the anger. He glanced at Aberdeen; she looked away.

"**Tell me another way to do this and I will,**" Adam challenged. He set his jaw defiantly. "**Give me another option.**"

Jarvis swallowed and said nothing for a long time. His eyes remained glued on Adam's. "I can't . . ." he finally admitted, looking away defeated.

"Alright then," Adam said calmly with resolve, ". . . I'll go pack." He took a deep breath. Again he looked at Aberdeen. Her eyes were filled with tears.

". . . I guess I will too," Jon added grimly. He looked at his watch. "But first I should check in with Deacon."

Jarvis watched the two brothers leave the room. His heart was heavy. He'd done many things over the years; compromised his principles more than once but there had always been a line he hadn't been willing to cross; until now. The kid was right, they needed to be stopped; permanently.

* * *

Adam's emotions were still raw and he was mad at himself for letting his guard down in front of the others. Although it'd been effective, he'd lost control and couldn't forget the look he'd seen on Aberdeen's face. He was hoping to avoid the others until he left but it was not to be. He entered the kitchen to find Shane sitting across from Jon. The big man motioned for Adam to take a seat, going so far as to reach over and pull out the chair.

"Sit down," he firmly insisted, "this conversation is long overdue." Adam looked from one face to the other and then at his watch estimating how long it would take to get to the airport. He took the seat.

"I know the score," Shane began, "the type of people we're dealing. The existence of those children is just one example." With tears in his eyes he looked at his first born. "I'm so sorry Jon . . . your mother was willing to sacrifice herself to stop Bergstein from creating more children. The day the Agency came for us I saw him die and I thought . . . it was over. I want you both to know I'm sorry that your lives have been caught up in this. I would give anything to change that." He looked directly at Jon. "I'm so sorry . . . ." Shane paused considering his next words.

He took a deep breath. "Anyway just so you know . . . I'm not stupid . . . I have no delusions as what operatives do and truth be told I haven't had the luxury of being as principled as Daniel. Situations dictate actions, sometimes there are no choices. This is one of those situations." He paused again switching his focus to Adam.

"I know haven't earned the right to tell you anything," Shane admitted, "but like it or not you are my son and I want you to listen to me. What's happened in the past doesn't have to make you who you are. Epsilon and the Agency did this to you; move on or you'll self destruct. It doesn't have to define you. If it does they win. We're not the enemy and we have no hidden agenda."

Adam knew his father was right but he was filled with doubt. He looked down at the table. All three men were quiet, lost in their own thoughts. "She had sad eyes," Adam said surprising himself and the others. "When I was young I would try to draw them but could never get them right." He closed his eyes and pictured her face. "Even when she smiled at me her eyes were sad." Adam inhaled deeply and remembered. "She smelled like lilacs and was always singing. Even when she was mad, her voice sounded musical." He stopped, shaking his head and took another deep breath. Softening his eyes, Adam remembered her laugh and the way she would blow on his soup to cool it. He shared with them his memory of her and the loss that surrounded it. All three were quiet for a long time. Then Adam got up from the table. "Jon, we need to go soon," he said almost whispering. He touched his father's shoulder before he left the room.

The two remaining men sat motionless, shaken by the experience.

* * *

"Blithe is a slippery character; very smart and very careful," Adam stated. The two brothers were on their way to the airport. "He was my main contact with Julian." Adam closed his eyes and considered their prior meetings, going over each detail in hopes of getting some insight into how to deal with him. "We've crossed paths eight times."

"Do you think he'll recognize you?" Jon asked hitting the turn signal as he made a left turn.

"I'm counting on it." Adam replied closed and determined once again. He listened to the recording of Thomas Blithe's voice again, concentrating on each intonation, practicing its meter and pitch. His brother sat amazed.

Jon waited outside the Omaha hospital where their target was finishing his final interview with one of the lab technicians. Only one guard and one lab tech had been admitted for treatment. Their charts stated that injuries were incurred during a car accident. Jon looked at his watch. Adam said 25 minutes; 8 had already passed. With the receiver in his ear, he listened to his brother's footsteps echo down the hospital's corridor.

Jon understood from the beginning of his activation that the greater good outweighed the individual and that collateral damage was inevitable. What he hadn't considered were men like Joseph Dresner. He'd read his brother's file and knew it was incomplete. His assignments for Julian were absent. Adam had many talents but his specialty was *"Personnel Mitigation."* The Agency tried to make it sound palatable but in reality he'd been an assassin and a very good one. His unwillingness to openly interact was not surprising. He'd always been alone; the Agency had made sure of it.

Adam wore a white coat and walked with purpose. No one questioned his credentials or impeded his progress. Room 407 was on the 4th door to the right of the elevator; *34 steps.* The ride from the main floor had taken exactly 32 seconds. He'd made a metal note of the three nurses and the cleaner visible from the hallway. A uniformed man outside room 407 sat uninterested until Adam approached.

"He's a little busy right now," the guard stated, rising to his feet.

"So am I," Adam replied, arrogant and aloof, "and my shift ends in exactly 6 minutes." He quickly assessed the man in front of him and considered the options. Looking down at the chart he'd brought, Adam stepped forward and opened the door.

"I said he's busy right now," the guard insisted coming between Adam and open the door, but it was done. Thomas Blithe was on his feet, anger flashing in his eyes but the moment he spotted Adam his demeanour changed.

"What's going on?" he asked.

"This arrogant prig thinks the world revolves around him sir," the guard replied glaring at Adam. "I'll take care of him."

"Let him in," Blithe responded as he waved Adam into the room. "That'll be all for now," he dismissed the flustered man back into the hallway. Adam went directly to the IV drip hanging from a stand next to the bed. Blithe's partner stepped in to stop him. "Stand down Pete," Blithe ordered. Adam emptied a syringe into the clear tube and within moments the lab technician on the bed slipped into a deep sleep.

"I thought you were dead," Thomas Blithe stated calmly. His hand slid into his pocket cradling his gun.

"You thought wrong," Adam replied, playing his role to perfection, emotionless and robotic. "We need to talk." He looked at the second man as if considering whether or not to wait until alone with Blithe. "Julian wanted me off the Agency's radar but he's been silent for weeks and my passcode is now invalid." Adam paused. "I assume he's dead . . . I need to know how to proceed." Thomas Blithe and Pete Garrison traded looks.

"Proceed with what?" Blithe inquired.

"What to do with Stevens," stated Adam.

"Where is he?" Garrison asked, a sense of relief filling the room.

"Contained."

". . . and the girl?"

"Terminated."

"That's unfortunate," Blithe quipped, "now that the lab has been destroyed she was more valuable alive." He was trying to think fast; how could he use this new turn of events to his advantage. ". . . and what of her mother?"

"Terminated . . . those were my instructions." Adam took a deep breath, decoding everything and fighting to suppress his anger. "How should I proceed?"

"Take us to him," Blithe instructed, hoping Adam was still under Epsilon control. He was thrilled, with this new weapon in his arsenal he began to realize the possibilities how he might take control of the entire program. He dismissed the hallway guard and headed toward the elevator. Garrison followed close behind.

"Tom," he said, "this guy makes me nervous."

"Good," Blithe replied.

Once in the parking lot Garrison slid behind the wheel of a dark sedan. The two other men got into the back seat. As Adam closed the door he felt the barrel of a gun against his temple. He fought the urge to neutralize the man who held it. Garrison pulled out of the parking lot and headed toward the address Adam had given.

"My mother was a wise woman," Blithe said. "She told me if something seems too good to be true it probably is." Adam slowly straightened his body and placed his hands face up on his lap. Garrison watched through the rearview mirror. "Empty your pockets one at a time," Blithe demanded, "Put their contents on the seat between us." Adam slowly complied. "How did you find me?" the man with the gun asked.

"Once Stevens told me of the attack on the lab," Adam explained, "I was able to track the investigation. Without instructions from Julian you were my next logical contact. I know the stakes in this. I need to know how to proceed."

"How did you find Stevens?" Blithe asked.

"I focused on Dallas." Adam replied. "It wasn't hard to 'persuade' an orderly from the Health Center to enlighten me to a few details that led me straight to Sophia Munroe. It was only a matter of time before Stevens showed up." Adam again fought the urge to grab the gun as Blithe, aware of the passing motorists began to point it at his ribs.

Jon followed the sedan. He knew where they were going so the heavy traffic wasn't an issue but the way things were unfolding for Adam was of great concern. He couldn't see the gun pointed at his brother but he could hear the sinister tone of Blithe's voice. There was a long pause in the conversation coming through Jon's receiver. He increased his speed, overtook the sedan and headed to the meeting place.

"You know the danger of taking things for granted," Blithe voice transmitted into Jon's earpiece, "There's too much at stake to take any chances. How do I know I'm not stepping into a trap?" he asked, trying to decide whether or not to trust Adam.

"You don't," Adam replied. "How do I know you're not going to kill me once I take you to Stevens?"

"If you're still with Epsilon you're way too valuable to me for that." The sedan turned down another street moving toward the old industrial district. A large abandoned warehouse loomed before them.

"Go to the back of the building," Adam instructed. "He's in a small storage shed behind the abandoned bus." Garrison parked behind the warehouse and waited for the two men to exit the car. He then followed close behind, gun drawn.

Adam walked slowly hoping that Jon was ready. Dead bodies with bullet holes were not the way he wanted this to play out. He listened carefully to the sound of the footsteps behind him calculating their distance. He could tell Garrison was scanning the area, looking for others that might be hiding in wait. Blithe's gun was pointed at Adam's back as they approached the old bus. Once out of Garrison's line of sight, Adam propelled himself forward, twisting his body away from the gun. It went off as he brought his elbow up under the other man's jaw.

Garrison heard the gun shot and quickly took cover. Jon who was nearby froze and held his breath. Both peered out from where they hid and waited.

"I knew it was too good to be true," Blithe's shaky voice exclaimed. "Pete get over here, I think he broke my leg."

Jon watched Garrison rush behind the bus to his partner's aid and crept forward. Through his ear piece he heard a small commotion and then a moment of silence. "Jon," Adam winced, "I've been shot."

"Is it all clear?" Jon called as he approached the bus.

"Yes." Adam was sitting on the ground with his back against the bus, knees up. His face was pale and drawn with pain. He held his right arm tightly against his side. **"I knew I should have taken them out in the hospital parking lot."** He winced again. **"It's just above my hip. It wasn't bad until I took down Garrison."** Aware of his own shallow breathing Adam licked his lips. "I felt something tear."

Before going to his brother, Jon checked the two fallen men and moved their guns a safe distance away. Garrison was dead. He rolled Blithe onto his stomach and pulled on his sleeves until there was enough slack to tie them together. He then rolled him back onto his back and turned his attention to Adam.

He knelt beside his brother, quickly moving his hands up along each leg and then up the length of Adam's left side. He checked the neck and the back of the head. The injured man watched with his jaw clenched, trying to breathe normally. Jon then focussed on Adam's right side. He carefully but quickly moved Adam's arm and slid his hand in to continue pressure. There was a lot of blood; too much blood.

* * *

Flynn had maneuvered his way into the school. His landscaping position had been expanded to include Wednesday late night custodial and Sunday morning kitchen help. Enoch Borden preferred a limited staff and was careful to do extensive background checks on each one. Flynn's background as a high school custodian and his brief time in the military implied that he could do the necessary work and not question authority. In truth Flynn had done neither.

The rest of the group in Akron continued to get a handle on the workings of St. Thomas'. With the heightened security it was not easy but they had plenty of time. No one could make a move without Jon and Adam and as long as there was no risk of the children being moved the more they knew the better it was. They still hadn't identified all of them but they were getting close.

Munroe hacked into the City data base to see when the Academy's next building inspection was due. It was slated for June; more than two months away. This allowed them to supersede it and gain access to the entire school premises. Munroe sat at the meeting table. He'd acquired the appropriate city paperwork and was discussing the timing of such an unannounced visit. Jarvis and Shane were with him. The three were going over details when Shane's phone rang.

His face instantly went white and he closed his eyes to hide his thoughts. His two friends waited while he asked a few quiet questions into the receiver. They were only able to quickly decode that it was Jon on the phone and something had gone terribly wrong.

"Okay Son," he said, "let me know." Shane shut off his phone and rubbed his temples. "Adam's been shot."

* * *

Chapter 14

THE PAIN WAS EXTRAORDINARY. As Adam slowly remembered what happened, he touched his right side. The bandage covering the wound was moist with blood. He was disorientated and when he opened his eyes, they wouldn't focus.

"I wouldn't move too much," he heard his brother say. "You've lost a lot of blood. The bullet went right through the fleshy part but nicked your abdominal wall. You tore it open when you took down Garrison. You're lucky you didn't bleed to death."

Adam blinked several times. The room was small and stuffy; it smelt like stale cigarette smoke. He was lying on his left side facing a window whose curtains were faded with age and ill fitting. Next to it was a door. The hotel's room check-in and check-out times were plastered to it.

"If you weren't hurt so bad Adam," Jon said half joking in a low voice. "I'd punch you in the face . . . You should have waited for me." He moved his chair into Adam's line of view; in his hand was a juice box. "Drink this," he insisted, gently placing it into his brother's hand. Adam struggled to swallow.

"**He surprised me . . .**" Adam admitted looking ashamed, **"for a moment I thought . . .**" He took another drink.

"**Welcome to being human little brother,**" Jon replied. "**Staring death in the face will do that to you.**" For the first time he could see Adam for what he really was; lost.

"How long have I been out?" Adam asked. Jon helped him move and propped him up with pillows behind his back.

"18 hours."

". . . and Blithe?"

"He wasn't very cooperative but I got what we needed," Jon replied. He pulled Blithe's phone from his pocket. "It's rung twice; both times it was from Harris."

"And the pass codes?"

"Everything is here," Jon pulled a small notepad from his pocket. "We still have to return his rental, the contract is up tomorrow."

The brothers studied each other, neither giving too much away. There was a small connection and it felt good. Jon put his hand on Adam's shoulder wishing the circumstances of the moment were different. "You need more fluids," he said aloud going over to the small fridge next to the TV.

"I most certainly do," Blithe's voice weakly agreed, "perhaps some food . . . please."

Once Jon left to get food Adam carefully reached for his phone on the nightstand. He still felt lightheaded and took a moment to recover from the effort. He looked the phone for a long time before dialling.

"Adam?" a voice answered.

"Hello Jarvis," Adam said weakly. "Everything will be delayed for a couple of days but its still a go." There was a pause at the other end of the phone.

"I suppose this is your way of saying your okay."

"I suppose it is," Adam continued awkwardly. ". . . I'll be in touch."

Jarvis put down his phone and shared his relief with the others.

"Weeeeeeee," Flynn said quietly to himself.

"Weeeeee?" questioned Shane.

"Exactly . . . weeeeee!" the other man replied with a mischievous grin. "I didn't much like the last part of this roller coaster ride but this part's not bad and I'm going to enjoy it while it lasts." Shane laughed. Aberdeen sighed deeply.

Jarvis looked at his daughter's tortured eyes. "Aberdeen," he asked, "are you okay?"

"No . . . yes . . . Dad . . . I'm sorry," she replied looking away. "It doesn't matter how hard I try; I can't help myself. You were right he's dangerous." She took a deep breath and bit her lip, "but he's stuck in my head and then when he was hurt . . ." She shook her head.

"What happened between you two?" Jarvis asked gently.

"Nothing," Aberdeen replied exasperated, "absolutely nothing . . ." She bit her lip again. *But **more** than Adam thinks,* she thought to herself.

*   *   *

Harris picked up his phone and looked at the incoming number. *Finally,* he thought to himself. "I've gotta take this Darlin'," He said to his wife as he got up from the table. The pot roast was dry anyway. Closing the door to his den he pushed the button. "Blithe, where the hell are you? I've been trying to reach you for days."

"Gee, its nice to hear you too," Blithe's voice answered. "Sometimes being led through the middle of nowhere leaves cell coverage a little sketchy; besides my battery ran out after the first day."

"You found them?"

"It didn't go well Russell," Blithe's voice got very serious. "They had no intentions of being caught alive and we were totally caught off guard. They'd set up in an abandoned mine site near Boulder. It was quite sophisticated. They must have realized there was nowhere to run."

"How many?"

"Seven, I think the woman was already dead before we got there. Reznikov was with them," after a pause Blithe's voice continued. "He killed Pete Garrison . . ."

". . . Any survivors?"

"No."

"Did they know about the children?" Harris asked.

"They must have after all they destroyed the lab, but I don't think it goes beyond here." There was a bump and a cuss. ". . . give me a minute here I'm on the phone," Blithe's voice insisted, there was a pause. "Sorry Russell . . . we may have found something . . . I'll call you back." Adam turned off the phone.

"You walk like an old man." Jon said carefully; realizing their relationship was still a little shaky. It was Adam's first real attempt to get moving. It'd been two days and he'd regained his strength but his muscles were stiff from inactivity. He walked down the hall of the hotel over and over. First using the wall for support and then gradually on his own. He kept at it, graduating to the stairs and finally, covered in sweat, he returned to the room.

Adam sat on the bed and checked his wound. Jon's stitches were holding and there was no sign of bleeding. His brother passed him a bottle of water. After a long drink he picked up Blithe's phone, punched in the pass code then dialled Harris' number; 45 minutes had passed since the last call.

"What took so long?" Harris asked.

"Again its good to hear your voice too." Adam replied concentrating carefully on his articulation and tone. Jon listened on the speaker phone. "We found a cache of passports and paperwork. It took a while to go through. It looks like they were eventually headed overseas. We found intel on the Omaha Lab but nothing about the school." Adam paused purposefully rustling some papers. "I don't understand how they couldn't have known."

"Anything about the kid?" Harris asked. Adam looked at Jon.

"Nothing, where is he?"

"His last contact with Deacon was from Madrid. They're keeping track of him daily." Russell sighed. "Maybe they knew he was entrenched with the Agency and they couldn't take the risk of him tipping them of," Russell considered. "Anything else?"

"We found the names of two others," Blithe's voice replied, "We tracked them down and took care of them. We just left an address we extracted from one of them and cleaned up the rest of the mess."

"Do you think we've stopped the bleeding?" Russell asked.

"I think so . . ." Adam answered. ". . . I need to follow up on a few things before I'm sure . . ."

"We need to meet to discuss the future of Epsilon," Russell decided.

"It's a good thing they didn't go public or there would be no Epsilon." Adam added. "The damage is contained, local authorities have no idea what's gone on and the press hasn't gotten a hold of this. We may have been lucky; this may not even cause a blip."

"With the lab and the girl both gone it most certainly will," replied Harris. "How long before you get back to Washington?"

"It'll take at least a few more days to clean things up here," Adam replied "Probably Monday. I'll call and let you know in a couple of days with a full report." He ended the call and took a deep breath.

"Now we wait for Johnson's call to see what Harris does next," Jon said, "but in the meantime let's get Blithe's rental car back." Just as the two were about to leave Jon's Agency phone began to vibrate in his pocket. He typed in his pass code and read the text. "It's pick up instructions at an address in Madrid," Jon said concerned. "They must be bringing me back."

Adam began to cycle through the options and finally looked at his brother. "Will they be watching?"

"Not normally," Jon replied.

Adam took out his phone and dialled a number.

"Hola," the Spanish speaking voice answered, "qué puedo hacer por usted?"

*   *   *

It was obvious Danielle was struggling. She all but stopped eating and remained closed to those around her. There'd been a lot to do to keep her mind off the harsh reality of what Epsilon had done but it'd become a waiting game and there was more time to think. Flynn had taken pictures and they were added to the wall in the briefing room. Several were of the playground during an outside break for the children. Danielle would steal away and stare at the small faces. That's where Shane found her. She heard him approach.

"For a long while I thought it was just my first 13 years that had been stolen, and then Agency started to manipulate me to its own ends. Now I find out they'd planned it all . . . but this . . ." Tears flowed freely down her cheeks. "I can't even look at Jon . . . I don't know what to say." She continued to look at the pictures. **"How can people be so evil . . . so thoughtless with no regard for others?"** She was quiet for a long time. Shane waited, his heart aching for her.

Danielle finally turned with softened eyes. She needed someone to understand and knew he would. She let him see all the pain and anger. His thoughts then drifted to the past, to a small room with his beautiful Elena. He let Danielle see the pain involved in that fateful decision so many years ago and the reasons for it.

Danielle turned away. "She thought it would end but it didn't end, did it?"

"No," Shane admitted. " . . . Once Elena was gone I thought it was over . . . and then when Bergstein died . . . again I thought . . . I'm sorry . . . I was wrong."

"As long as there's one of us left," her eyes flashed, "and someone who knows, it will never be over." She turned and walked away her words lingering.

* * *

"You don't have to go back," Adam said as the two brothers pulled into the airport parking lot. He put the car in park and looked at Jon. The Agency had called him back to Phoenix but there were many uncertainties. If Epsilon had decided he'd become a liability Jon would be in great danger. Both men knew the ramifications but it was Adam who said them out loud. **"There is no guarantee that there isn't a termination order on you."**

"I'll have time to get out if I have too," Jon assured. "The plane from Madrid lands at the busiest time of day. It will be easy to disappear in the crowd if I need to." They both new it was wishful thinking and that Jon's cavalier attitude was a front.

Adam was at a loss; he sighed trying to think of what to say. "Jon . . ."

"Adam," Jon interrupted, "we both know this has to play out. If we don't end this right it will never be over." His eyes were piercing as he looked at his brother. "The others need us, both of us." It was both a warning and a promise. Jon narrowed his eyes. "It can't end like this."

Adam set his jaw and returned his brother's gaze. "It won't, but this doesn't make any sense." His brother would not be convinced. He stayed in the parking lot a long while after Jon left, forcing himself not to rework the plan and consider the "if this; then that" options. The "if this" was not going to happen. Failure was not an option and Jon would be fine. Adam had every intention of seeing his brother again.

* * *

Hours before everyone had been so confident. Earlier in the day, Dr. Erikson had called with the news that the ranch would be ready for the children. The renovations were almost complete. Jarvis and Munroe would be heading to St. Thomas' the next day to get a good look around and another call from Jon with a positive update on Adam's recovery put the group in good spirits. Things were coming together and within a few days it seemed they would be ready. It all came down to Harris and how long it would take Adam and Jon to get to him. The intel was in and it was only a matter of time. If they could somehow convince the school that Russell Harris wanted to move to the children, it could as easy as going and picking them up. Everyone was about to sit down to eat when Shane's phone rang again. Jon had been recalled to Phoenix and the mood in the room instantly changed.

*   *   *

Jarvis and Munroe were met at the school gates by two guards. After showing their ID they were met by other guards who accompanied them to the Dean's office. Security was tight.

"Hello Gentlemen," the quiet, unassuming man behind the desk welcomed. Neither receiver was fooled; Enoch Borden was in complete control and ran things with an iron fist. "These men will be joining you on your inspection," he informed them. "Our students belong to some of the most powerful people in the country. We don't take any chances with their safety."

"Of course," Jarvis replied. He put his toolbox on the desk so it could be searched. "Here is a list of the areas we'll focus on." He handed the Dean a list. "If your men can direct us to the areas of concern we can get through this as quickly as possible." Borden gave one of his men the list and nodded.

"You must have some very special students attending this facility," mused Jarvis.

"All of our students are exceptional," Dean Borden replied. Jarvis had discovered long ago that if you ask the right question, the unspoken ambient thought surrounding the answer could say more than the words expressed aloud. He could decode that the Epsilon children hadn't yet started to exhibit any particular abilities and that testing had intensified in the last few weeks for the older children. Borden thought that very soon something extraordinary was going to occur.

The Academy was expansive; it's brick clad walls covered with ivy. The green leaves climbed skyward framing the windows and gently blew in the breeze. The grounds were landscaped, as any prestigious private school with well trimmed scrubs and grassy areas intermittently fenced with colourful flowers. Its driveway looped from the gate to the main entrance and then back to where it began. A small side road led to the back buildings that looked like miniature versions of the main structure. At the rear of the main building was the playground, tennis courts and sports field.

The equipment was painted bright colours and the scent of freshly mowed grass filled the air.

The inside was just as impressive. Everything was clean, bright and modern. St. Thomas' had attracted the children of some very affluent and powerful people for a reason. Jarvis and Munroe were able to check out a few of the empty classrooms to assess the sprinkler system and other basic structural concerns. They also toured one of the school residences looking for smoke detectors and fire escapes.

* * *

Most of Jon's work with the Agency had been information gathering. His ability to "read people's minds" made him invaluable during interrogations and reconnaissance. There'd been little danger involved except for his time with the Van Hussen Group so although the Agency had given him the best training he hadn't used much of it. Dealing with Blithe had been difficult although he would never admit it to Adam. Killing a man wasn't an easy thing to do.

Jon was headed straight for trouble and he knew it. He considered his options. All he could do was put on a good show and play dumb. It would be difficult considering what Epsilon had stolen from him.

Although it wasn't a long plane ride, he'd thought a lot about the children and about Danielle. She could hardly look at him. They'd always been very different but as children it was the differences that had kept them grounded. For many years all they'd had was each other and now when they both were struggling with what Epsilon had done, they seemed so far apart. He knew that of all the unfinished business he had, Danielle was not something he could put aside. He took out his phone and began to type. Jon struggled a long time with exactly what needed to be said but by the time his plane landed he was satisfied and hit the send button.

Jon didn't have to wait long until the plane from Madrid landed. He sat in the chairs next to it's arrival gate and kept an eye out for the Agency. It became evident no one was watching and after the plane arrived he headed to arrivals. Caleb was waiting for him.

"Any news of my father?" Jon asked as he embraced his friend. He could tell that the younger man knew nothing. Caleb had never lied to him and it had become apparent to Jon that the Epsilon had been very careful to keep the young man in the dark so there'd been nothing to hide.

"They haven't told me anything," Caleb replied, "but you're to meet with Deacon when we get back to base." He led Jon to a waiting car and they both got in the back seat. As the car pulled away from the loading zone, Caleb looked at his friend. **"Something big is going on Jon and I don't think its good."** Jon frowned and nodded. Caleb usually only focussed his thoughts to communicate when on assignment, that fact that he was doing it now made Jon nervous.

"I'm sorry Jon," George Deacon said, his eyes filled with concern. Jon Stevens sat in his handler's office; his face masked with grief and his eyes shielded by glasses. "So you're saying it was this Luka guy and the girl." He shook his head and flipped through the pictures laid out on the desk in front of him. ". . . And that they went willingly." Caleb sat next to him. Jon picked a photograph of Luka Reznikov and Alison Mitchell standing in the Lobby of the hotel in Edinburgh. It showed a very intimate moment. It was a moment that was so out of character for his brother. Jon shook his head remembering he was looking at Luka not Adam.

"Neither of them is known to us and neither can be traced." Deacon continued. "The fact they made it into the Conference under our radar is of great concern and gives us pause to wonder who they were working for." He looked at Jon. "I know this is hard for you and I am truly sorry about this . . ." Deacon took a deep breath, ". . . you sensed nothing?"

"Everything coming from the Russian told me he was exactly who he said he was." Jon replied attempting to be stoic. He looked at his friend who nodded back at him. "I only saw the girl once or twice and there really was nothing unusual." Jon put his hands to his face. "I knew he wasn't happy . . . I knew he was hiding something." He swallowed and rubbed his eyes. "I thought it was the headaches . . ."

"We think Danielle knew what was going on all along." Deacon added. "She most likely got caught up in it all because of her mother." He looked at Jon again. "No one wanted it to end this way."

*   *   *

Adam closed his eyes and took a mental inventory of everything he knew about Russell Harris. The surveillance had paid off and he was on his way back to the Capitol. Harris had no doubt been Joseph Dresner's right hand man. His bio was impressive yet disconcerting; he was another survivor. He'd spent 5 1/2 years at a Vietnamese POW camp and was welcomed home as a hero. Although there were rumours from fellow prisoners of complicity with his captors in order to elicit preferential treatment; nothing was ever proven. He'd survived; just like Dresner, many hadn't. Only 25 years old upon his release, Russell Harris rose through Army ranks and had become a consultant to the Joint Chiefs of Staff. Where'd he met Dresner was unknown but they'd forged a relationship over time, one that had made Epsilon possible.

Adam was getting tired of travelling. His body was sore and his side hurt. He hadn't been able to run for more than a week and it was taking a mental toll on him. He was glad he didn't have to go back and face the others. Jon's recall would've hit them hard. He needed to distance himself. Dale Johnson met him at the airport and took him to a small office. Inside, two men wearing earphones sat at desks taking notes.

"It seems that Epsilon is even more secretive then we thought." Johnson told Adam. "I'm beginning to think that Joseph Dresner was the only one who knew all the players. Harris, Blithe and Borden are well acquainted but Harris is scrambling to identify the others and get a peg on who knows what." He passed Adam several pieces of paper. "As you expected no one knows much." The papers showed assorted communications with five individuals including Jonah Ackerman and George Deacon. There were also several calls to a private number in Akron. It seemed to be associated with some sort of research and testing facility. "Jarvis will check it out; it could be important. Harris refers to it as 'Rupert Street.' The others all seem to be a bunch of 'yes men' following directions but without the intel to know what's really going on."

"Dresner took advantage of the covert nature of the Agency." Adam observed. He quickly scanned the communications between George Deacon and Russell Harris. They had focussed their attention on Luka and Alison, a few details were given and a risk assessment of Jonathan Stevens was ordered. One line got his attention, *'do to matters of extreme sensitivity, reassignment may be necessary.'* Adam read between the lines and put his hand on the desk in front of him to support himself.

"Are you okay?" Johnson asked.

Adam shook it off and nodded. He took a deep breath and tried not to think about his brother. Adam began to assess things. Harris was circling the wagons and shutting down all unnecessary aspects of Epsilon. With simple phone calls, those not directly associated with the children or Jon, were unceremoniously discharged and told to destroy all evidence of the program. Harris was unknowingly making Adam's job a lot easier.

Adam looked at his watch; it was well after 9 pm. "I need to eat something and get some sleep." Johnson nodded to the others and went to the door.

"I booked you a room nearby," he said. "We can stop and get some take out on the way."

Adam slept but fought nightmares all night. Early in the morning he showered, shaved and put on the uniform Johnson had left for him hanging in the closet. It was army dress greens and identical to the one Harris' driver wore. He spent a few minutes fine tuning his look and looking over Russell Harris' day plan. He memorized each route then glanced at his watch and headed to the car waiting for him at the front on the hotel.

"His regular driver has been reassigned," Johnson told Adam as he opened the driver's door for the young man. "I'll expect your call." Dale nodded and turned crisply, walked quickly away from the car and disappeared to the left down the 1st intersection.

CHAPTER 15

THE MOMENT HE SAW Russell Harris, Adam disliked him. His Colonel's uniform crisp and pressed; it was part of who he was. Unlike Joseph Dresner, Adam could tell he was self serving and motivated by the need for control and power. Dresner had done what he'd done in order to stop a similar evil to what he'd survived from ever happening again. Harris' intentions were more sinister. He wanted to impose his ideas on others and change the world so it would conform to what he envisioned. Russell Harris was a very dangerous man.

"Where is Fox?" Harris asked as he approached the car.

"I don't know, Sir," Adam replied and saluted. "Private First Class Ryan Bell, reporting for duty, Sir." He opened the back passenger door and stood at attention. "I was told to be at your disposal for the next few days, Sir."

"Bell, eh . . . ," the Colonel saluted back and climbed into the car. "I don't like being late Private, get me to my meeting."

"Yes Sir."

Adam drove Harris to a government office near the US Capitol Building. He waited 47 minutes in the car for him to return and just as the Colonel left the building Adam sent him a text from Blithe. It was a simple message, just enough to get him thinking so Adam could get a better peg on things. It was also his way of trying to keep his brother alive.

'DONE—CONTAINED—REPORT TO FOLLOW— NEED TO TALK TO STEVENS.'

As Harris approached the car Adam could decode every thought. A feeling of great relief surrounded the man but his reaction to the mention of Jon caught Adam by surprise. Harris had come to a decision. *The kid is a liability,* the Colonel thought. *It'll be a loss for the Agency but it just might worth having a look inside that head of his. Rupert Street can do what they want with him after Blithe has a chance to interview him.* He paused for a moment before continuing toward the car. *Then Blithe has to go too,* he smiled; *he's too smart for his own good.*

"Colonel, Sir." Adam saluted as Harris reached the car.

Adam spent the rest of the day driving Harris from place to place. He watched the man carefully, making note of his body language and getting a feel for how he communicated with others. The Colonel's daily schedule showed his routine to be predictable and other than his weekly meeting at the Pentagon his absence for a few days wouldn't be out of the ordinary. That meeting was in two days. Adam had to be careful, if he missed one detail it could be disastrous.

"You're with me," Harris said at the last stop of the day. Adam followed him into a small cafe where they sat at a table occupied by Corporal Andrew Hunter, Harris' personal assistant. Adam sat quietly, sipped his coffee and observed.

* * *

Jon Stevens was frustrated. Deacon had confined him to base until further notice and there was no way to communicate with the others. Caleb wouldn't let him out of his sight and Jon could decode that his friend was under orders to keep an eye on him. Someone was very nervous.

George Deacon was a good man and followed orders without question. He put down the phone and sighed. Losing Jon would be a blow to the effectiveness of his department but as he expected the young man had been transferred. Deacon had no choice. His department head had made it very clear from the beginning that Jon belonged to another program that took precedent and now they were recalling him. *Perhaps its for the best,* he thought, *Jon needs a change after everything that's happened.* He sighed again. The helicopter would arrive within the hour and he still needed to tell Jon. Deacon grabbed the pair of glasses from his top desk drawer and left to find the young man.

*   *   *

Adam followed Harris' assistant to a gym. Andrew Hunter didn't live on base and Adam had waited patiently outside his house for 2 hours and 17 minutes. It'd paid off. It was still early evening and he could use a run even if it was on a treadmill. He made a point of being in near proximity of his target without acknowledging him. He took it easy; the injury to his side made sure of it. Adam hoped Hunter would make the first move and he wasn't disappointed.

Andrew had a closed life and not many opportunities to socialize. He jumped at the chance to start a conversation. Adam jogged for 30 minutes while the other man used the gym equipment. Blithe's phone began to vibrate in his pocket and as he stepped off the treadmill, Andrew approached.

"Hey," he said, "I haven't seen you here before."

Adam looked at him confused and then allowed recognition to cross his face. "Ah . . . coffee with the Colonel, right?"

"Right."

"I was transferred in from Akron last week," Adam replied. "I'm still trying to find my way around, this place isn't bad." He looked around the gym. Hunter smiled. Andrew Hunter's life revolved around his boss so it was easy to bring the conversation around to the Colonel and by dropping key words and phrases was able to glean enough from the other man's reactions to decide what to do next. By the end of their encounter Adam determined Harris' assistant knew nothing of Epsilon.

Arriving back at Johnson's office to check in, Adam received confirmation of his brother's relocation. Russell Harris had made the call; Jon was going to Rupert Street. There was no way to stop the transfer. He was probably already in the air. Adam carefully looked through the transmissions made by Harris. The one to Blithe was among them, all it said was, "CALL." Once he finished carefully going over them all he reached for Blithe's phone and nodded to Johnson as he dialled.

"It's about time," Harris answered

"A simple hello would go along way Russell," Blithe's voice replied. "No wonder I don't call more often." Adam smirked looking at Johnson. "I'll be catching the plane to Phoenix tomorrow night to interview Jon Stevens and will arrive in DC in a few days."

"He'll be at our new facility in Akron," Harris returned. "They're expecting you there. Text with your arrival time in Akron and I'll make sure a car is waiting for you at the airport." There was a pause. ". . . and Blithe . . . keep me informed." Before Adam could reply the call ended; he looked at Johnson.

"Get a hold of Jarvis," Adam said, "we're going to need help."

* * *

Rupert Street was reputedly owned by a wealthy businessman whose main offices were in New York. It was touted as a corporate executive training facility and retreat. There was a helicopter pad at the back of the property with a small warehouse adjacent. A parking structure large enough to hold a small bus and several cars sat across from the main building which was in the process having a wing added to the east side. Construction was about 85% finished and the landscaping was clearly almost complete.

Jarvis and the others met in the briefing room at the Akron house. Spread on the table before them was a crude hand drawn map of the Rupert Street complex. It showed approximately where the security cameras were placed along the perimeter fences and where the buildings were situated on the property. It was the best

Jarvis could do with the little information he had. The building plans submitted to the city didn't match what had actually been built and there was still some construction going on at the sight.

"Whatever this place is its not finished and not fully staffed," Jarvis explained. He looked around the room. Emotions were raw; no one made eye contact. Shane had his head in his hands. He hadn't said a word since the news of Jon's transfer.

"We know exactly what this place is," Danielle said attempting to remain stoic. Her face was pale and she inhaled deeply. "We can't leave him in there." She tried to hide her terror but failed. The young woman's hands shook uncontrollably.

She'd received his text earlier. It'd taken a long while for her to muster enough courage to read it.

Danni,

Right now I'm on a plane heading back to Phoenix. I don't know what awaits me but I do know that of everything that's happened, your pain angers and hurts me the most. It's been hard; I didn't know what to say to you about the children, our children. We should face this together as we have so many things in the past. I don't know what'll happen, maybe we still will, but that doesn't seem likely. Be strong.

As for me, it doesn't matter. I'm sorry I'm not there . . . and the children. I'm torn— angry that they exist! But its not their fault. They need help; they need to be safe and to grow up with people who care about them. They deserve better than what we had. Thank you for saving me so many times just by being by my side. Love always Jon.

He was now alone facing who knew what and Danielle was trying so hard to be strong.

*   *   *

Jon knew something was wrong the moment Deacon arrived at his room with the news but it wasn't until the helicopter landed at Rupert Street that he truly understood the gravity of his situation. Two burly men wearing glasses escorted him along a beautifully landscaped pathway into what appeared to be the lobby of a luxury hotel. There was no one behind the front desk and when they entered the elevator, one of the men put a key card in a slot and the doors closed. It began to descend and Jon felt a knot form in the pit of his stomach.

To the right, a lone door stood at the end of a long, brightly lit hallway. Each footstep echoed. He'd been in similar rooms many times questioning the person sitting in the chair in which he would soon sit. As he entered the room the lights flickered causing him to feel a little disorientated. Then the door closed behind him with a loud click.

"Empty your pockets," the man to Jon's left ordered. He motioned to an empty plastic bin on a table. As the young man complied he tried to read the others and failed. Their glasses hid everything. He switched his attention to the room. It was no bigger than a large closet. One metal chair was bolted to the floor. In front of it was a small table also metal with two chairs facing the first. A long fluorescent light protected with thick metal mesh flickered from the ceiling. "Face against the wall, arms up," the man demanded. He roughly patted Jon down. "Sit," the other man ordered. Again Jon complied.

The two men left with the bin holding the items from Jon's pockets. The light flickered again. Soon the young man's head began to ache and random reflective smudges appeared, confusing him further. He closed his eyes and as he regained control he tried not to panic. The flickering frequency of the light was no coincidence.

After several hours the two men returned and although neither wore glasses Jon couldn't read them. As the visual overload from the flickering lights began to confuse him again, he closed his eyes absolutely exhausted.

"We have some questions for you Jon," a voice echoed in the small room.

"What is this about?" asked the confused young man, holding his head. He looked at them but his vision blurred and he was unable to focus. Again he closed his eyes.

"I don't think you understand Jon," the larger of the two men stated. "We're the ones who get to ask the questions." He slammed his fist down on the table in front of Jon forcing the young man to open his eyes.

With sweat beading on his forehead and under extreme duress, Jon sat up straight and made eye contact. His breathing was shallow and he struggled to keep from passing out. "I . . . don't understand . . . what's happened . . . ?"

*   *   *

Adam stood next to the car outside of Harris' house. The uniform rubbed uncomfortably against his skin and the anticipation of the next few hours remained hidden behind his set jaw and piercing eyes. He saluted, and then opened the door as his target approached. As Harris took his seat, Adam jammed a syringe into the Colonel's right leg, emptied its contents and closed the door. Both back doors locked with a loud click.

Harris cursed, grasping his leg. "What's going on Bell?" he questioned as he tried the handle several times. Adam's passenger noticed the privacy glass between himself and the driver. Colonel Russell Harris realized he was trapped and weakly took out his phone only to find no signal. He was at the mercy of the young man behind the wheel.

Adam turned to face him in order to decode his thoughts. Satisfied, he put the car in drive and pulled away from the Harris house. He could hear the muffled sound of the Colonel's angry rant until the trapped man finally succumbed to the drug that had been forced into his system. The back windows were tinted. No one could see the unconscious man as the car made its way out of the city.

Harris awoke restrained to a chair in a darkened room with duct tape over his mouth. A dim lamp stood on a table a few feet in front on him. Also on the table were his cell phone, wallet and house keys. There was no other light in the room. He sat for a long time trying not to let his imagination get the best of him. Many things went through his mind and unbeknownst to him the man sitting quietly in the dark could decode each one.

"Hello Russell," Adam finally said. He'd seen enough and only needed a few questions answered. "You know there's only one reason you're here," he continued, "let's not waste time." He'd deepened his voice for effect. It made him sound older and it was a voice Harris wasn't familiar with. Adam stepped forward still staying in the shadows but reaching down and taking the cell phone from the table. He watched the man in the chair carefully and dialled a number.

"Hello Hunter," he said using Harris' voice. Adam put the speaker phone on. The Colonel's eyes widened in disbelief. "We are running behind schedule Corporal and something has come up."

"Sir," Andrew Hunter replied frustrated, "they won't start the meeting without you."

"I've been called out of town," Adam stated abruptly. "Its unavoidable." Hate filled eyes glared in his direction. "Cancel all my appointments for the next few days. I should be back Friday."

"Sir . . . you have a meeting at the Pentagon Thursday afternoon," Hunter reminded the Colonel.

"I'm aware of that, Soldier," Adam barked, "give my regrets . . . and tell my wife I'll be away, I don't have the time to deal with her questions right now. Am I understood?"

"Yes Sir."

Adam ended the call and placed the phone back on the table. He took several steps back into the darkness and waited. Harris was well disciplined and didn't outwardly react but his thoughts were a tangled mess of uncertainty.

Are these guys Agency? Did they discover Epsilon? That fool Blithe . . . Do they know about the children? Assorted images of meetings and phone calls passed through the Colonel's mind as he tried to determine what he was dealing with.

"Things aren't what they seem," stated Adam. He took three steps to the right.

"Stevens and the girl were never in the Colorado desert," Blithe's voice boomed. Again Adam moved positions.

"I want you to think Russell," Joseph Dresner's voice urged, "How much of what you know . . . do you *really* know?" Harris' face turned toward the voice and he became more confused. Adam moved.

"We moved the children from St. Thomas' weeks ago," Enoch Borden's voice interjected. Adam retraced his steps.

"Again Russell," Dresner asked, "how much are you certain of?" The restrained man took in a deep breath and shook his head. Imagines raced through his mind as he tried to figure out what was going on. He thought back to his last face to face encounter with Thomas Blithe. It'd been months ago during a meeting with Dresner and so much had happened since then . . . or had it? He felt the knot in his stomach tighten as things became more and more uncertain.

Adam was now confident of all the details except for Rupert Street. He considered his next actions carefully, wanting to learn as much as possible about the Akron facility. He took a deep breath.

"Have you figured it out yet Russell?" asked Dresner. Adam took several steps to the left and recalled the voice of Harris' contact at Rupert Street.

"Construction funding was suspended as of the 1st of last month," the voice echoed. "Only the first level of security is complete." Adam moved again watching the Colonel's thoughts.

"There really was no point in sending the Stevens kid there," George Deacon added. Adam gave his full attention to the turmoil raging in Harris. Images of a long hallway below ground flashed before him; there were faces interspersed with the memory and a set of large metal doors. It was done; he needed nothing further.

Harris would never be found. An old car left on blocks covered his grave in the backyard of the old farm house. Adam and Johnson erased all evidence of any recent activity in the house or yard. The two men worked silently aware of the little time they had before both had to catch a plane.

* * *

CHAPTER 16

IT WAS WELL AFTER midnight when they arrived at the Akron house. Although he'd slept on the plane, Adam was exhausted and knew that dealing with the others would be an emotional strain. His own reaction to Jon's relocation had been difficult and he continued to struggle with remaining detached. It was a battle he knew he'd already lost.

Jarvis met the newcomers at the door. He shook Johnson's hand and then switched his attention to Adam. He looked lost and afraid.

"Are you alright?" Jarvis asked placing his hand on the young man's shoulder. Adam fought the urge to breakdown. He straightened his frame and set his jaw. He took several deep breaths pushing back his emotion. His countenance changed and his confidence returned.

"I have to be," Adam replied. "What am I walking into?" He looked into the other man's eyes.

"It is what it is," Jarvis answered. "They're waiting in the briefing room."

Shane looked up as the three men entered. Adam could decode his relief but also the fear. He looked at the other ashen faces of those who sat around the table. Aberdeen met his gaze; he faltered for but a moment. Adam took a deep breath. He stood tall, emoting a strength and confidence that he didn't possess.

"Harris has played into our hand," he lied with a grin. "He's given us direct access to Rupert Street." He looked around the table, fire in his eyes. "It's the last stronghold of Epsilon; it'll be the last domino to fall." Adam took another deep breath. He knew getting Jon out alive was unlikely but he kept it to himself. "Is everything in place at your end?" he looked at Flynn.

"Yes," came the answer. "We'll be ready tomorrow. It's a long weekend so there are no classes on Friday. Doctor Erikson says the ranch is ready to go."

"Good." Adam stated. "I'll call Dean Borden in the morning. We can make the move on Rupert Street at the same time. They'll be picking up Jarvis, Johnson and I at the airport at 1:35 pm. I called from DC." The group so much wanted to believe his optimism. He'd been able to plant a seed of hope but he was physically fading. Adam rubbed his face, hiding his own concern. They'd be walking into a fortress with no guarantees that any of them would get out. The exhausted young man quickly glanced over at Jarvis, desperate and spent.

"Let's regroup in the morning," Jarvis suggested recognizing the urgent plea for help. "It's late and there's nothing more we can do tonight." He put his hand on Adam's back and led him to a bedroom at the back of the house. Once away from the others, Adam began to shake.

"I don't know how to deal with this," he whispered leaning against the wall. His eyes softened and he became transparent. **"Jarvis . . . I don't know if we can do this."** Jarvis could see confusion and uncertainty. The young man had no prior experience with the emotions he was going through. **"What happens if we fail?"**

"You can't think about that." Jarvis replied. **"Remember . . . you told me failure isn't an option."**

"It might not be an option, but its a real possibility." Adam closed his eyes. He'd known this was going to happen. Attachment led to weakness and that's exactly how he felt, weak and powerless. "I need to figure this out," he whispered.

"I don't know if you can, Adam," Jarvis admitted, "and no one expects you to. You can't take the weight of all of this on your shoulders. The only certainty is that it will be over and that in itself is something." He looked at the young man who'd been through so much in the last few weeks. Adam's whole life had changed and so had he. Jarvis hoped Adam would have a chance to enjoy the things that the Agency had stolen from him but for now he needed to get through the next few days.

"Get some sleep Adam," Jarvis suggested. "There is nothing left to do until morning." He turned to leave.

"Jarvis," the young man whispered. "Thank you."

*   *   *

With the early morning light peeking through the window Adam headed to the shower. His mind still racing as it had all night. Careful to protect his stitches from the cascading water, he allowed the warmth to envelop him. He closed his eyes and remembered what Dr. Erikson had told him on that first day. *You have the skills to deal with this . . . fall back on your Agency training.* He began counting backwards from 20, first in Russian, then Greek and finally Mandarin. When his clarity of mind returned, it was like he'd flicked a switch.

As expected, Enoch Borden was full of questions. Adam sat at the kitchen table. Harris' cell was on speaker phone and everyone listened intently to the frustrated voice coming from the other end of the line.

"I thought you said Blithe had contained the problem?" Borden questioned.

"There've been other developments," Harris' voice answered. "We have reason to believe Epsilon has been compromised." Adam paused for effect. "Tighten security and be careful. Shred everything. The bus will arrive at 3:30pm; make sure the children are ready and not in their uniforms. They can each bring one small bag of personal items." He paused again. "We'll regroup as soon as we can assess the severity of the security breech."

"Understood," Borden answered, "they'll be ready."

"Good," Adam answered. "The most important thing right now is the safety of those children."

"Agreed."

Adam ended the call abruptly, cleared his throat and had a drink of water. "That's that," he declared. He turned and looked at Flynn. **"Are you ready?"** The stocky man nodded. **"Are you sure?"** Again he nodded.

"We have 45 minutes," Jarvis informed Adam and Johnson. "We need to get ready."

* * *

Adam looked in the mirror. It'd been a while since he'd worn a black suit. It fit well. He stood tall and fixed his hair. Smirking a little, he realized he looked like Johnson had on that first day at the Compound. He headed for the briefing room.

Aberdeen was in the hallway. She'd just spend a few precious minutes with her father. She didn't want to admit it might be the last time she would see him. When she looked up it took her a moment to recognize Adam coming down the hall. Every time she saw him he seemed to be someone else. She searched his face hoping for a response.

Adam didn't have to decode Aberdeen's thoughts to see she was terrified. He approached to pass, uncertain of what to say and knowing he should just keep walking. He didn't. He stood next to her, too close, but said nothing; not trusting himself. Soft wisps of hair gently fell about her shoulders. Adam's heart began to pound in his chest as he met her gaze. He wanted to protect her; he so much wanted things to be different. He tried to remain stoic.

"Tell me everything's going to be ok," she pleaded. Her eyes looked tortured but she remained closed. Adam took a deep breath not knowing how to respond.

He touched her hair, gently moving a strand from her cheek. His hand remained, cradling her face. He ran his thumb slowly along the length of her jaw. "When I close my eyes," he whispered,

"I see your face. When I'm alone . . . I imagine how your hair frames your features and how soft it felt brushing against my cheek." His voice shook. Adam looked away embarrassed with his confession. He felt weak yet somehow empowered. Again he looked into Aberdeen's eyes. Time stopped . . . then voices from the briefing room made Adam come to his senses. He withdrew his hand.

"I don't know how all this is going to end Aberdeen," the struggling young man admitted. His eyes said what needed to be said, as did hers. They held onto the moment as long as they could then Adam took a deep breath and turned toward the briefing room. As he walked away she stayed back not wanting the others to see her tears. Things needed to unfold quickly . . .

* * *

The goodbyes at the house had been brief; no one wanting to admit the danger they all faced. They'd gone over all the details one last time before everyone headed out to their assignment.

1:12 pm

Flynn positioned the highway maintenance truck so it blocked the entire left lane. The hazard lights flashed and in front of it, a sign with a flashing arrow instructed cars to merge right, limiting traffic down from two lanes. Both Danielle and Aberdeen held traffic signs stopping vehicles intermittently. They wore orange hard hats and high visibility vests. Those picking up the others at the airport needed to be late.

1:30 pm

After delaying the traffic for 10 minutes the two young women got in the truck with Flynn and proceeded down the highway. He dropped the girls of at a mall parking lot, texted Jarvis and then continued on his way. He needed to switch vehicles and get to

St. Thomas'. Aberdeen and Danielle would be waiting for the bus elsewhere, ready to transfer the children into other vehicles before continuing on to the ranch.

* * *

The three didn't speak as they drove to the airport. There was nothing left to be said. When they arrived at the terminal Jarvis took out his phone and read the text from Flynn,

'ETA 15 MIN, 1 DRV—1 PASS'

It was perfect timing; the plane they should have been on had just landed and they could wait in the chairs at arrivals. After 10 minutes Jarvis took a deep breath and phoned Rupert Street.

"We are at the airport . . . waiting," he said abruptly. "Where is your car?" he asked curtly then listening to the answer. "They have 10 minutes, after that we make our own way." He ended the call not waiting for an answer. They'd effectively put Rupert Street on edge and had the upper hand.

* * *

Ken Munroe and Shane Stevens walked around the bus one last time. They had more than an hour to wait until they needed to leave for the school to pick up the children. Shane wore a blue bus driver's uniform. Both men had altered their appearance in order to not be recognized. Munroe looked at his watch then started to pace.

1:48 pm

Flynn climbed behind the wheel of a landscaping company pickup. Several shrubs and potted flowers filled its box. He'd removed his hard hat and high visibility vest and left them in the highway truck. Looking at his watch Flynn put the pickup in gear and headed for the school.

* * *

As their contact approached Jarvis stood and looked at his watch. The young man was flustered and out of breath. He extended his hand. It was ignored.

"We're short on time," Jarvis disclosed gruffly. He quickly proceeded toward the exit without further comment. Johnson and Adam followed. All three wore sunglasses to complete the look of inapproachability. The contact hustled to keep up.

"The car is waiting just out front," the young man said trying to regain a sense of control. Jarvis continued to push forward, nearing the car.

"What's your name?" Jarvis asked sharply. His tone demanded a quick response.

"Darcy Lockwood, Sir."

"How long's the drive?" Again the question was barked.

"About 45 minutes Sir," Lockwood answered awkwardly. He opened the back passenger door. Jarvis climbed into the back of the car; Adam followed and Johnson went around to the other side. They were in control. The two men in the front were unimportant but Jarvis hoped he'd set the stage for once they arrived at Rupert Street.

* * *

2:24pm

Flynn passed through the gate with ease. Although security had increased, all efforts had been made to maintain normalcy at the school. He was known at the Academy and nothing seemed out of the ordinary. He drove directly to the garden shed and joined the other landscapers. Flynn was careful to stay close to the main building and within sight of the gate. He mentally went through what was expected and tried to emotionally prepare himself.

* * *

Shane was having a hard time remaining focused. Because of the upcoming long weekend the traffic was worse the usual. He took a deep breath and accelerated the bus in order to change lanes. He looked at his watch then concentrated on getting to the Academy on time.

* * *

As the car pulled into Rupert Street, Adam studied every aspect of the property. The main building was fenced by an immaculately trimmed hedge and an ornate courtyard greeted the visitors as they made their way down a cobble stone pathway and through heavy wooden doors. *56 paces,* Adam counted. He could hear the sound of hammering and electric tools from the rear of the building.

The interior had the atmosphere of a high end spa with an expansive lobby welcoming its clients with luxury and opulence. A huge marble desk stood empty and the two fountains were dry. The retreat was a work in progress. Adam looked for residual light signatures. There were none.

Jarvis glanced at his watch and sighed with impatience. He gave Lockwood an unimpressed look. Then he nodded at Johnson who looked at his own watch. Adam studied the reaction of the two men leading them toward the elevator; both were flustered but well trained. Lockwood's partner entered first and slid a key card into a slot in the button panel. The elevator clicked loudly as it engaged. Adam counted as they descended, *11 seconds.*

"This is quite the facility," Jarvis commented.

"It is," Lockwood replied, "and you haven't even seen it yet." Adam took note of the young man's thoughts. He was able to catch glimpses of the layout and of the man they were about to meet.

To the right of the elevator there was a lone door at end of a long brightly lit hallway; to the left a door. They went left. Again Lockwood's partner used his card key and there was a loud click. *Five steps to the door.* Beyond it was a small reception area. *A file cabinet to the right,* Adam observed, *desk to the left . . . camera . . . three chairs along the back wall.*

"He's on his way," the pretty receptionist smiled. *Two metal security doors, large panel . . . table with coffee maker.* Adam soaked in every detail, *three security cameras . . .*

The metal doors opened as a large man in a grey suit entered. He was 50ish with a Roman nose and dark eyes. *Small scar below right eye . . .* The man stood looking at the three newcomers with a grimace. *Sweat beading slightly on forehead.*

Jarvis glanced at Adam, **"He doesn't want us here."** Focussing on this new player Adam agreed. The man felt they were imposing on his territory and wanted them out as soon as possible. Jon had been forced upon him unexpectedly and . . .

"My name is Ambrose," the deep voice boomed. "We were expecting Blithe. This is a sensitive area." Adam listened carefully to the intonation of each word.

"My is Costane," Jarvis replied. He looked toward Johnson then Adam, "Brown and Hastings. Mr. Blithe was needed elsewhere." He looked again at his watch and then back at the large man standing before him.

"We'll talk as we walk," Ambrose continued. He dismissed Lockwood and his partner with a nod. *11 steps to the security panel.* Johnson and Adam followed behind the two men. "We have developed an oscillating light source which interferes with the cartal gland enhancements." *Palm print scan.* The metal doors slid open. "Of course it was designed for the children." A similar brightly lit hall was revealed leading to the right but it was lined with several doors on the left, each with its own palm scanner. "We started the session before we knew you were coming," Ambrose informed them. "It seems its had some negative effects," he added almost sheepishly. *Three doors . . . 24 steps . . . 25 . . .* Adam's focus changed instantly and he looked at Ambrose.

Jarvis also stopped short. "What kind of negative effects?"

* * *

3:27pm

Flynn spotted the bus enter through the Academy gate. They were right on time. He would wait 15 minutes, then make his move.

Shane parked the bus at the loading area in front on the main entrance. Munroe rose and headed toward the door. He looked at the big man behind the wheel.

"Take a deep breath Ken," Shane suggested. **"Remember say only what's necessary."** Munroe inhaled deeply and nodded.

The door opened and he stepped out to greet Enoch Borden. Two large guards stood on either side of him. It was obvious he didn't like the idea of moving the children; it was against his better judgment. There was fear coming from Borden; fear for the children's well being; fear that Harris was making a mistake.

"Where is Harris?" he asked. "I've been trying to reach him."

"We were told to transport the children," Munroe answered, "nothing more."

Borden frowned. He was unsure; something didn't feel right. He looked at Munroe and then at the man driving the bus. Munroe decoded his suspicion and indecision.

"Look," Munroe said glancing at his watch and thinking fast. "Tom Blithe is expecting us in 25 minutes. We've got to get moving." He hoped that mentioning Blithe would ease the other man's distrust. It did. Borden turned and motioned to someone inside the school. "What did you tell them?"

"They think they're going for examinations and assessments," Borden answered. "I hope your people know what they're doing. Interrupting their training now will set us back."

"We were told to transport the children," Munroe repeated, "nothing more."

The door to the school opened and a young woman, followed by a group of children, filed out of the building. They waited in line for instructions. Each child had a small bag. One little girl hugged a small stuffed bear tightly around its neck. They said nothing and looked straight at Borden.

"You are all to be on your best behaviour and follow instructions." The children nodded almost in unison. "Ms. Hebert, will you please get them settled," he asked the young woman. He turned back to Munroe. "Be on your guard, these children are very valuable."

"There should be 14, where are the others?" Munroe inquired. He looked at the Dean for answers.

"Collateral damage," Borden replied.

The young woman led the children aboard the bus. As she passed Shane, he could see her thoughts. There was nothing unusual. She had no idea. She settled a pair into each seat, sometimes straightening a collar, other times giving an encouraging smile. After tucking loose hair behind the ear of a small girl with braids, Ms. Hebert, smiled and headed back to the front of the bus.

"Remember," she reminded them before leaving, "your best behaviour."

* * *

"The Doctor is assessing him now to determine the severity of the damage." Ambrose replied. "He was only exposed to the lights for 3 hours but they caused great discomfort that hasn't yet subsided." They arrived at the lone door at the end of the hall. Ambrose scanned his palm print in the panel next to it. The door slid open.

Adam was having difficulty staying calm and focussed. *42 steps down the hall.* His heart rate increased and there was a tightening in the pit of his stomach. The room they'd entered was circular, with observation windows and doors around its perimeter. *five doors; four windows.* In the middle of the room was a bank of computers with a security guard manning either side. *To the right eight monitors devoted to the holding rooms; to the left twelve that cycled through images of the entire facility.*

Ambrose continued toward one of the observation windows. Adam forced himself to remain back, carefully studying the layout and details of the room before him. He had to stick with the plan. It would up to him to find a way out. Directly across from the door they'd entered, another palm scanner was fixed next to another metal door. *Two cameras.* The other entryways were different, each one leading into one of the four holding rooms. Adam stepped to the left in order to scan the images on the other twelve monitors. They continued to cycle through the whole facility. He absorbed each image and filed it to memory. He took note of the sequence and estimated how much time passed between the images of his present location. *57 seconds . . . Holding cell door release panel to the left . . . Camera control upper right.*

Jarvis stepped forward and looked inside the first holding room. Jon lay on a bunk curled in the fetal position. His hands covered his eyes; his body tight. Jarvis just caught a glimpse of a doctor's back as he left the room. Something had gone terribly wrong. Jarvis looked over at Ambrose with venom in his eyes.

"That looks a lot more serious than severe discomfort." His voice was a accusing but remained calm and professional. "If he's unable to answer my questions, Harris won't be happy."

Adam looked at Jarvis. He saw the deep concern in his eyes and the rage. The young man felt his own anger rise and took a deep breath to maintain control. Johnson stepped forward and whispered something in his partner's ear causing the other man to break eye contact with Adam.

"Time is short," Jarvis demanded quietly, "I need to speak to the kid now." Ambrose nodded and cleared his throat. He looked through the viewing window.

"Jack," he said to one of the men at the computers. "Get Dr. Bergstein in here right now.

* * *

Flynn slipped away as he spotted the bus leave through the Academy gate. His hand wrapped around the small cylinder in his pocket. Timing was everything. The cameras in the hallways cycled through a loop activating each one in a regular pattern. He slipped into Borden's office unnoticed and waited.

*　　*　　*

The children were silent as the bus made its way through the city. Ken Munroe sat in the front seat to the right of the driver. He watched the small faces of his passengers. They didn't seem like typical children. There was no chatter, no laughter. Each sat straight with hands neatly folded in front.

Twelve children, their ages spaced over 5 years. The nine years olds were two sets identical of twins; one set male, one set female. The little girl with the stuffed bear had a five year old male counterpart and the 4 seven year olds were all boys. The two oldest were girls and almost eleven.

"Shane," Munroe said aloud to get the driver's attention at a red light. **"Two children are missing,"** He inhaled deeply. **"He said they were collateral damage"** There were tears in his eyes.

"Keep it together my friend," Shane replied quickly. **"One thing at a time. We need to focus on these 12 right now."**

Munroe swallowed hard, blinked and looked back at the children to find a ten year old girl with long, dark braids staring at him. Her gaze unnerved him. She turned away hoping she hadn't given herself away.

He paused reaching inside his pocket for his glasses. "Things just got a whole lot more complicated." Munroe whispered to the driver. "You'd better put your glasses on." He spent the last part of the journey trying to decide what to do. Things had changed yet again.

Aberdeen and Danielle were ready. As the bus approached the large bay door opened and then closed behind it. They could see small faces through the window and they both took a deep breath.

"Are you ready?" Aberdeen asked her friend. The other woman nodded and they both stepped toward the bus. Munroe emerged and he looked concerned. He told them about the missing children. ". . . And at least one of those children can decode and she observed Shane and I communicate." He rubbed his face. "We need to decide what to do. I don't want them to think we're deceiving them. Besides I caught a glimpse of fear in her eyes. They must be terrified."

Shane watched as the three spoke quietly with their backs to the bus. He could see the children through the rearview mirror. They faced forward patiently waiting for what would come next. It made him wonder what the Epsilon had done to them; what they'd told them. Aberdeen boarded the bus.

"Hello," she said looking at each small face and smiling. "My name is Aberdeen and this is Shane." She motioned toward the large man behind the wheel. "We'd been looking for him and others for a very long time." She paused. "We wanted to help them get away from some people, some bad people." She smiled. "We not only found them but you as well."

The children sat wide eyed and although Aberdeen couldn't read any of them she could see fear on their faces.

"There are nine of us who have a special ability called decoding. All we want is to have normal lives, but there are people who have others ideas." She hoped they understood. "They will do everything in their power to stop us. Our abilities are very valuable to them."

"Are you from Epsilon?" A young boy near the middle of the bus asked with a shaky voice. He was afraid; they were all afraid. The children knew more than it was thought.

"No," Shane answered with certainty. "It's Epsilon we're trying to get away from." He looked at the girl with long dark braids. **"You're going to have to trust us."** She looked away nervously. Shane took a deep breath. "We are going to take you to a safe place, away from Epsilon." He looked at the girl again. "Are there any questions before we leave?"

"Where are we going?" the little girl with the bear asked.

". . . To a ranch with horses and sunshine." Aberdeen replied. "Where there are people who care about you and want you to grow up happy and strong." She hesitated. "You will be safe there until we figure out what to do next. We don't want you to be afraid. We know that at least some of you can already decode and that you've kept it from the people at the school. That was very wise."

* * *

Borden closed his office door and took several steps toward his desk before he saw Flynn. He immediately recognized him as one of the ground keepers.

"What are you doing in my office?" he challenged.

"Harris . . . ," Flynn said ominously. "Is it done?" The Dean froze.

"I've done everything he wanted . . . it's all gone . . . destroyed . . . they've taken the children." Borden began to shake, realizing he was just another loose end. ". . . I've always done everything they've asked." He began to hyperventilate.

"Hmm," Flynn nodded stepping closer. "You really shouldn't have." As he took another step he retrieved the small cylinder from his pocket and swiftly positioned it onto Borden's chest. A shock just strong enough to stop a beating heart entered the terrified man's body. Flynn stepped back.

Borden clutched his chest and fell to his knees. It was done. The authorities would conclude that Dean Enoch Borden of the St. Thomas Academy died of a heart attack. It was Flynn's turn to shake; he'd never killed anyone before.

* * *

CHAPTER 17

JARVIS HELD HIS BREATH and turned away from Ambrose. *Bergstein is alive;* he thought to himself, *if he recognizes me . . . we're all dead.* He looked over at Adam. **"Adam . . . he can't see me?"**

"There's 57 seconds between the camera surveillance cycles." Adam communicated quickly, trying to ease Jarvis' concerns. **"As soon as the door closes behind Bergstein, we'll act at the beginning of the next cycle."** He nodded slightly. **"Step back; let Dale take the lead . . . Don't worry . . . we've got this, it'll only be a matter of moments."**

With a quick whisper in his ear from Jarvis, Dale Johnson knew exactly what to do. They'd worked together long enough that little needed to be said. He knew of Dr. Bergstein and understood his partner's apprehension at being recognized. He scanned the room, his eyes finally resting on Adam. They shared a look, both concerned about Jarvis; both uncertain how he would react to seeing Bergstein after so many years.

The door slid open. A figure bent over with age entered but Anthony Bergstein still an air of influence about him. His thoughts were focussed but he struggled with a weakened body. He'd once been physically powerful but over time his muscle mass had deteriorated and his skin now hung loosely on his tall frame. He wasn't what Adam expected. He was frail and laboured just put one foot in front of the other. In a sense he reminded Adam of Joseph Dresner, a mere shadow of what he must have once been.

"Is he able to answer some questions?" Ambrose asked the Doctor. Bergstein stepped toward the observation window. Adam could see Jarvis' body tighten because of his proximity. The door closed.

"**35 seconds until the next camera loop begins**," Adam informed Jarvis. "**Hang in there.**" He readied himself.

"There've certainly been some unexpected complications," Bergstein replied. *29 seconds.* "The lights have over stimulated his cartal gland and there seems to be significant swelling. It's a good thing its him and not one of the children. I thought I'd gotten the right oscillation frequency. It could have been disastrous." *21 seconds.* The doctor looked from Johnson to Adam and then at the back of Jarvis' head. "He is in distress and unable to see," Bergstein notified them, "I don't think he's in any condition to do anything."

Anger rose in Adam's chest as he continued to count down. *18 seconds . . . 17.* He mentally ran through what needed to be done, visualizing each step. *13 . . . 12 . . .*

"Harris won't be happy," responded Dale. "Will he recover?" Adam held his breath waiting for the answer. *10 seconds.* Jarvis turned his ear toward the doctor also waiting. *9 seconds.*

Anthony Bergstein turned to look through the observation window. *7 seconds.* "I really can't be sure," he answered. "There should already have been some improvement and there hasn't been. Its as though he's shutting down." *5 seconds.*

"**4 seconds . . . 3 seconds,**" Adam looked at Jarvis' reflection and then at Johnson. Assured they were ready, he looked back over at the monitors, waiting for the images of their present location to disappear. Instantly he made his move.

Adam moved quickly to the left side of the computer bank. He jammed his foot behind the wheel of the security guard's chair, yanking up on its arm. It pivoted momentarily then crashed to the floor. Caught unaware the guard tumbled out, lying helpless on the ground. Adam brought his heal down hard to the man's temple. Once . . . twice . . . three times. *54 seconds.*

The young man then looked over at the others. Johnson had dropped the second guard and was holding Doctor Bergstein against the wall. Jarvis struggled with Ambrose, restraining him from behind but unable to bring him down. *50 . . . 49 seconds.* He winced as his opponent jammed his elbow to his ribs. Ambrose reached for an alarm button on the control panel but Jarvis pushed him back. *46 . . . 45 . . .*

Adam stepped forward. He reached up from behind to grab Ambrose by the chin and shoulder. He wrenched the man's head around but the big man twisted his body. Adam left his feet, swinging just off the ground. *40 seconds.* As his body hit the wall, he felt extreme pain to his right side. Using the wall as leverage, Adam wrenched Ambrose's neck again. He heard the snap. Both crumpled to the floor. *33 seconds.*

"Who are you people?" Bergstein asked as Jarvis helped roll a motionless Ambrose off of Adam. "What do want?" the doctor demanded. He was terrified. Johnson slammed him against the wall and told him to shut up. *30 seconds.*

"I've got to get to the control panel," Adam demanded struggling to his feet. "We've got to shut down the cameras before the beginning of the next cycle." *25 seconds.* He felt a sticky warmth spread across his right side. "Camera controls . . . other end of the panel . . . upper right." *21 seconds.* He staggered toward the computer bank. *19 . . . 18 . . .*

Adam took a deep breath and set his jaw. His training took over as he quickly accessed the controls and shut down the two cameras. *That should buy us some time.* Leaning against the panel he took another deep breath and calmed himself.

Running his right hand down his side, Adam assessed his injury. He must have pulled some stitches. Things needed to happen fast and he didn't have the luxury of being hurt. Cleaning the blood off his hand with the inside of his jacket he buttoned it to hide the injury from the others. He unlocked the holding room doors and turned to Jarvis.

Jarvis' thoughts were filled with rage. He stared at Bergstein. There was no recognition in the doctor's eyes and beads of sweat streamed down his forehead. He was still backed against the wall even though Johnson had let him go.

"Who are you?" he asked staring back.

Jarvis stepped closer to the old man.

"We don't have time for this." Adam insisted.

"I've got this kid," came the answer. Jarvis continued to get closer to Bergstein. **"Get Jon."** There was no point arguing with him. "Dale . . . go with Adam." His voice was deep and ominous.

"Daniel . . ." His partner looked at him with concern.

"Go . . . now," Jarvis replied abruptly, "The good doctor and I need to have a little chat."

* * *

Flynn had finally stopped shaking. He'd ditched the pick up near the bus station and was now on his way the Rupert Street. His work overalls were gone, replaced by a black suit. Jarvis would contact him when it was time to make a move but until then it would be a waiting game. He so much wanted this all to be over. He parked a couple of blocks from his destination and checked his messages again.

* * *

"They put them in our arms," a little boy informed Shane. His twin nodded rolling up his sleeve to show a small linear scar on his right forearm. The children had come to terms with what was happening and Munroe had boarded the bus to scan for GPS implants. He held the same device Jarvis had used on Adam at the Compound.

"We need to remove them." Munroe looked at the girl with the braids. **"What's your name?"** he asked. She turned away. "I know you understand me," he insisted gently. His eyes didn't falter. **"At some point you're going to have to trust us."** She didn't respond.

"Her name is Emily," the girl next to her replied, **"and mine is Hannah."** The two girls were almost opposites. Hannah was fair, her blonde hair cut short and the spitting image of a younger

Danielle. **"Don't mind her,"** she said, **"she only talks to me."** The girl stood and rolled up her sleeve. "Let's get this over with." Munroe stepped forward, and ran the scanner along her arm. The device squealed. He put the extraction apparatus to her skin. "Ready?" Hannah nodded and closed her eyes. Munroe pulled the trigger and the young girl showed no reaction as the small implant was drawn out. A small trickle of blood appeared from the tiny incision. She turned to Emily.

"Your turn," she said, taking the girl's hand and pulling her to her feet. Emily complied and soon all 12 children were scanned and their implants removed. None reacted or complained. It was apparent they were not strangers to similar experiences. Munroe also scanned their belongings. They exited the bus in pairs once he gave them the all clear. Aberdeen cleaned and bandaged each wound as they gathered next to the waiting vans.

Danielle was struggling. The young woman couldn't bring herself to engage and her hands wouldn't stop shaking. She couldn't help thinking of Jon or the missing children. *This is stupid,* she thought, *get over it.* She leaned against the far wall, away from the growing activity next to the bus and looked over at her father. He too was overwhelmed. They all were. Shane looked dazed, forcing himself to stay focussed on the task in front of him and Aberdeen had sprung into overdrive. No one wanted to think about what had happened to the missing children or give into the idea that the others were up against almost impossible odds at Rupert Street.

Danielle didn't notice the little girl with the bear approach until a small hand touched her arm. Jon's big, blue eyes looked up at her.

"I'm sorry you're sad," the tiny 5 year old voiced. "My name is Paige and when I'm sad, Snuggly makes me feel better." She lifted her bear, offering it to Danielle. The young woman was taken by surprise and a single tear slipped down her cheek before she forced a smile.

* * *

Jon couldn't bear anymore. He felt like he was being pulled under water and was about to drown. It was becoming increasingly difficult to breath and he was afraid to open his eyes. A sharp, unbearable pain replaced the dull ache whenever he tried. Besides, it was over. Bergstein's voice had brought that realization home. There was no way out and if there were he was helpless to do anything about it.

The future had been so promising but now all hope was lost and he sank deeper into despair. Jon brought his knees closer to his chest and wrapped his arms around them, holding tight. He tried to breath, it was getting harder. It was too shallow and he couldn't fill his lungs.

Something caught his attention. His name . . . someone was calling his name but it was too far away for him to be sure it was real.

Adam's side throbbed as he knelt beside his brother and called his name again. The tightly curled figure didn't respond and it was obvious he was in great distress and slipping away. "Jon," he said again next to his ear. "Jon." He pried one of his brother's arms from around his legs. Adam opened the clenched hand and laid it open on his own chest. He inhaled deeply. "Feel the way I breathe Jon . . . feel it . . . you need to breath."

Adam felt the panic rise in his chest. His brother was dying, slipping away. He closed his eyes, going back many months; back to the Sudan. He needed to detach, become someone else. Failure was not an option. Doctor Jacob Morris, a member of Doctors Without Borders. He'd performed under the most hellish of conditions. Adam took another deep breath and flicked a mental switch.

Dale Johnson watched as Adam's demeanour instantly transformed. The young man's shoulders went back and his breathing changed. His face became unfamiliar; so much so that no trace of Adam remained. He sprang into action, forcing the injured man's legs straight, rolling him on his back and tilting back his head. Jon gasped for air.

"Jon," a voice that wasn't Adam's ordered, "snap out of it." Jacob Morris pinched the gasping man causing him to flinch.

"Jon come back." He ran his hands over the length of his patient's body. He found nothing but heard a low moan and watched as Jon brought his hands to his face and pushed against his eyes.

"Its alright Jon," Adam had returned. "Its us. We've come to get you out of here."

"Bergstein . . . . uh . . ." Jon replied almost hyperventilating. "Got to . . . uh . . . get out." His voice was a whisper and he began to bring his legs back up to his chest. "I . . . can't see . . . and my head . . . uh . . ."

"Dale is here," Adam said. He waved the other man over and looked at him. "He's going to rip some sheets and pad your eyes then tie around a blindfold so that pressure will be against your eyes but your hands will be free." He put his hand on Dale's shoulder. "Do you understand?" There was a quick nod. "It's time to call Flynn, I'll be back."

He stepped out of the holding room and glanced at Jarvis. Bergstein was still backed against the wall but the old man was unswerving, resolved with a self righteous belief that everything he'd done was justified. Joseph Dresner had inspired him to do what needed to be done. There were no apologies; no regrets. Jarvis seethed.

Considering all the options Adam went to the fallen Ambrose and took his gun from its holster. "This is Ambrose," he said aloud. Deepening his voice he repeated, "this is Ambrose . . . this is Ambrose our visitors will be leaving." He continued to practice the voice as he went to the computers and picked up the phone. He pushed the button labeled reception. A woman's familiar voice answered.

"Hello, Reception."

"This is Ambrose," Adam announced. "Our visitors will be leaving soon. Advise the front gate a black sedan will be arriving in the next few minutes to pick them up."

"Yes sir," the pleasant voice replied. "Is there anything else?"

"No." Adam hung up.

He watched the security cameras scan through their cycle and calculated the risk of shutting down another camera. Sliding his hand inside his jacket and touching his side, Adam knew there was no other option. The bleeding had to be stopped. He deactivated the camera to the infirmary.

"Jarvis," Adam interrupted, "get a hold of Flynn, its almost time." He stepped between the two men, grabbing the doctor by the throat. "You and I need to go on an errand," he whispered to Bergstein. There was fire in his eyes. Behind him Jarvis inhaled, exasperated. Adam turned to him, still holding the doctor. **"You'll get no satisfaction from him . . . get a hold of Flynn . . . we're going to have to move fast."** Jarvis continued to stare at Bergstein and then suddenly turned away, pulled out his phone and texted Flynn. He got an immediate reply.

"He's on his way," he announced.

Adam looked at his friend. **"I need you to help Johnson get Jon ready to move."** Jarvis looked from Adam to Bergstein and then back again. **"He's my problem now."** The older man hesitated; torn. With one last hateful glare at Bergstein he backed off.

"You'll never get out of here alive," the man in the white coat goaded the young man who had his hand against his neck.

"I know *you* won't," Adam replied calmly, "but first we have business in the infirmary."

"Why should I help you?" asked Bergstein. "Do you think I'm a fool?" Adam looked deeply into the old man's eyes and waded through his thoughts. He chose his next words carefully.

"A fool . . . no," Adam responded. "but you have this misguided notion that if you can stay alive long enough someone will save you." He smiled, narrowing his eyes. "For some reason you think you're so valuable to them that they'll do anything to save you." The doctor swallowed. "Shall we test your theory?" Adam grabbed Bergstein's hand and pulled him toward the control panel next to the door. He winced as he twisted the old man around like a rag doll. "You can either cooperate or we can see how much damage I can inflict while you're waiting to be saved. Truth be told all I need is your palm. Shall I remove your hand and leave the rest of you here with Jarvis?" The door slid open as the doctor's palm was scanned.

"Who the hell are you?" Bergstein asked as he regained his balance and tried to regain his composure. There was fear in his eyes. Adam took him by the arm and they entered the hall, quickly heading toward the infirmary. "Who are you?"

"Didn't you get my mother's Christmas cards?" Adam asked sarcastically. "Wait . . . You weren't on her list." The old man was confused but the venom in the young man's voice made its point. Inside the infirmary Adam released the doctor, pulled the gun and pointed it at his head. A young woman in a white lab coat looked up from her desk. "I need a suture kit and absorbent bandages . . . now!" Adam barked.

She fumbled through one of the cabinets and produced an armful of supplies then deposited them on the examining table. She trembled with fear. Bergstein studied Adam, noticing first the blood on the young man's hand and then the darkened portion of his black jacket. Adam was pale and starting to shake.

"You're hurt," the doctor observed with satisfaction. "I told you, you'd never get out of here alive."

The injured man smiled and stepped forward; the old man cowered. With one swift motion Adam dropped the doctor to the floor. He looked at his watch. 3 minutes had already passed since he'd left the others. He was running out of time.

"What is your name?" he asked the terrified woman.

"Isabelle."

"Isabelle, I need your help," he said softly. Adam put the gun down on the examining table and weakly smiled at her. It was calculated and effective. He opened his jacket. Both his shirt and the inside of his coat were saturated with blood. She gasped. He unbuttoned the shirt and gingerly opened it. His eyes never left hers; assessing her reaction. Several of his stitches had ripped and blood seeped from the jagged gash. "You need to stop the bleeding." He'd planned on doing it himself, but this was better. She looked at the doctor and then back at Adam.

"You killed him," she said with tears in her eyes.

"I *stopped* him," Adam replied feigning emotion. "He was an evil man." He knew she agreed. Tilting his head he grimaced for effect. A low guttural noise came from his throat. Deep blue eyes pleaded with her. With shaking hands she put on some gloves and approached the injured young man.

* * *

As Adam buttoned up Bergstein's ill fitting shirt, the bulge of bandages at his right side pushed against the fabric. A blanket covered the doctor's body as it lay crumpled on the floor. The young woman was washing blood from her hands. Adam took a deep breath and looked at his watch and then over at her.

"My friend needs a wheelchair, the "good' doctor's last patient can no longer walk." She knew who he was talking about and looked over at the storage room.

"When I started working here I had no idea," she confessed. "Then they wouldn't let me quit." The young woman frowned. "I know too much."

They stayed near the left wall limiting the cameras' view. At the metal doors the girl scanned her palm and the door opened. The others were waiting, concern on their faces. Jon sat in one of the guards' wheeled chairs, his eyes covered with strips torn from a sheet. Agony contorted his features. Johnson held onto him firmly so he wouldn't fall. Jarvis was at the computers attaching a small round cylinder to one of the processors. He pushed a small button on its side and the small device began to break through the network's firewall in order to implant a virus. It would destroy the entire database and any computer that logged onto it.

In one of the holding rooms the two guards were bound, gagged and gunless. In the corner Jarvis' jacket was strewn over Ambrose's upper body and head. Adam exhaled deeply. He couldn't stop shaking. Jarvis and Johnson shared a worried look and then both looked at the girl.

"Has Flynn arrived?" Adam asked with a raspy voice. Jarvis nodded. "Good," the young man responded. "Time is running out.

Once we leave this room we've got to make it back to reception in less than 20 seconds or the cameras will see us coming. We'll have to hurry. I counted 42 steps on the way here. Is everyone ready?"

"**Adam?** . . ." Jarvis began.

"**Save it, I'm fine,**" Adam lied with a grimace.

"**. . . and the girl . . . Bergstein?**"

Adam glanced at the young woman in the lab coat. "**We need her to get past security.**" Changing his focus to the computers he began to calculate the timing.

". . . and Bergstein . . . ?" Adam looked at Jarvis, showing him what he wanted to see. The older man nodded. Johnson and the girl put Jon in the wheel chair and fastened the straps. "**Then he's really dead.**" Jarvis concluded. He scanned the room and each face. "**Let's get out of here.**" Adam began a countdown in his head.

"Is everyone ready?" he questioned. The girl studied his face and then looked at the others. With a deep breath, she nodded. Adam returned her nod. "Remember after my mark we have 20 seconds. We move in 8 . . . 7 . . . 6 . . ." Johnston pushed the wheelchair closer to the door and Jarvis took the young woman by the arm. She scanned her hand and the door opened. "3 . . . 2 . . . 1 . . . Move!"

The group hurried down the hall. *19 seconds . . . 18 . . .* The pain in Adam's side increased and he struggled to keep up. He needed to stop but knew he couldn't. *15 . . . 14 . . .* Things were getting blurry as he looked down the hall. He blinked his eyes twice, bringing things back into focus. Johnson left the wheelchair and came back for him. *11 seconds . . . 10 . . .* With an arm over Johnson's shoulder, Adam battled the rest of the way. *7 . . . 6 . . .* All three men shared a look and took a deep breath. *4 seconds . . .* They drew their guns. *3 seconds . . .* Jarvis nodded, and the girl scanned her palm. The door opened and before they stepped in Adam shot out the cameras; once inside, the door closed behind them.

The reception area was empty except for the pretty young woman behind the desk. Fearing she'd hit an alarm button, Jarvis approached quickly, reached forward and pulled her away from the desk. She screamed, twisted and headed for the exit. The girl in the lab coat stayed by the metal doors and made herself small.

"Stop or I'll shoot you," Adam warned the receptionist. She didn't stop. A bullet whizzed by her head. She froze, terrified. "We don't want to hurt you," he assured her. "We just want to get out of here." Jarvis stepped forward and grabbed the young woman by her arm.

"And you, my dear are going to help us." His voice was menacing. "Where is your card key?" She didn't reply but her thoughts drifted to her purse. Adam rifled through the bag and found it.

"Keep her quiet," he instructed Jarvis. A hand was placed firmly over the receptionist's mouth. Adam hit the intercom.

"Lockwood here," the speaker crackled.

"Find out what's going on at the west wing," Ambrose ordered. "Those idiots must have cut through a wire or something. We've having nothing but problems with the electrical down here." Adam took a deep breath. "We keep losing security cameras and I don't like it."

"Yes Sir," the voice replied. "I'll send Cooper and Davis to investigate." Adam pushed the button again ending the exchange.

"How many security on site?" questioned Jarvis removing his hand from over the receptionist's mouth. She didn't respond. He shook her slightly. "How many?" he demanded. He looked into the young woman's eyes and behind the hate he found the answers he needed. Continuing his firm grip on her arm Jarvis turned to the others. "6 guards . . . 2 stationed in the lobby; two at the front gate."

Adam checked on his brother. Jon was conscious but his breathing was laboured. Adam said some reassuring words then stepped close to Bergstein's assistant. "Isabelle, you need to get out of here as soon as you can," he whispered in her ear. "Don't leave any trace that you were ever here and then disappear for a while." He looked in her eyes making sure she understood. She nodded.

* * *

Flynn was directed by the guards at the front gate to park near the main entrance and told not to get out of his car. He carefully surveyed the area from where he sat but couldn't easily see beyond the decorative hedge. There was only one opening in the thick foliage. Back towards the road he had a clear view of the gate. He was getting antsy. The longer he waited the more concerned he became.

* * *

The receptionist's terrified face disappeared as the elevator doors closed. Adam leaned against the wall and tried to refocus. He knew he'd lost a lot of blood and it was taking its toll. The young man felt weak.

The trio had correctly anticipated that Darcy Lockwood and his partner would be waiting in the lobby. As the elevator door opened, Jarvis stepped out with purpose. He looked at his watch and then back at the others. Adam lagged behind pushing the wheelchair.

"If traffic is busy we're going to miss our flight," the man in the lead complained.

"Just a minute Sir," Lockwood said. "I need to confirm your departure with operations." He noted the injured man in the wheelchair. "Jack," he said into his radio, "Jack, do you copy?" Jarvis looked at his watch again, flustering the two men between him and the door. "Jack?" Lockwood repeated into his radio.

"You two get Stevens in the car," Jarvis spoke over his shoulder. "I'll wait here." The others started toward the door.

"I'm sorry Sir," Lockwood said apologetically. "You're all going to have to wait." He and his partner moved forward so they were blocking the others. Jarvis and Johnson shared a look. Adam got ready to make a break for the door.

Jarvis went left and Johnson went right. Both targets were caught off guard, unable to defend the first blows. Lockwood fell to the ground and slid along the highly polished floor. He got control of his gun and took a shot. Although blood and tissue exploded from Dale's right shoulder he kept moving forward. He kicked the gun from Lockwood's hand and the weapon skidded across the floor. The young guard looked up in disbelief. He watched as Johnson thrust his foot toward his face. It caught him just under the jaw. He saw a flash of red and then nothing.

Jarvis took down his man quickly. A well placed blow to the temple followed by an upper cut to the chin was all that was needed. The skin tore and the jaw fractured. The moment before the young man fell, their eyes met and Jarvis fought off the rising guilt he felt for inflicting so much damage. The feeling was short lived as gun shots from down the hall erupted.

Adam made it as far as the door when the gun fire began. From behind he heard Johnson's verbal reaction to the pain of being shot and a moment later the volley of bullets from the hallway. He safely deposited Jon in a small alcove just outside the door, drew Ambrose's gun and turned back to help the others.

They were pinned. Out of the shooter's view, Adam watched Jarvis and Johnson hide against the outside corner of the marble counter from the barrage of bullets. Dale was hurt and there was a smear of blood along the floor. Puffs of dust and bits of marble tumbled to the floor as bullets collided with the ornate desk. Jarvis and Adam locked eyes. Something was wrong.

"**Adam** . . ." Jarvis took a deep breath. "**I'm hit** . . ." There was no need to explain. His eyes were glassy and the colour draining from his face. Behind him, his partner watched in disbelief as a large puddle of blood began to form. Johnson tried to help; to apply pressure but his right arm was useless. Adam's eyes burned while he watched the realization of the inevitable set in. The anguish on Dale's face mirrored his own.

"**. . . I'm sorry Jarvis**," Adam gulped. "**. . . I tried** . . ."

"**It's not your fault**," replied Jarvis. He flinched at the sound of another shot. "**None of this is** . . . **Get the others out** . . ." He licked his lips. The dying man looked at his partner and smiled weakly, then gave a firm nod of encouragement. His eyes returned to Adam. **"Keep her safe."** He began to fade. Licking his lips again, his eyes flickered then he slowly went limp. His life drained away.

The remaining men shared a moment of profound grief across the room. Then Johnson reached awkwardly with his left hand and took his partner's gun. Closing his eyes, he took a deep breath and crouched ready to move. Adam nodded and flipped a mental switch.

Things became slower. He looked in his gun clip; eight shots. Clicking it back in place, he carefully peeked down the darkened hall and searched for the shooters but only observed flashes from each discharge. Adam concentrated. *Click . . . muffled whispers . . . a shoe sliding on the floor . . . gunshot.* He began to calculate distances and frequency. *Click . . . silence . . . heavy inhale.* They were getting ready to move.

Adam looked at Johnson, nodded and held up three fingers . . . then two . . . He levelled his gun . . . then one. At the next discharge, Adam took two quick shots exactly 5 1/2 inches behind and 1 inch below the flash. The first, hit the shooter's three lower fingers where they wrapped around the gun. The second caught him in the forearm as he recoiled from the pain. There was a scream and an echo as his gun dropped to the floor.

Johnson sprang to his feet, letting off three shots down the hall as he ran toward the door. Adam kept his gun levelled ready to fire and counted . . . *one* . . . *two* . . . *three.* He aimed higher, anticipating from where the second guard would fire. The bullet caught the corner of the wall, taking off the plaster and dusting the guard's face with dust. It was effective. Johnson opened the door and escaped. Adam followed keeping an eye on the hallway but not wanting to waste any shots.

5 bullets left, Adam thought to himself. Johnson stopped and turned to him, but said nothing. He was breathing heavily. Adam assessed his shoulder. There wasn't much blood but the damage was extensive. *Click . . .* Adam quickly turned, levelled his gun and took one shot at the man who'd followed them from the lobby. Through the small crack of the open door Adam's bullet hit its mark. The guard fell forward, blood dripping from a small round hole between his eyes. Adam pushed him back inside and closed the door. *4 bullets . . .*

"Get out of the car!" ordered a man's voice from the parking lot. Adam motioned with his eyes for Johnson to stay with Jon. The injured man leaned against the building and nodded.

"Give me a gun," Adam said. *4 bullets in mine . . . 5 bullets in his . . .* He paced quickly toward the noise in the parking lot, a weapon in each hand.

A guard approached Flynn's car with an automatic assault rifle in hand. He pointed it straight at Flynn demanding he get out. It was clear the others had made their move and it wasn't going well. *First the gun fire from inside the building,* Flynn thought, *now this.*

From the corner of his eye Flynn saw movement near the hedge. Suddenly, four gun blasts exploded. The guard with the rifle fell to the ground. Adam appeared at the opening between the hedges. He walked toward the car, guns in hand. He tucked them in the back of his pants as he scanned the area. There was blood on his shirt and hands; his face emotionless. The young man walked over to the fallen guard and took his rifle.

With a quick look he said, **"Wait here,"** then walked toward the front gate. Flynn barely recognized him. Without hesitation Adam riddled the gate house with bullets until the gun was empty. Throwing down the depleted weapon he reached back and pulled out his two hand guns then disappeared behind another hedge.

Flynn waited wondering where the others were. He heard shattering glass, a single shot and then two more. He held his breath. Moments later Adam reappeared wiping blood from a cut on his forehead, another rifle in his hand. He ran back toward the main building with urgency. Flynn got out of the car and followed.

He was taken aback at what awaited him. The two men he approached looked like they'd been in a war zone. Jon sat, strapped in a wheelchair, barely coherent. His eyes were wrapped with ripped bandage. Dale was covered in blood. It had darkened as it dried and he'd rubbed his face smearing some across his brow.

"Where's Daniel?" Flynn asked.

There was no time for Flynn to react to the answer. It wasn't until they sped away in the car that the reality of his friend's death set in. He's gone. Flynn blinked, glancing over at Jon next to him in the passenger seat. From behind he heard Adam.

"I need a safe doctor in Akron Ohio," the young man said. ". . . Two subjects," he continued, ". . . gun shots . . ." His phone rested on his lap as he tried to dress Johnson's shoulder. ". . . The west side . . ." he paused to look at a street sign, ". . . near Dumont and 5th. Call me back." Nodding at Dale he reached in his pocket for Blithe's phone then dialed the CIA.

"CIA, Agent Ferguson."

"Agent Blithe, security clearance 901" Adam croaked into the phone. "Code 7 at 317 Rupert Street, Akron, Ohio; Priority One, Agents down."

"Priority One?"

He ended the call, took a deep breath and waited for his phone to ring.

CHAPTER 18

THE TRAVELLERS WERE TIRED when they reached the ranch. After leaving from different airports the children had arrived in two separate groups. Any bed would have been a welcome sight and they settled in quietly for the night staying close to each other, still unsure. The adults gathered in the sitting room to talk things through and decide how to proceed in the morning. They waited for news from the others.

After a time, no one said much. There was nothing left to say. Shane began to pace. Sophia was next to her daughter and Aberdeen sat curled up in an armchair next to the fire. She stared at the flames mesmerized. It was just after midnight when the phone finally rang.

* * *

The others arrived early, before the children awoke. They went directly to the treatment room; Dr. Erikson, his assistant and Shane met them at the helicopter. Danielle waited for them inside. Adam needed help; his strength had left him and after repeated damage to his side, infection was setting in. He was feverish and lethargic. Jon was brought in on a gurney. The sedative given to him in Akron hadn't worn off. The Doctor checked him quickly and then turned his attention to Adam. Danielle remained by his side. Flynn went to find the others.

The stinging pain in Adam's side was nothing compared to the mess of emotions he was going through. It confused him that he could be in such agony yet feel numb at the same time. He felt broken inside. He'd emotionally shut down at Rupert Street but once he'd reached the ranch and the adrenaline wore off, it was like a flood gate opened.

The Doctor's voice became garbled as he sat the young man down on an examining table. Adam watched everything move slowly and his vision blurred. He saw the pen light flash in his eyes and recognized his father's voice echoing in his ears. His eyes filled with tears. There were more garbled words and he was aware of being laid onto the table. He felt the IV go into his arm and his shirt being cut away.

"There's another through and through GSW on his left upper arm," the Doctor's assistant observed removing another saturated dressing. "He's lost a lot of blood."

"Shane," Erikson ordered. "Find a chair and role up your sleeve."

*　*　*

Flynn arrived to update everyone. He was in shock like everyone else. He told them what he knew about Jon and that Jarvis hadn't made it out of Rupert Street. Also that Dale Johnson had been shot. He was on his way to a safe clinic in New York. His wife would meet him there. He'd need extensive reconstructive surgery.

"And Adam?" inquired Munroe.

"He's in bad shape." Flynn replied. "The doctor in Akron took one look at him and wanted to admit him to a hospital. The lad wouldn't have it. He said it wasn't safe and insisted on getting back here as soon as possible. Other than that he hasn't said two words." He paused and looked at Aberdeen.

She still sat in the arm chair. The fire had burned down but her gaze never left the dying flames. She'd drifted off to sleep at some point in the night and someone had placed a blanket over her petite body. She stirred when Flynn arrived and now tightly hugged herself with the blanket. The young woman had spent a lot of time thinking.

Her father tried to prepare her and in the back of her mind she'd known. The news hadn't really been a surprise. Tears trickled gently down her face and she imagined them together; her mother and father. They'd been apart for so long but no longer; Aberdeen was the one left behind.

"Lassie," Flynn said gently as he approached. He kneeled and put his hands on her lap. "I'm sorry."

"We all are," she replied with a weak smile. "We all are." Flynn brought a chair next to her and they both looked at the fire.

* * *

Sophia took over once the children started to wake up. Her health had improved and she was in her element. She wore glasses to protect them from the devastating events of the day before. Everyone agreed that a positive first impression was important. They responded to her well and even Emily had a smile.

Breakfast was the first priority. Extra staff had been hired to help and a larger eating area set up. It wasn't prefect but it could be worked on. Afterward a tour: inside and out, then the horses and swimming pool. Munroe joined them. It was a beautiful day. Things went well but the children were uneasy. It was to be expected. They were careful not to get caught up in it, to enjoy themselves too much. After lunch it would be time for questions and a discussion of the future. It was hard to know how much they would understand or how much they already knew. It was evident though, there could be no secrets.

* * *

Shane interrupted the silence in the sitting room. Both people staring at the fire turned toward him as he entered. They'd been lost in their own thoughts. His face was drawn and his shoulders tightened by stress, worry and grief.

"How are they?" Flynn asked.

"The Doctor is still with Adam. He's not in good shape." He shook his head. "Jon's resting," the huge man replied seeming small. "He woke up briefly mumbling something about Bergstein." Shane inhaled. "The Doctor gave him a shot to ease the pain." He looked at Flynn incredulous. "He was there Flynn. Bergstein was there." A chill went through both men. "Once the pain dulled he was able to explain what happened." Shane told them about the lights and the interrogation . . . and about the terror Jon went through when he'd heard Bergstein's voice.

"And his vision?" asked Flynn.

"Erikson said the frequency of the lights caused swelling of the cartal gland," Shane answered. "He hopes it will go down with time." Shane ran his hand through his hair and shook his head. "The pain's excruciating and when he opens his eyes its unbearable even with the pain killer. Jon said all he can see red and bright flashes." There was a long silence. Aberdeen turned back toward the fire.

"Is Bergstein dead?" Flynn asked.

"He didn't know and Adam's in no condition to talk." Shane took a deep cleansing breath and shook his head. He'd aged 10 years in twelve hours. Flynn arose from his chair and hugged his friend.

* * *

Flynn joined the children by the pool for hot dogs. Some of them recognized him from the Academy. He had to explain why he'd been at the school. It took some time before they began to relax. After lunch some of the staff led the younger children to the small play area near the pool deck. Initially they were nervous, not wanting to separate from the others. Sophia reassured them. They wouldn't be far and could return whenever they wanted. With a smile and nod from Hannah, the little ones went off to play.

"We want to be entirely honest with you," Sophia began, "but we really don't know where to begin or what you already know."

They knew a lot. Hannah told them everything; the nightmares and the plans to get away before they were sent to Rupert Street. She even mentioned Bergstein. Emily had been taken for a visit to a small testing facility near the school. Tears flowed as Hannah told them of when the oldest boy was sent to Dean Borden's office never to return and not long afterward another also disappeared. The adults were stunned. No wonder children were terrified yet so willing to come with them.

Emily began to tremble. She looked at Sophia. **"There was a room with a light . . . Doctor Bergstein . . ."** Hannah took the shaking girl's hand. **"It flickered and . . ."** She couldn't continue. Munroe sat next to her and took her other hand. They waited but she began to rock back and forth. Hannah's anguish filled eyes looked at the adults and she took a deep breath.

"What we don't understand," Hannah said, "is why we are. You talked about this special ability that is so valuable." She looked at the other children. "Why are we so different than others? Why are you?" Are there more?"

Munroe made a decision. He looked at Flynn and Sophia. They both nodded. "It started a long time ago in a clinic that was probably a lot like the testing facility you were brought to. Dr. Bergstein was there too." He went on to give a quick summary of the events that led up to the present. He told of the enhancements and of Bergstein's escape with Sophia and the others; of how long it had taken to find them and get them away from Epsilon. He briefly explained that while looking they'd discovered the children. Hannah was satisfied . . . for now. They knew there'd be more questions. There would be difficult times ahead.

*   *   *

Adam's heart was heavy in his chest and he knew there was no way out. The building was surrounded and it was getting harder to breath. Thick smoke filled the room as it poured in from under the door. It made his eyes burn. The familiar sound of a helicopter pounded in his ears. He looked over at the four small windows lining the wall.

"Adam . . . Help me!" Aberdeen's voice echoed in his ears.

He rushed to the row of windows and peered inside each one. In the last, a small figure crouched in the corner. Her hair draped forward, covering her face. The lights flickered. She sobbed. Adam coughed as smoke filled his lungs. He rattled the handle of the door. It was locked.

"Aberdeen!" he screamed, pounding on the door. "Aberdeen!" She looked up, her hair falling from her face. The lights flickered again. Adam pulled at the handle. He looked through the small window again and saw her face. He gasped. She had no eyes.

Sweat poured from Adam. He awoke to an unfamiliar place. He rubbed his eyes trying to erase the lastest nightmarish installment from his memory. He felt like he'd been hit by a bus. Reaching down to his side he noticed the IV in his arm; then remembered and a great heaviness took over.

"You gave me a scare," the old man sitting next to the bed stated. "I'm not sure you realize you're not invincible." Dr. Erikson took Adam's vitals and placed a few pillows behind his shoulders. "A half hour longer and you would've died." He helped the young man sip some water from a cup and then phoned for a tray of food. "You need to eat something."

"How's Jon?" Adam asked. His voice was low and raspy.

"I'm hopeful he'll recover fully, but I don't know for sure." the doctor replied. "The swelling caused some damage. There's been small improvement each day."

"Each day," Adam repeated. "How long have I been out?"

"This is the fourth day and its just before dinner." Erikson paused and got very quiet. "Is he dead?" he whispered. "Is Anthony Bergstein dead?" Adam studied the old man's face.

"Yes."

"Are you sure?"

"Positive," Adam replied. He was tired and it frustrated him. There was a gentle knock on the door. It was Shane with a tray of food. The Doctor smiled.

"I'll check in on you later," he said leaving the room.

The two men sat silently; neither knowing what to say. Adam picked at his food and finally pushed it away in frustration. His eyes burned. He felt like his chest was being crushed. Shane felt the same way.

"You're a lot like him Adam," Shane said breaking the silence, "Strong in character, careful with words and very private." He smiled slightly. "Daniel was a thinker." Adam tried to blink away tears but failed. "He knew how to read people and how to reach them."

"How can I hurt so much, yet feel so numb?" Adam asked. "I feel burnt inside." The tears readily flowed. The young man looked lost, ". . . and Aberdeen."

"Everyone dies son." Shane searched for the right words. "Every mother, father, husband, wife, child . . . ." He paused, ". . . friend. Everyone." He inhaled deeply experiencing his own grief. ". . . and for those left behind it hurts like hell, but its part of life." Adam nodded fighting for control of his emotions. Shane swallowed. **"One of the hardest parts is watching others you care about go through it."** He put his hand gently on Adam's shoulder. **"None of this is your fault.** You did what you did. Exactly what you thought was best at the time." He shook his head and sighed. **"You're going to go over what happened a million times** . . . if you haven't already, **and second guess everything."** Looking at Adam, Shane narrowed his eyes. **"I've been there; done that. It doesn't help."** The young man could still see years of past pain and guilt in his father's eyes.

"I can't help it," Adam admitted. **"It never should have happened."**

"The odds of any of you getting out alive were slim," Shane reminded him, **"remember that."**

Adam knew his father was right but it didn't help. The young man was exhausted and found himself struggling to stay awake. Shane gently took the extra pillows from behind his son's shoulders put them on the chair in the corner. By the time he turned back,

Adam had already drifted off. He stayed a while watching him sleep, relieved he was alive.

The next day Shane brought Jon to visit. He wore dark glasses and held his father's arm as he was led to the chair next to the bed. Shane described the room and brought the other chair closer to the bed before taking a seat.

"He's starting to see shadows, but is very light sensitive." Shane transmitted. "As soon as he heard you were awake he insisted I bring him."

Adam struggled to stay composed and shifted in his bed. His body was getting stiff. "I'm glad you're doing better," he said awkwardly.

"I'm looking forward to a good long run with you soon little brother," Jon quipped with a smirk. Adam was instantly disarmed. "You must like getting shot, its becoming a habit." Adam smiled; he couldn't help himself. His mood lightened but it was difficult not being able to connect visually. Decoding had changed the way Adam communicated.

Jon leaned forward. "Adam," he said; his voice resolute. "I need to know what happened." He cleared his throat and inhaled deeply. "I need to know what happened to Bergstein . . . and to Jarvis."

Adam swallowed. For a moment he imaged he was in another dream; that he would wake up covered in sweat, hyperventilating. He didn't. He lay on his bed stunned, propped up by pillows and his eyes started to burn.

"Adam . . . ?" Jon's voice prompted. The words began to spill out and Adam's wall crumbled. Shane watched, reliving it with him. Outwardly, the young man remained calm and precise but his father could see fractured images. *The elevator opening to a long hallway . . . Ambrose and Jarvis walking, the observation room . . . Bergstein and Jarvis . . .* Adam continued. Each word was careful and concise; his face emotionless. Shane flinched at the image of Bergstein's broken body. *Jarvis holding the receptionist . . . Lockwood telling them they'd have to wait . . .*

Adam stopped and looked at Shane. The wall returned. "The shots came from down the hall," the young man gulped losing control. "I heard them from the alcove outside." He paused; his eyes burning. "They were pinned by the front desk . . . I couldn't get to him . . ." He was speaking quickly, trying to get through it as fast as possible. "Dale tried to stop the bleeding . . ." Again he paused, breathing heavily. ". . . He died in Dale's arms," Adam became very quiet and covered his face with his hands.

* * *

It took two more days before Adam felt strong enough to get out of bed on his own but he wasn't ready to leave his room. Around him life went on. Everyone's emotions were raw with grief but as each day passed the children brought laughter and life to the ranch. His father visited daily and Munroe and Flynn took turns delivering his meals. They all tried to engage but Adam said very little. He longed for and yet dreaded a visit from Aberdeen. It never came.

He focused on getting strong. At night when no one was around, he'd carefully walk the hall, using the wall for support. It was a slow and excruciating process. Adam's body fought him with every step. During the day he'd work his left arm, struggling through the pain. Dr. Erikson noted his progress but said nothing.

Then one afternoon he took a shower and shaved. It was time. Two weeks had passed and Adam couldn't hide any longer. The fear he experienced almost amused him. He was facing no danger yet he was terrified. He felt fractured and uncertain. He'd considered leaving but only briefly.

The little ones were playing outside. Their structured study sessions were finished for the day. Aberdeen sat in the sun enjoying the warmth and the sound of their laughter. The older girls were horseback riding and some of the boys had gone with Flynn and a ranch hand to mend a fence. Every day the numbness of loss eased just a little. Occasionally she still heard her father's voice in the next room or his steps coming down the hall, but she knew better. He was gone.

She heard a noise from behind and turned toward it. Adam stood in the doorway. He looked at her sheepishly. He'd lost weight and leaned against the door heavily.

"Sophia told me you were out here," he said. His voice cracked and he looked away embarrassed. He fought the urge to fall back into his past pattern and shut down. He inhaled and set his jaw then suddenly his face softened. **"I'm so sorry, Aberdeen."** His approach took effort, both physical and emotional. He sat in the chair next to her.

They silently watched the children play. Adam spoke first. "He loved you very much." She turned and studied his face. The cut above brow was almost gone. Only a thin red line remained. His cheeks were sunken slightly and his skin pale. Their eyes met and she touched his face. He involuntarily flinched but took her hand before she could withdraw. He brought it to his lips and kissed it gently. She smiled thinking of Luka. He saw her thoughts.

". . . that's why I can't do this," he smiled back. **". . . I'm not Luka."** Her eyes questioned him. **"I'm not Adam either. Adam doesn't exist. He's just a collection of parts that don't know how to fit together or if they even should."**

"I don't understand," Aberdeen said taking her hand from him. **"What are you saying?"** She was hurt and confused. He gingerly brought his arm around and held her hands in his. Every movement still hurt.

He inhaled, softening his eyes. **"I need to put the pieces together but I can't do it here. It's all too much. I'll come back."** He let her go. **"I need you to understand."** She looked back at the children.

After a long pause she spoke. "I do." Their eyes never left the children. "When will you go?"

"Not today," he replied, "I need to get stronger."

"I'll convince you to stay," she warned.

"You'll try."

A small girl approached from the play area. She had big tears in her eyes and was holding one of her fingers. A scruffy little stuffed bear was tucked under her arm. Aberdeen went to her. The young woman blew on the little finger and smiled. The big blue eyes looked through tears over at Adam.

"Is that Adam?" she whispered. Aberdeen nodded. The little one ventured forward until she stood directly in front of him. "Hi Adam," the little voice sung. "My name is Paige." She held the stuffed toy out to him and smiled. "This is Snuggly Bear, he's been waiting to meet you."